S0-BZG-693

EX LIBRIS

SOUTH ORANGE
PUBLIC LIBRARY

DISCARDED

Sandra Wilson

Alice

NEW YORK
ST. MARTIN'S PRESS

LONDON
ROBERT HALE & COMPANY

© Sandra Wilson 1976
First published in the United States of America 1976

All rights reserved. For information, write:
St. Martin's Press, Inc., 175 Fifth Avenue,
New York, N.Y. 10010

Library of Congress Cataloging in Publication Data
Wilson, Sandra. Alice
1. De Longmore, Alice, Lady—Fiction.
I. Title. PZ4.W7538Al3 [PR6073.I474] 823'.9'14 75-10003

First published in Great Britain 1976

ISBN 0 7091 5536 0

Robert Hale & Company
Clerkenwell House, Clerkenwell Green, London, EC1

Printed in Great Britain by
Clarke, Doble & Brendon Ltd.
Plymouth.

Books Consulted:

EDWARD II: THE PLIANT KING, Harold F. Hutchison, 1971
THE LIFE AND TIMES OF EDWARD II, Caroline Bingham, 1973
THE POLITICAL HISTORY OF ENGLAND, VOL. IV, T.F. Tout, 1918
THOMAS OF LANCASTER, J.R. Maddicott, 1970
THE SEVEN EDWARDS OF ENGLAND, K.A. Patmore, 1911
KINGS OF MERRY ENGLAND, P. Lindsay
THE SEVERN BORE, F.W. Rowbotham, 1964
A MEDIEVAL SOCIETY – THE WEST MIDLANDS AT THE END
    OF THE 13TH CENTURY, R.H. Hilton
THE GOLDEN BOUGH, Sir J.G. Frazer, 1922

for Bob and Sheila

ONE

"BERKELEY must not be alerted, of that we must be certain!" The Earl of Warwick's rough voice sounded even rougher as he signalled to one of his knights to ride closer that they might confer.

The strange funeral procession wended its slow way down the rolling slopes of the western edge of the Severn valley, towards the silver strip in the distance which was the river itself. The Forest of Dean was behind them now, the land more open, more exposed . . . more likely to reveal their presence to enemies. The sun had already begun to sink towards the blue-purple mountains of Wales, and there was no warmth in the blood-red orb which drifted closer to its November bed beyond those ragged peaks. The winter of the year 1307 was bitter and cruel.

Warwick leaned closer to the knight, his dark face in shadow. Beside him Lady Alice de Longmore rode silently, her own face bereft of expression. She was eighteen years old, a tall slender girl with golden eyes and dark red hair. Beneath her fur-lined travelling cloak she wore a velvet gown of dove grey. Her clothing was fine enough, but nothing to match the splendour of Guy Beauchamp, Earl of Warwick.

Now he glanced quickly at her, his grey eyes sliding over her body as she swayed to the movement of her mount. He was exactly twice her age, a fine looking man with iron grey hair and a thick beard, but his fine looks were marred by a certain coldness in his eyes, a hardness.

"Well, Madam, we shall have to see that you are more suitably attired once Longmore is reached."

She turned her head, stubbornly away from him. Jesu, but she despised this man above all others. Angrily she pulled her hood further forward over her face to shield herself from his sharp eyes. More suitably attired indeed! Aye, because she was now a widow. A widow. Was it possible then to be a widow when one had never truly been a wife?

As if to emphasise her thoughts, the rumbling of the oxen cart

9

behind them came more loudly to their ears as they entered a small ravine. Alice felt compelled to look behind at the crude oak coffin which was lashed to the cart. Inside that narrow case lay the body of Sir Robert Beauchamp, her husband since she had been thirteen, and Warwick's nephew.

Bleak thoughts engulfed her, the anger and spite she seemed always to have known fighting back to the surface. Her lips straightened into a sullen line, resentment clouding her loveliness. The Beauchamps had much to answer for. They had murdered her father, and then forced her into an unwelcome marriage . . . and all so that they could become masters of Longmore Castle.

Longmore. Her home, and the home of her family for more than two centuries. It stood four miles south of Gloucester on a small wooded hill which was surrounded on three sides by a lazy curve in the River Severn. It was not a large fortress, nor yet did it command an important ford over the river, and to many it was impossible to see the significance attached to it by one of the mightiest families in England. But vital it was, to an Earl whose main lands were near Warwick and Elmley, and whose only rival in the rich acres of Gloucestershire was Holy Church . . . and Sir Thomas Berkeley. Earl Guy needs must keep a finger upon the pulse of Gloucestershire close to the large tracts owned by the Berkeleys, and Longmore provided a place for him to test that pulse. It was close enough to Berkeley Castle itself to enable the Beauchamps to watch in safety the comings and goings of their neighbours. There was no outright antagonism between the two, indeed Sir Thomas was forced to bow to the superior strength of the Earl, but Berkeley was powerful enough to cause the Earl more than a moment's apprehension.

The unexpected death of Robert Beauchamp had left Earl Guy without Longmore. Alice was the heiress to the castle. Now the unwanted wife who had been so badly treated by Robert had become once more of prime importance. She must be restrained until such time as she could safely be married to another member of the Earl's family. Alice knew that if she wished to escape from Beauchamp clutches, then she must do so hastily. But there was no opportunity. Not even a momentary chance had been afforded for escape.

She stared into the misty, flat landscape before her to where she knew Berkeley Castle stood, but although she strained her eyes she could see nothing. Even if Sir Thomas knew what had happened, would he come to her aid? She thought about him, recalling his thin, stooped figure and receding hair . . . she also recalled his smiling deference to the Earl whenever they had chanced to meet. No, she thought, he would not dare to openly defy Guy Beauchamp. Not even the chance of seeing Longmore pass into more friendly hands would cause him to risk aiding her.

They were close to the river now, and the cart clattered alarmingly in the winter still. For so great a river, the Severn was ominously silent, eery in its soundless strength as it licked its muddy banks. The water was peculiarly low for mid-winter because there had been little rain to swell the flow. The distant Welsh hills were gripped in snow and ice, and as yet had not melted sufficiently to feed the greedy river. On the opposite bank they would soon see the towers of Longmore, and Alice was strangely uplifted at the thought for she loved the castle which had caused her nothing but pain and unhappiness.

But she should have known only joy. Her eyes dwelt lovingly upon the straight back of the knight now engaged so deeply in conversation with her tormentor. Gareth. His hood was pushed back from his head, revealing the tight sandy curls she loved so much. He moved as one with his horse. *He* was to have been her husband, her father had always intended as much. But for the politics and strength of Warwick, the dream would have been realised.

Sir Gareth ap Llewellyn was 19 and the only son of her father's oldest friend, and the two men had been well pleased at the prospect of joining their families in such a marriage. But then came Earl Guy, the death of her father, and the ruthless harrying of Gareth's father's lands. The Welshman was no match for the might of the House of Beauchamp, and before such a dangerous adversary he stepped down and agreed to every demand. Not only did he withdraw from the betrothal of his son with Alice, but he also gave Gareth into Beauchamp's custody until the boy reached his majority at the age of twenty-one. And so now Gareth served Earl Guy, and was bound to do so by his own father's oath and pledge.

"My Lady, I see Longmore ahead." The quiet little voice of Morvina, Alice's maid, came from just behind her and she started, so deep had she been in her thoughts. She narrowed her eyes but could see nothing but the darkening shadows and the encroaching mist. A fire crackled on the opposite bank, sparks and smoke drifting across the hurrying waters. The peasants who tossed dead reeds upon the scarlet flames paused in their work to stare at the procession which moved so hastily. They whispered together, looking now at the red and white banners of the Earl of Warwick.

The Earl saw their glances and gave an angry exclamation as he realised that he had forgotten to conceal the banners which had afforded protection on their long journey through the unruly Welsh marches. Now he spoke curtly to Gareth. Flushing at the tone used, Gareth turned his mount's head away and rode back to tell the men to take down the banners. He smiled quickly at Alice as he passed.

Warmth surged through her and she turned in the saddle to watch him. She saw Morvina's elfin face. "Morvina, I cannot see Longmore, how I wish my eyes were as piercing as yours."

The maid smiled her strange smile. "Perhaps it would be more true, my Lady, to say that I *feel* Longmore ahead." Morvina was Welsh, and had brought with her from that land many secrets and powers which were beyond Alice's comprehension. She knew of herbs for cooking, herbs for healing . . . and herbs for poisoning. She knew in the morning if it would be sun or rain when evening came. She knew which days would be good for fishing in the river, and which would be fruitless, although to Alice's eyes the weather was identical upon each day. She knew too when the tidal wave called the Severn bore would sweep up the river. Many had been the times when she had lifted her head from her work and said simply that in half an hour the bore would be there. And always, always, it was.

Alice had long since forsaken attempts at drawing forth suitable explanations from her and now she merely accepted without question. Morvina had come to Longmore from the lands of Gareth's father, and was his kinswoman.

Warwick's great horse stumbled in the failing light, its breath standing out in a silver cloud in the cold air. He cursed crudely and dragged its mouth as he sought to steady it. The water lurked eagerly, silently, and Alice wished that he had fallen into that dangerous current. But he survived, kicking his heel into his mount's side and urging it forward more quickly.

"We shall not be able to ride through Gloucester, I fear, for darkness is almost upon us and the citizens of the city are always in a hurry to close the gates. We shall have to take a boat across the river at Stonebench."

Alice felt a finger of fear touch her. She feared this river at night, with its tides and mud, its eddies and silent ripples. "You

12

cannot be serious!" Her golden eyes were wide.

"When am I ever other than serious, Madam! We have passed the sleeping lookouts of Berkeley and I do not wish to draw unwelcome attention by riding through Gloucester when they are waiting to close the gates. There is a royal castle there and I have no intention of allowing you to slip away and seek refuge *there!* I am not so foolish, Lady Alice." He smiled mirthlessly.

Morvina touched her arm. "You can in truth see Longmore now, my Lady." Alice glanced across the river and at last could make out the tall stone walls she loved so much. Quickly she glanced up at the dark skies for she knew that Stonebench was a mere ten minutes ahead of them now, behind the hill upon which Longmore stood. Complete darkness was a little way off yet.

Gareth's horse passed her again, bringing with it the sweet smell of the oxen as they lumbered along with their unwieldy load. The shadow of Longmore spread high on their right as they followed the swing of the river until at last they could see the few tiny lights of Stonebench.

There was no real village here, it was merely a convenient place at which to cross the river which narrowed suddenly. Small jetties clung to each bank. Low tide here meant that many of the larger craft which plied their way upriver to Gloucester and beyond must drop anchor and await high tide: for Stonebench was as true as its name. A bench of stone jutted out beneath the water, reaching across two-thirds of the river. The keels of the boats were too deep for this evil ledge and many a captain, eager to receive payment for his cargo, had come to grief upon its hidden hazard. But now the tide was not too low, and they would merely be using a small rowing-boat. Alice was relieved that the light had not faded entirely.

The funeral procession halted at last, the horses stamping and sweating after the long journey from Wales where a hunting accident had ended the young life of Sir Robert Beauchamp.

The Earl ordered Gareth to wake up someone in one of the poor cottages so that they could be rowed across the river. He took two men with him and went to the nearest cottage. The door opened cautiously as his fist beat loudly upon the wood and Alice recognised the face of Bedith the cobbler peering out into the cold evening air. Gareth's voice came as little more than a mumble to Alice's ears, but she delighted in hearing it.

Bedith was nodding, turning back into his home for a moment and then returning with his winter hood. He rubbed his hands together to bring warmth to them as he dragged one of the two boats towards the jetty. Gareth ordered his men to help the cobbler who was no longer young. Tying an ancient rope to the jetty, they lowered the boat into the water, and immediately it swung away on the swift current, held by the taut green twine the old man had tied so expertly. He climbed down the jetty, stretching first one leg to the bobbing craft and then the other. He moved to the stern from where he unravelled yet another rope which he tossed to one of the Earl's men telling him to secure it beside the other twine. And so he drew the boat alongside the wooden posts of the jetty and looked up patiently, waiting for the first of his passengers.

Beauchamp dismounted and pushed Alice towards the landing. "You shall accompany me, Madam, for I shall not let you pass from my sight until we reach the castle! Llewellyn, you shall stay here and cross with the . . . coffin." His dark eyes went momentarily to the oak box on the cart.

Alice turned sharply. "You cannot mean to bring the *coffin* across in so small a boat! You are mad!"

He scowled. "When I wish for your opinion of my sanity I shall ask for it! The coffin crosses the river tonight. The fewer who know of my nephew's death the better. To send a funeral procession through Gloucester would be foolish in the extreme." He held her hand as she climbed down into the boat. Morvina followed her and then came the Earl himself.

The ropes were untied and the old man immediately dipped the oars into the water as it snatched the boat in its grasp. The jetty upon the opposite bank was downstream of the one they now left, allowing for the strong current. For a moment it seemed as if they would be carried past, but Bedith rowed with deceptive strength and skill. The other jetty was lit now by torches as the noise of the Earl's party had aroused the occupants of the cottages there. Strong arms reached down to secure the boat as it fled past.

Alice's legs were trembling when at last she stood upon the safety of the landing. She watched as Bedith returned over the river to bring the coffin. Beauchamp held her arm as if he feared she would even now escape from him.

An argument commenced at the other jetty and they could hear Bedith's voice raised in protest. The guttering flames of the torches threw a weak light across the darkness and they could see that the old man was refusing to take Gareth in the boat as well as the coffin. Gareth must wait. The task of lowering the heavy oak box

14

took longer than expected and darkness was entirely upon them when at last the ropes were untied for Bedith to cross.

The wind had risen unexpectedly, caught by the twist of the river and the hill of Longmore. Ripples appeared on the chilly water and for the first time they could hear the passing of the Severn as it slapped noisily against the wooden posts and the bank. The torches began to gyrate, hissing and spluttering. Bedith seemed unprepared for the weather change. He had been so intent on loading the coffin that he had not noticed the wind. The boat dipped and swayed dangerously as it struck the shallow, choppy waters over the bench of stone.

Alice put her hand to her mouth in horror as she realised that he could not control the boat. The prow bobbed severely in the wavelets and the oars missed the water. Bedith fell backwards against the ill-secured coffin. It was all over in a heartbeat. The boat capsized and with a horrible grating sound the coffin slid from its place and into the water. For a moment it seemed as if it would float, but the grinding noise which came to their ears told Alice that it was only the stone ledge which held the oak box above water. The boat drifted away downstream, its slimy keel upended to the skies, and already Bedith was being helped ashore by his friends. The Earl and Alice, however, had eyes only for the coffin as it dragged dreadfully upon the stone.

" 'Tis nearly at the edge," murmured someone and Alice licked her dry lips as at long last the water carried Robert's coffin to the sudden end of the stone shelf. It stood almost upright for a second before plunging down into the deep water beyond.

Silence reigned on both banks. Alice recovered first and looked quickly at the Earl. Beauchamp was staring at the spot where his nephew's body had slid to its final resting place, and beads of perspiration stood out on his forehead. He was afraid she thought in surprise.

"How deep is it there?" he asked, and his voice was only a whisper.

"Too deep to consider recovering my departed husband's body, my Lord." She enjoyed saying these words, enjoyed the thought that at least one Beauchamp would not enjoy a Christian burial.

He shivered in horror, but then recovered as quickly as he had weakened. His voice was as strong and harsh as ever when he cupped his hands to his mouth and called across to Gareth. "Ride on to Gloucester and present yourself to me in the morning."

15

Then without further ado he turned away and asked if there were any horses to be had in order that they might ride to the castle. Heads were shaken in unison; did he not realise, the faces seemed to say, that they were very poor hereabouts? He must do as they did . . . walk.

Morvina was whispering with one of the peasants, and Beauchamp pushed her forwards rudely. "Come along, Mistress, if we must walk then we have no time for gossiping!"

And so Alice returned to Longmore . . . a widow and the prisoner of her dead husband's uncle.

TWO

HOW little the castle seemed altered by the sudden passing of its lord. Alice's lips twisted wryly . . . maybe it was not so strange though, after all it was Warwick who was now and had been for many years the true master of Longmore. From the towers streamed the long red and white banners of Warwick, and the stone passages rang with the voices of his retainers. The Longmore family was almost stifled, a hollow echo half-forgotten by the castle which took its very name from them. Who could remember when the green and gold dragons of Longmore had streamed from the towers?

With an agitated movement she stood and paced around the small chamber, holding out her hands to the brazier which glowed dully in the corner. She was a prisoner in her own home, helpless and completely at Warwick's mercy. How long could it be before he forced yet another unwanted bridegroom upon her? At least she was spared the attentions of Guy Beauchamp himself, for he already had a wife. That he desired her she knew well enough, for his eyes told her that. Her skirts rustled and dragged against the rushes on the floor and her face was thoughtful. How could she possibly thwart him . . .

There was a loud screech from the far corner of the room and her eyes moved quickly to where Robert's falcon hurried restlessly up and down upon its perch. Its hooded head turned again and again, now listening, now shaking angrily, as it sought to be

16

the vague murmuring of the guards at the door. Morvina once again took to her casket of herbs. Alice resumed her restless walking, and eventually the falcon responded to her restlessness and began to match her.

Robert's falcon. How many times had she seen her handsome husband ride out from this very castle with the bird perched on his elegant wrist. Had ever there been a more handsome knight than Robert Beauchamp? She knew that she had had the envy of many a lady when he had become her husband, and for a brief while she had tried to bring a little warmth into the marriage. But her small efforts had come to nought, for he acted as if she did not exist. It had been left to Morvina to tell the new bride the truth about her husband, the truth that it was the company of men he preferred . . . and of one man in particular.

"The Prince of Wales? You jest!" Alice remembered her innocent reaction so well. She had not thought it possible that Robert could love a *man* in such a way. Morvina had smiled. "Is it not in your Bible about the love which was between David and Jonathan?" *Your* Bible, she had said, for Morvina was of the Old Religion and had little time for the Bible or talk of God. "You cannot come close to your husband because he is in love with Prince Edward and the Prince with him. That is why you are alone here so often and why you have been kept close in your own apartments when the Prince has visited Longmore."

Never again had Alice been able to look at Robert without the contempt showing clearly upon her face. Now his elegance took on new meaning, his love of peacock colours did not mean a mere love of fashion but a foppery which was somehow distasteful. His combed, prinked hair was effeminate, and the jewels he wore were gaudy and over-bright. She shuddered even now as she thought of him.

But two years ago Robert's fortunes had taken a sudden dive, from the pinnacles of joy and happiness to the depths of unhappiness and despair. The Prince of Wales had apparently forsaken him for another. Alice had heard this other's name mentioned only once. Sir Piers Gaveston, a Gascon knight in the Prince's household. Gaveston's father had been of service to the late King Edward I and in reward the King had taken Gaveston's son and placed him in the Prince's household. The old King was dead now, and the Prince had these past four months been King Edward II of England.

Robert's unhappiness had turned him at last to his young bride, but she could not suffer his touch. She spurned him, feeling physically sick at his closeness. Her proud Longmore blood could not endure his attentions. He salvaged what was left of his pride and left her very much alone once more. She did not regret this for she despised him too deeply now, not only for what he was but because he was a Beauchamp. Her hatred was complete. The bottom of the muddy Severn was a fitting resting place for Sir Robert.

Morvina moved to place another log upon the brazier and a shower of dust and sparks fell to the floor. She glanced at the narrow window which sucked and dragged at the fire. Outside the sky was black.

The sounds outside the door were muffled and so stealthy that at first neither of the girls heard, but then the maid's sharp hearing caught the change in the atmosphere. She looked at the door, her finger to her lips. Alice's heart began to beat more quickly. Slowly the door was opening! The bright torchlight from the passageway flooded in on the candle-lit room.

A strange but welcome sight met their eager eyes, for outside they saw the huddled shapes of their guards lying upon the floor, bound and gagged. Beyond them were many dark-clad figures whose faces were hidden by their heavy hoods. Morvina smiled. "It is Malcolm. Say nothing but do as you are told."

The tallest of the hooded men beckoned to them and they quickly stepped out into the passage. Alice felt a winter travelling cloak being placed around her shoulders and she reached up to tie it firmly. Her eyes were large as she gazed around her. A stocky, furious figure was struggling in the grip of two men, a figure which was mute because of a rough cloth which was tied about its mouth. But the angry, wild eyes which glared from that slightly ridiculous figure were those of Guy Beauchamp.

The tall man seemed to be the leader and must be Malcolm. He paused in front of the Earl. "And now, *my Lord Earl*, my instructions to you remain the same. If any of your men are so ill-advised as to attempt to thwart us, then this dagger shall snuff you out!" To emphasise the matter, he waved the dagger's sharp blade within inches of Earl Guy's nose.

They walked swiftly through the castle, finding that the Earl's guards soon fell back before them when they saw their master. Sometimes they were challenged, but then Malcolm told the guards that Warwick would die if they made a movement, and the Earl nodded his head to tell his own men to stand away. He was forced to suffer the further indignity of being dragged along wearing a loosely-tied coat and very little else.

The gale howled and whistled around the turrets, gasping down to the narrow courtyard with huge breaths. Alice's cloak billowed ound her. She felt almost sorry for the Earl as the bitter cold uck his virtually naked body. The drawbridge was lowered and nediately more of Malcolm's men rode in leading horses for the ty who had entered the castle. The Earl was pushed up on to a ck mare, with his head dangling down one side and his feet down other. He was to continue with them as their hostage to ensure at there was no pursuit.

Hoofbeats rattled loudly in the courtyard, flattening out to a dull udding as they rode over the drawbridge and down the hillside wards Longmore village where it nestled in a hollow. Not even a g stirred as they thundered past the tiny cottages, not even a dle was lit. Soon Longmore was behind them and they were ssing the width of the valley towards the distant ridge of the swolds.

Malcolm stopped them after a while, putting his finger to his Then he dismounted and took a scarf from his purse. champ raised his head to look, only to find the scarf placed ly over his eyes and tied sharply behind his head. His choked sts went unheeded. Malcolm was grinning as he took the of the Earl's mare and began to lead the animal round and in a circle. He then gave the bridle into the hands of one of tlaws who led the Earl away in the direction of Berkeley.

w he will not know which direction he travels in! I pray e grows sick with dizziness!" He remounted and grinned e vanishing Earl. "Sir Thomas Berkeley will have a vastly time persuading Warwick that he had absolutely nothing th this night's work."

rode on, soon climbing up the steady incline towards the Cotswolds. Woods concealed them at last, and the ground became softer and muffled the sound of their passing. The gale bent the trees savagely, and twigs were occasionally broken off and went spinning through the noisy air. At last they stopped once more, to rest the tired horses.

Alice thankfully slid to the ground, pulling her mount's bridle over its head and tethering it to a nearby holly bush. She saw the small figure of Morvina running into the embrace of the tall outlaw. As he put his arms around her, Alice felt a prick of

21

jealousy. It was not the mistress of Longmore who inspired such devotion, but her maid. Malcolm Musard was prepared to risk his life for Morvina, prepared to risk a terrible death if he was discovered as the kidnapper of the Earl of Warwick.

They came to where Alice stood and he pushed back the hood of his cloak. He was about thirty years old. She could not see the colour of his eyes in the darkness but his hair was Saxon fair and hung to his shoulders. He took Alice's hand and raised it to his lips in a manner which surprised her, for she had imagined him to be a low person, uncouth and as wild as his exploits suggested.

"And now we have you from Beauchamp's grasp, my Lady, what are your plans?"

For the first time she stopped to consider her position. She did not know what her plans were. All she had thought of was getting free of Warwick. What to do after that had not occurred to her. She bit her lip miserably, conscious of the grin on his face as he watched her confusion mounting.

Her stubborn will struggled against the seemingly overpowering odds. She looked away from him leaning against a tree and closing her eyes. Where might she find help? Indeed, who was strong enough in the whole land to be able to flout Warwick?

A sudden dazzling idea came to her and she opened her eyes. "I shall go to the King."

Malcolm threw back his head and laughed aloud. "That sweet boy? Jesu, Madam, you have unusual notions. Why should the King help the widow of a discarded lover?"

Morvina frowned at him and nudged him fiercely for his lack of feeling. "Have a care, Sir Outlaw, else I take a herb potion and end your blabbing forever. 'Diawch!'" The Welsh expletive slipped out in her anger.

Alice drew herself up to her full height and glared at him. "You show a tactlessness and coarseness which I would expect! I thank you for aiding me . . . if you will but provide me with a horse and two of your men to accompany me then I will take myself off your hands. My plans can be of no consequence to you."

His grin broadened at her stiffness. He was about to prod her further when one of his men shouted a warning and there was a sudden scuffle in the bushes to their left. Morvina grabbed at Alice and pushed her behind the tree, while Malcolm was already drawing his dagger from his belt.

The struggle was short and violent, but soon the dishevelled figure of a man was dragged out, writhing and cursing before they gagged him. They could all see the brilliant red and white of Warwick's badge emblazoned on his coat.

Darkness concealed his face from them as he was brought before Malcolm. "Well?" said the outlaw dangerously. "And which of Warwick's toads have we here? Bring a torch."

The man who had first shouted the warning pushed forward. "He has recognised us, there can be no doubt. He must die else we run into peril from his clacking tongue!" There was an immediate murmur of agreement from the others and they closed in menacingly.

A torch was lit and Malcolm snatched it to peer into his prisoner's haughty face. Alice gasped aloud, her hands flying to her mouth in horror. "Gareth!"

THREE

HOW she longed to touch his pale face, feel the damp curls which clung to his hot skin. Her hand reached out momentarily before she remembered the laughing, mocking eyes of Malcolm as he watched the scene before him. The outstretched hand dropped back to her side and she turned, disguising her anxiety.

"What will you do with him?" Her heart twisted with fear for Gareth.

Malcolm's expression became cool as his eyes slid from her back to the prisoner. "He has witnessed too much, I cannot afford to let him go free." His interested glance returned to her. "And why, pray, do you show such an interest in his fate? Surely that is not seemly in one so recently widowed."

Gareth's lips curled in a fury at the insolent tone. He renewed his struggles but was held too firmly.

A blush prickled at her face uncomfortably. "I do not mourn the loss of my husband. I am not so false as to pretend a grief I do not feel."

Malcolm folded his arms across his broad chest. "You protest overmuch, I think."

Alice felt a helplessness now, and she threw a look of appeal to

23

Morvina. Save him. Morvina was torn between her loyalty to her mistress and her love for the outlaw. Unhappily she hesitated, for she could not bear to plead for Gareth if by doing so she might endanger Malcolm's life.

Seeing the indecision on the maid's face, Alice spoke again to Malcolm. She must save Gareth, even if it meant begging to this . . . this . . . "Before my marriage to Sir Robert Beauchamp I was betrothed to Gareth. I am close to him, aye, but that is no concern of yours. Should you not speak with him first, before you kill him unheard. Perhaps he will pledge his silence . . . and besides," she looked slyly at Morvina, "He is Morvina's kinsman."

For the first time the smile faded from Malcolm's lips and his brows drew together in disapproval. "Is this true?" He looked at the maid.

She nodded, hanging her head dejectedly, for she knew that he prized loyalty above all things.

"Sweetheart, you disappoint me. It shames me to think that you would have stood silently by and watched the death of a member of your own family . . . for I must wonder if ever you would stand thus silently and watch *my* death!"

Morvina's pretty face was tormented as she ran to him. "Never, 'Cariad', never! It was for your sake that I held my tongue, *your* sake! You are everything to me and I would sacrifice anything for you!" She clung to his arm, seeking desperately for a sign of kindness in his stern face.

"Nonetheless, your silence was a shameful thing." But he did not remove her hands, indeed he allowed her small fingers to clasp his own. He looked over her bowed head to Alice. "You would have me speak with him then?"

Gareth's crude gag was removed and for a moment he licked his dry lips, spitting out pieces of cloth. His eyes dwelt lovingly on Alice before his attention was drawn sharply to the tall outlaw. "What have you to say then, Sir Gareth?"

"Say? You ask me for my silence in return for my life?" Gareth's fiery Welsh spirit rebelled instinctively against this smiling man whose slightest word could end his life.

Alice stepped between them hastily, putting her hand on Gareth's chest. The fool, could he not see that his attitude would inevitably harden the outlaw? "No Gareth, *I* would have your silence. Malcolm has rescued me from Longmore, and you would dishonour me if you told of what you now know." A thought occurred to her. "How did you come upon us?"

"I chose to return to Longmore by riding through the night. I went around Gloucester and rode across the causeway over the marshes. I was just about to ride up to the castle when you all rode out. I realised that there was something odd about it all and so I followed you. I saw the Earl being led off to Berkeley, and I kept on following your main party. I did not realise that you were accompanying the outlaws voluntarily. At first I thought that they had captured you. My own clumsiness gave my presence away, and the rest you know." He grinned suddenly, the smile showing the unexpected charm which was his. "Musard, you should not chide my kinswoman for remaining silent . . . she knows well enough that I would have held my tongue in a like fashion for Alice!"

Morvina did not move her head, but the outlaw snorted in disgust. "What family devotion! I'faith the Welsh are barbaric! So, Sir Gareth, wherein does your true loyalty lie? To Warwick, whose colours you wear? Or to the Lady Alice, whom you profess to love? Well? I am anxious to know if indeed you understand the meaning of loyalty at all."

Gareth contained his anger this time. "There can be no doubt that I wear the red and white of Warwick, it would be useless to deny it. I am bound to serve Guy Beauchamp by the word of my father, and I would be a poor son if I so sullied my honour by putting aside my father's oath. I cannot aid Warwick in any way by telling him your identity, for if he knew he would still have to catch you . . . which I understand to be an impossibility! So my lips are sealed and my honour unblighted. My loyalty to Lady Alice is unwavering and will always be thus. If she wishes my silence, then I have no hesitation in agreeing." He smiled again, his face boyish in the softening light as dawn approached.

Malcolm put his fingers to his mouth thoughtfully, his eyes narrowing. The other outlaws murmured uneasily amongst themselves, and the one who had first discovered Gareth edged forward again. "Malcolm, I don't trust him! Let's have an end of it now!"

Morvina spoke at last. "There is no need for all this. You heard what Gareth said, and he spoke truthfully. I know. He will hold his tongue." She glanced shamefacedly at Alice, as if to resume their former friendship by her words.

The outlaws seemed a little mollified, for they knew that Morvina risked her own life if Gareth betrayed them. That she was so

25

adamant as to his reliability told them that Gareth's word could be counted on.

Dawn was changing the heavy skies to a pale grey now, and Malcolm became restless. Daylight meant the risk of recognition. The wind had not abated as the wild western storm continued to bluster. The outlaw spoke to Alice. "We must make haste else we are discovered, my Lady. You are still determined to ride to the King?"

"I am . . . there is no other course. Warwick is powerful, and so I must seek the protection of one whose power is greater. The King offers my only hope." .

Gareth touched her arm and turned her to face him. "Is it wise to take yourself to Robert's former love? It could be that he has no wish to be reminded of the past."

"He may well be right." Malcolm was serious.

She stared at the swaying holly bush where her horse was tethered. The bright shiny leaves reflected the lightening skies. Some berries decorated the tips of the branches, dancing in the wind. "Can you suggest another who would be able to protect me? None of the great Earls would wish to cross Warwick, even the old King's adviser Lincoln would rather avoid my petition I feel. The King's cousin, Lancaster, would most certainly turn me away as he is Warwick's friend. There *is* only the King himself. Perhaps if I sought his mercy and begged him to place me in the household of some great lady . . . with the Dowager Queen Margaret perhaps . . ." Queen Margaret! Of course! Warwick would not dare cause unpleasantness *there*. She smiled for the first time. "There is my answer. Queen Margaret is renowned for her kindness and will almost certainly extend her protection to me."

"It is settled then." Malcolm remounted. "Some of my men shall accompany you, for I dare not ride openly to London at the head of so many men. My name is infamous even in England's capital."

"I shall ride with you." Gareth was determined.

"And so shall I." Morvina looked unhappily at Malcolm who scowled blackly.

"Why, sweetheart? You have no need to remain with Lady Alice."

"I am her maid and I will go with her. There is time enough for you and me, Malcolm."

Alice saw that Malcolm was unwilling to accept this. "Morvina, are you sure that is your wish? I will not stand between you and Malcolm."

"It is my wish to accompany you." Morvina was final. Without a word Malcolm turned his horse's head and with most of his men he rode away from them.

Gareth untied Alice's horse, putting his hands on her waist to help her to mount, but instead he held her for a moment. "Sweetheart, there is another way in which you can be safe. You are free now, not only of Warwick but also of an unwanted husband. We can marry if you wish."

She smiled gently. "Gareth, for you to marry me would be to sign your death warrant. Warwick will rid himself of you as he once rid himself of my father. Besides, you are still bound to him and he could force you to his will, by law if necessary. I love you, my dearest Gareth, but I will not allow Longmore to fall into his hands again, and neither will I put your life in jeopardy." The words were somehow rather too easy to say and she was conscious of an unexpected glibness. She was puzzled at herself, but there was no time to probe deeper into her heart at the moment.

His green eyes searched her pretty face. "Is Longmore your whole life then? Can you not put aside your inheritance for me? One day I shall have lands of my own, lands in Wales where the laws of England are not so easy to enforce. We could be safe there, both from English law and from the wrath of Guy Beauchamp. I do not place my loyalty to him above my loyalty to you." There was reproach in his voice and she was miserably conscious of it. As she did not answer he contined. "Longmore is but small, it carries no great fortune beyond its usefulness to Warwick. It has already cost your father his life and you an unhappy marriage. Do not let it come between you and your chance of happiness now." His fingers clasped hers.

She could not meet his eyes. Her heart was in a turmoil. Why was she so hesitant in reaching out to take what he offered? Was this not what she had so often dreamed of? She must say something. "I cannot decide so abruptly to cast aside my father's inheritance. As you owe a loyalty to your father, so I owe a loyalty to mine." At last she raised her eyes to his motionless face.

"Very well, Alice, I must accept your decision." His voice was clipped, hurt, and he lifted her quickly on to her horse.

They moved off swiftly in the direction of London. The woods sped past them in the watery morning light, and the wind whipped up the dead leaves of autumn in a rust-coloured cloud beneath their horses' hooves. Gareth rode in complete silence, a silence which

27

grew more and more oppressive with each mile they covered.

Alice's spirits were dampened, and she endeavoured to draw him into conversation when the opportunity presented itself. "What will you do when Warwick requires an explanation of you for your lengthy absence?" She edged her mount alongside his as they paused by a stream. The horses drank the chill waters.

For a moment it seemed that he was not going to answer. Even Morvina looked at him. But eventually an answer was forthcoming. "I shall tell him partly the truth, that I escorted you to London. I shall not tell him that I knew you to have escaped or that he himself had been kidnapped. He will not be able to disprove my words, even if his suspicions are aroused."

She could say no more to him for he urged his horse forward across the broad stream, the water splashing to a white foam. From then on he presented only his back to her. She retreated further into her own uncertainty. She looked at him and then down at her horse's flying mane. Why did she not accept him? Could it be that some of Morvina's disapproval had found a resting place? Or could it be that she loved him only because she could not have him, and now that she was faced with the opportunity . . . No, that could not be the case, for she had always loved Gareth and he her. It *must* be as she had told him, that she could not lightly put aside her father's memory.

But she was still miserable as they rode on towards the capital.

FOUR

AS they left the Cotswolds behind them, so the storm diminished. The day was dull and overcast, and the sun could not break through the cloak of cloud. The horses were very tired and only moved at a slow canter.

Alice ached in every limb. Never before had she ridden for so long and at such a pace. Oh to lie in a fresh bed, and close her eyes . . . and sleep. Gareth had maintained his surly silence, his face stern and almost that of a stranger. She could see no way out of her predicament. The way in which she now felt was no way in which to marry him. The doubts were clamouring to be recognised.

"We are almost there." Morvina was excited as she pointed ahead to the towers and spires of London rising from the distant landscape.

Alice glanced behind as if expecting to see the red and white banners of Guy Beauchamp bearing down on them. Even now he could capture her. Her heart almost faltered as her horrified eyes saw that an enormous calvacade was fast coming up behind. Fresh, fleet-footed horses carried the newcomers swiftly. Her fingers clenched upon the reins and she swallowed with fear. In her alarm she did not glance at the colours borne by this calvacade; if she had her anxiety would have been quelled.

Morvina's sharp ears caught the sound of the strange horses and she turned. At the same moment Malcolm's men became aware of the danger they might be in. Their confidence in Gareth's promises was not sufficient to hold them and with one accord they sheered away to the left, kicking their heels into their weary horses' flanks. Alice, Gareth and Morvina were suddenly alone with the horsemen who were upon them in a moment.

For the first time Alice thought of looking at their banners, and she saw that they were not red and white but blue and silver, not bears but birds. She searched in her memory for the owner of those blue and silver birds, but her mind was hopelessly entangled with fear.

Gareth steadied his frightened horse and smiled at the fine nobleman who rode at the head of the cavalcade; a tall, thin man with a hooked nose and dark, straggling hair.

"My Lord of Pembroke, I greet you."

Pembroke! Of course, now she recognised the banners. Aymer de Valence, Earl of Pembroke, an important and respected nobleman.

"You are Warwick's man are you not?" De Valence's voice was curiously thin, somehow seeming to match his appearance. Idly he flicked his long fingers at the mane of his stamping horse, his eyes watching Gareth closely. He did not much like Guy Beauchamp, this much was apparent in his cool demeanour.

"I am, my Lord. Sir Gareth ap Llewellyn." Gareth bowed slightly.

"I am overcome with curiosity, Sir, as to the conduct of your escort when we approached. Their departure was hasty to say the very least." Pembroke leaned forward, his hands resting elegantly on the pommel of his saddle.

Alice smiled brightly at the Earl. "My Lord of Pembroke, they were outlaws." She heard Morvina suck in her breath sharply. "They had intended to hold me to ransom. Sir Gareth was escorting me to London when we were set upon by brigands."

De Valence surveyed her. "And you are?"

"Lady Alice de Longmore, widow of Sir Robert Beauchamp."

"Ah! Now I understand. Sir Richard de Longmore, your father, was a good and faithful friend to me." The distrust evaporated and Pembroke held out his hand to Alice, grasping her fingers and pressing them to his lips. "It seems then that I have arrived at a most opportune moment."

"Indeed, my Lord." She caught a glimpse of Morvina's face. "I wish only that we knew the identity of the outlaws, but they were from hereabouts."

"They shall be discovered. It has come to a sorry pass when travellers such as yourself cannot ride in safety across the King's realm." He was again flicking his horse's mane. "You are on your way to London?" He did not wait for her to reply for he looked closely at her as her previous words struck him. "Robert Beauchamp's *widow*, you say? I did not know that he was dead!"

"He died but recently, my Lord. A hunting accident in Wales." Her tone betrayed no hint of feeling and he could not help but notice.

"Why are you journeying to London?"

"I go to enter the household of the Dowager Queen." Alice's words were ambiguous. Pembroke was almost certain to assume that she was expected.

"Then I may be of further service to you. It so happens that I ride to London myself and that I shall shortly be attending the Queen as my wife is at present in her service. I shall be only too pleased to lend you my protection for the remainder of your journey." He smiled graciously at her, the smile fading as he looked at Gareth once more. "Sir, your master will no doubt have need of you. You may relinquish your duty to the Lady Alice."

Gareth's face reddened at the abrupt dismissal, and Alice felt keenly for him. "My Lord of Pembroke, I have every reason to be grateful to Sir Gareth, his kindness and thoughtfulness have upheld me in a time of great stress." She looked from Pembroke back to Gareth. He reluctantly met her gaze, but the hurt was deep within him and he could not forgive her her coolness towards him. And I deserve it, she thought miserably, I deserve the reproach I see in his eyes now. "Sir Gareth?" She smiled at him. "Sir Gareth, you will visit me? Our friendship is of long-standing and must not be allowed to fail because distance separates us."

He inclined his head briefly. "I shall be pleased to attend you, my Lady." Oh, the distance which yawned between them now. She bit her lip and stared at her hands which twisted the reins. Oh Gareth, forgive me, forgive me . . . When she looked again he was already riding away, the hoofbeats of his passing muffled by the grass verge. He did not look back.

Pembroke grunted. "A surly fellow, I declare! You are well rid of so disgruntled an escort."

Morvina looked at Alice's miserable face. The maid was more than a little surprised at the sudden disintegration of the friendship between Gareth and her mistress. It had been a friendship which had endured the years, a hidden, secret thing; a love of touching hands, soft smiles and concealed meetings. Morvina was sad.

Already the Earl's company was reforming, and Alice rode at Pembroke's side. He remembered again that Robert Beauchamp was dead. "A hunting accident, you say? How did it happen?"

"I am not certain, my Lord. My husband's horse moving in the bushes was thought to be a stag. The arrow was straight and true."

He took a deep breath. "You are well rid of a Beauchamp spouse!" His eyes studied her reaction to this sweeping statement. Seeing no flutter of resentment at what he said, he felt encouraged to continue. "Your father had no such husband in mind for his only child, that I know! I seem to remember that he had arranged a match for you with the son of an old friend . . . a Welsh knight, I believe."

She smiled suddenly, and with perverse pleasure she said, "Yes, my Lord, I was to have married Sir Gareth ap Llewellyn."

Pembroke's sallow face coloured, and he discontinued the conversation.

The Palace of Westminster was full of noise and merriment when they entered at last. Evening was long since upon them, the darkness broken only by torchlight and reflections upon the waters of the swift-flowing Thames as it swept by towards the sea. The barges and rowing boats with their flaring lamps plied their way in every direction over the river which was the main thoroughfare of London.

One of the barges brought Pembroke and Alice. They had paused at his lodgings for Alice to rest. She had been grateful for the chance to change, although the Countess of Pembroke was certainly of a more portly build than Alice. He had told the ladies who

31

remained at the lodgings to see to Alice's comfort, and they had endeavoured to do this, but as to clothing . . . She glanced down at the heavy dark grey folds of the Countess's gown. It had been the only suitable one in the wardrobe, but it hung limply against her more slender figure. Her dark red hair was plaited and coiled over her ears and then hidden beneath a black headdress and veil. She must try to look as if she mourned the passing of her husband. She pulled a face in the darkness. Jesu, I look more like a crow than my father's daughter!

Morvina sat meekly behind her mistress, her eyes wide as she looked around at the magnificence of London. The myriads of torches and lanterns revealed the immensity of the city, and to Morvina, who had only ever visited Gloucester, the size was hardly comprehensible.

Alice clung to the rail of the barge, her stomach heaving sickeningly at the lurching of the small craft. The November wind blew freely upriver, rippling the water into sharp waves. Her teeth chattered.

Aymer de Valence, watched her carefully from his seat. He was suspicious of her somehow, for she had never once mentioned a semblance of sorrow at being widowed, and never had she produced any letter from Queen Margaret. And her story of the outlaws ran a little thin on closer inspection. He pursed his lips thoughtfully. He knew a little of the struggle over Longmore Castle, but not much. If Alice was suddenly a widow, it was peculiar that Beauchamp allowed her to ride across England unattended but for that Welshman of so surly a manner. And she had no baggage with her . . . He sighed to himself. He was not about to pry further into her affairs for he feared that he would unearth something which was better left. Beauchamp of Warwick was a savage man to cross, and de Valence felt in his bones that he had somehow crossed Warwick by escorting this girl to London. He pulled his cloak tighter around his thin body and slouched, as if to hide from anyone who might look.

Inside the Palace, smoke from the torches filled the air, and her eyes stung. Her heart was thumping with excitement, but how she wished that Pembroke would leave her now. She did not wish to seek an interview with the Queen and thus let him realise that she was not expected at all. But he obviously intended to shepherd her right into the royal presence!

A drunken knight lurched along the passage towards them, his peacock blue satin coat stained with wine and his hand clutching a goblet which splashed with each step he took. His curling golden hair shone, each curl painstakingly combed and placed in position. His eyes were bright blue and he smiled happily at Pembroke.

"Aymer de Valence! How . . . very . . . p-pleasant to meet with you once more." He clapped his free arm around Pembroke's shoulder, the wine slopping down the satin yet again. The blue eyes swivelled glassily to Alice and he leered cheerfully at her. "I'faith, Pembroke, you're a cunning fox! Where did you find this pretty wench? I'll vow the Countess Beatrice knows nothing of this . . . "

"She does not, because there is nothing to know! Arundel, you have imbibed rather too much . . . again. You see before you Lady Alice de Longmore, a lady, and certainly not to be termed a 'pretty wench'!" Pembroke's voice was pinched with anger, and he slowly disengaged himself from Arundel's sticky grasp.

Arundel leaned suddenly against the wall. "De Longmore?" He frowned to himself through the alcoholic vapours which clouded his mind. "I had thought the l-last Longmore to be wedded to Robert Beauchamp." He leered at Alice again, his blue eyes moving suggestively over her. "Beauchamp has my envy if you are his wife, although perhaps *I* could serve you better!" He sniggered loudly into the goblet, the sound smothering noisily as he drained the wine and then tossed the costly goblet away. It rolled against Morvina's skirts and she stepped aside, her large eyes staring coldly at the unsteady knight.

Pembroke took Alice's arm and pushed her past and she heard Arundel hiccup loudly. De Valence was angry at the behaviour of the young Earl of Arundel. "Take little heed of him, my Lady, he is always in his cups."

She glanced behind to where he still slouched against the wall. He perceived her gaze and raised his arm in salute, seeming to find this very amusing and commencing to laugh drunkenly. He slid to the floor, laughing even more loudly. Yes indeed, Edmund Fitzalan, Earl of Arundel, was far gone in drink.

The Queen's apartments were quieter than the rest of the Palace. Alice found that her heart was beating almost unbearably fast now, and she rubbed her damp palms in the dark grey folds of her gown. She swallowed as Pembroke told a page to announce them. Then she was walking into the warm, tapestried rooms, seeing vaguely the small groups of ladies who stood around, talking. Some played chess, while others were busy at their embroidery frames. A minstrel

33

played soothingly at his lute. A roaring fire crackled in the huge hearth.

Morvina stopped, staring around in amazement at the sumptuous apartments. She had thought Longmore to be fine, and had marvelled at Pembroke's town lodgings . . . but *this* . . .

Alice kept her eyes downcast, for at last her nerve was deserting her and she realised the enormous impertinence of what she was doing. The Queen would surely dismiss her without hesitation. She bit her lip miserably, walking reluctantly in Pembroke's wake.

The Earl turned at last to take her hand and draw her to his side. They stood before two distinguished, richly-clad ladies. The smaller, rounder one could only be Pembroke's wife: Alice recognised the figure for which the dark grey gown had been stitched.

The other lady must be Queen Margaret, widow of King Edward I, and step-mother to England's new King.

FIVE

QUEEN Margaret was French, and the country of her birth had written its name indelibly upon her. She was small and dark, with an olive complexion and almost black eyes. Her hair was thick and lustrous, the heavy plaits shining with an almost bluish light in the dim room. She was a young woman still, having been married at the age of seventeen and widowed six years later. Her husband had been dead for only four months and the marks of sorrow were easy to see in this lovely, gracious princess. She had found her place in the hard, military heart of her husband.

Now she looked quizzically at Alice and then at Pembroke. "Lord Aymer, I pray that your journey was not too arduous in this inclement weather . . . " She glanced again at Alice.

Pembroke raised Alice's hand before him. "Your Grace, I would present to you Lady Alice de Longmore, the widow of Sir Robert Beauchamp." He gave no further explanation.

Alice's face was a blaze of unhappy scarlet now. She fervently wished herself back in Longmore, even under the watchful eye of Guy Beauchamp. "Your Grace, forgive my audacity in coming uninvited, but I seek your kindness, your . . . " Her voice trailed away and she was conscious of the interested eyes of the entire room on her. Tears pricked the back of her lids and she stared at the Queen's folded hands.

"My kindness, my Lady? In what way?" The Queen smiled gently at the unfortunate girl before her.

Alice glanced around the room. "Your Grace, if I could speak with you in private . . . "

Margaret's eyes were perceptibly cooler now. "What reason would I have for giving you a private audience, Madam?"

It seemed to Alice that her tongue had swollen to twice its normal size and that it more than filled her dry mouth. With great difficulty and acute discomfort she forced herself to continue. "My words will concern someone of considerable importance in the realm, Your Grace, and he would not be pleased if the tale became common knowledge."

The words sounded firm enough, and convincing, for Margaret looked troubled. She looked first at Pembroke's wife and then at Pembroke himself. The Earl indicated that he deemed it wiser for Alice's tale to be heard in private and so Margaret nodded. "Very well, my Lady, but I think Lord Aymer and his wife shall listen." She clapped her hands and dismissed the others from the room, and with disappointed faces they departed. Morvina reluctantly left her mistress.

Margaret walked to the fire, warming her hands at its heat for a moment before speaking to Pembroke. "Lord Aymer, this lady accompanied you. How came it that you did not elicit her reasons for coming?" There was gentle rebuke in the dark eyes.

De Valence shifted his stance awkwardly. "I thought from what she said that you expected her, Your Grace. I did not question her further on matters which I thought did not concern me."

The Queen looked then at Alice. "My Lady, you have much to explain, I think."

Alice took a deep breath. "Please forgive me, but I come to seek your protection . . . to beg your protection . . . "

"We shall see, my Lady. Proceed." Margaret sat close to the fire.

The long, sorry tale of Longmore Castle and Guy Beauchamp's plottings came pouring out. And when Alice had finished Margaret stood, tapping her fingers on the beads of her rosary. "What proof have you of the Earl of Warwick's interference in your family's affairs?"

"None, Your Grace, save the knowledge that I speak only the truth. I am a widow now, and seek only a widow's right to live her own life. With the death of my husband died also any right the Earl of Warwick had to Longmore Castle."

The Queen nodded. "I sympathise with you, Lady Alice, but the Earl of Warwick is, as you yourself said, a man of considerable importance, and not one whom I would gladly thwart."

Pembroke's personal dislike of Guy Beauchamp manifested itself now. He cleared his throat. "Your Grace, Warwick would not dare question any action of yours. As Lady Alice says, he has no rights in this, and he knows it as well as anyone. He is no fool and will do nothing."

Margaret looked to Pembroke for help and counsel. She was a foreigner, even though she had once been England's Queen, and the English still resented the interference of foreigners in their affairs. She must tread with care. "Should I grant the Lady Alice my protection then?"

"Of a certainty." Pembroke relished the thought of confounding a for once trapped Warwick. He despised Beauchamp, and had enjoyed the friendship of Alice's father, and in this situation knew himself to be safe enough.

Alice looked gratefully at him. She felt a little weak with the surge of relief which swept over her as Margaret nodded her agreement.

The Queen smoothed down the rich folds of her gown, smiling. "Be of good heart, my Lady, for your ordeal is almost at an end."

"Almost?" The ominous word crept dully into Alice's head. Must she endure still more then?

The French Queen looked embarrassed and glanced unhappily at Pembroke. "Why yes. I must present you to the King and tell him of my intentions. And to do this I must also explain exactly who you are . . . or to be precise, who your husband was . . . "

Alice closed her eyes. Robert. She opened her eyes again. "But I don't understand. Robert was dismissed from court . . . by the King himself . . . "

Again Margaret looked at Pembroke. "That is true . . . up to a point . . . You see, my Lady, Robert was dismissed at the instigation of another, one whose power over the King is immense and unshakeable."

Pembroke was scornful, his lip curling unpleasantly. "The Gascon squire!"

36

Alice realised who he meant then. "Sir Piers Gaveston?"

He snorted. "Now Earl of Cornwall, no less! A royal title for a Gascon knight!"

Margaret smiled gently. "Oh come, Lord Aymer, Piers should not be spoken of so disparagingly. He is a Gascon, true, but his family is of very noble birth. Confess now, it is not the man himself you dislike so, but the nickname he has for you! Joseph the Jew! We must all accept that Piers is established now, for he has his great earldom and the hand of the King's own niece in marriage. Lady Alice, I fear that it is to the new Earl of Cornwall that you must look now. *He* was behind your husband's dismissal from court, and it could be that he will have no wish to see Robert's widow so close to the King, reminding him of a lost love."

Alice's spirits plunged to a new, infinitely lower deep now. Robert had been petty and childish in his loves and hates. What if Gaveston were of the same ilk?

The Queen saw her distress and took her hand gently. "Take heart, Lady Alice. It could be that I malign Piers, for he has never shown himself to be a mean lord . . . but then I have never seen him when his security is in any way threatened. Let us be done with it immediately. We shall go to the King at this very moment." She led Alice from the apartments.

SIX

MIDNIGHT had passed when they came to the King's rooms, but the sounds of merry-making reached their ears long before the great double-doors barred their way. The doors were opened to the Queen and they stepped into Edward Plantagenet's private domain.

The mark of the new young King of England lay over the rich rooms in many ways. The colours were soft, the walls painted with gentle pastoral scenes and brilliant imaginary flowers and beasts. Curtains hung over the windows, curtains which were draped exquisitely, falling to definite patterns and resting elegantly in folds upon the freshly-strewn rushes of the floor.

Before the glowing fire lay a white greyhound bitch with a

37

litter of puppies. A young man crouched beside her, stroking the fine head and pulling the velvety ears. The puppies slept fatly by their dam's side. On a perch close by a monkey sat, a golden chain from its leg keeping it firmly in its place. Its bright little eyes watched the room intelligently, and its long tail curled around the perch.

The noise came from a group of four men who were clapping and stamping their feet in time to the music of a pipe. They cat-called loudly as a fifth man, dressed in a woman's gown, danced ridiculously to the uneven rhythm, holding up the skirts and showing his ankles like any coy girl.

Margaret's name was announced and the noise was snuffed out like a candleflame. The man in the gown blushed furiously as Margaret gazed bleakly at him. The awkward silence reigned until the Queen was led by a diminutive page into the inner rooms where the King was. Immediately that the Queen was gone the noise and hubbub broke out again.

Alice waited wearily for Margaret's return. Her eyes were sore and her head thumped with the ache of lost sleep. She had not slept for two days now and was exhausted, both physically and mentally. So much had happened. So much was yet in the balance. Her pathetic figure drew the curious glances of the men who saw the ill-fitting gown and bedraggled appearance, and yet could also see the tall beauty which lay beneath the outer covering. She was glad of the black veil which obscured her face from all but those who stood close.

Queen Margaret returned, and her black eyes were flashing with anger. "The King will see you now, Lady Alice. Alone. He is most insistent." Her lips were a firm line of disapproval of this arrangement.

The page was bowing to Alice and she followed him towards the inner rooms.

Two men were in the small room; one tall and golden, the other more slender and dark. Each was dressed as finely as the other. They glanced at one another as if sharing some secret, and then the fair man stepped aside and seated himself upon a small table, elaborately choosing a wrinkled apple from the wooden dish beside him.

Alice's golden eyes fled from him to the dark man who stood facing her expectantly. She had heard that King Edward was handsome, but never had she dreamed of seeing such perfection in one man. He put Robert's pretty looks in the shade. He was broad-shouldered, but his waist was narrow. His long velvet coat was of a mustard colour, trimmed with black fur. His dark hair was long and curled loosely to his shoulders. His face was clean-shaven and very handsome, and his eyes were of the deepest brown. He smiled and raised his eyebrows as if awaiting her.

"Your Grace, I . . . I am Alice de Longmore . . . "

He smiled, revealing his even white teeth, and she had the uncomfortable feeling that he was laughing at her. Robert's name brought no reaction at all, his dancing eyes did not flicker.

Behind her she heard the Queen's cold voice as Margaret entered the room. "My Lord . . . "

Now the dark man did laugh and Alice's eyes filled with tears. How right Gareth had been! This unkind King was merely mocking her.

Again Margaret spoke, her voice shaking with anger. "I suspected some such foolery as this. Your Grace, the play-acting has gone far enough I think! She is but a child and knows nothing of your court. She has come to seek a place in my household and by your present actions you cast a slight upon *me!*"

"You are right, sweet, sweet little mother, 'twas a cruel trick to play on one so tender!" It was the golden-haired man who spoke. He raised himself from the table. "Forgive us, Lady Alice, be assured that no real unkindness was intended . . . never, never unkindness to a lady!"

She dropped a confused and hasty curtsey to King Edward, the golden Plantagenet who towered above them all. He was a giant, strong and muscular. His hair was curled profusely, as was his beard, and there was that slight effeminancy about him which Alice could recognise. A distant echo of Robert Beauchamp stood before her in England's King.

She looked back at the dark man who had helped to trick her. He was different, that she could tell instantly. There was a love of clothing, a care of his handsome figure and appearance, but nothing of that strange womanish air which distinguished Robert and Edward. He smiled again. "Piers Gaveston, Earl of Cornwall. Your servant, my Lady. For ever would I serve such beauty as is yours." He took her hand and raised it to his lips. It was as if the veil was transparent as he looked at her, his eyes lingering on the dark red hair. The touch of his lips distracted her.

The King came immediately to his side, as if to share every

39

moment of his favourite's day. "You call yourself Lady Alice de Longmore. Why is this when I know you to be the wife of my . . . of Sir Robert Beauchamp?"

Alice turned sharply to look at the Queen, and realised that Edward was still unaware of Robert's death. She returned her glance to Edward's clear blue eyes. "I was his wife, Your Grace. Robert died less than a week ago in a hunting accident . . ." She stopped as she saw the stricken expression in those blue eyes.

"Robert dead? Sweet Jesu!" He crossed himself with shaking fingers. Alice could not help herself as she looked swiftly at Gaveston's face. Now she would know if her fate was sealed. He showed none of the petulance one might have expected from him on seeing Edward's so obvious grief at the loss of a lover. Neither did he show pleasure at the death of a competitor. Nothing. The handsome face was devoid of expression.

He spoke. "And so the heiress of Longmore Castle flees from the Black Dog of Arden?" He looked meaningfully at the troubled Edward, exerting his will over him.

The Queen frowned. "You would be well advised, my Lord of Cornwall, to subdue such epithets. They are not well received. Grin not so, Sirrah, for I know well enough of what I speak!"

Gaveston snapped his fingers expressively to the air. "That for Warwick and his kind! I do not fear him and find his lack of wit singularly tiresome."

The King was visibly forcing himself to recover from the shock of Alice's news, and Gaveston's light talk was drawing attention away from him. The blue eyes were still pained as he spoke to Alice. "You wish to enter my stepmother's household? Why?" His voice trembled slightly.

Alice learned her lessons quickly and enlisted Gaveston's own words to aid herself. "It is as my Lord of Cornwall says, Your Grace. I flee the Earl of Warwick." She saw the quick smile which crossed Gaveston's face as he detected her strategy. Once more she told the tale of her life, being careful not to mention her distaste and hatred for Robert.

Edward succeeded for the moment in completely hiding his grief. He sighed with great feeling as Alice finished and he remembered the squabbling over Longmore Castle. "Ah yes, that so-small fortress in Gloucestershire by which Beauchamp set such great store!"

Alice's anger was touched. "And would you speak so, Your Grace, if Beauchamp decided to set great store by Windsor Castle?

He has just as little right to your possessions as he has to mine!"
She bit her lip fearfully as the hot words spilled out. She had
been rude, and at a time when she must guard her tongue.

Edward's eyebrows shot up in surprise, but Gaveston laughed
easily. "Ned, you must agree that she shows spirit . . . and a
justifiable anger." He added these last words carefully.

"Perrot, you approve greatly of the lady, I perceive!" For a
terrible moment Alice thought that Edward was going to be
jealous, but instead he turned to his stepmother. "My mother, if
Perrot believes the lady's actions to be justifiable then I heartily
approve of your taking her into your household. Come, let us join
the merriment in the outer chambers. Perrot?" He held his hand
out towards Gaveston.

Although Gaveston followed the King, he did not take the
proffered hand, choosing instead to usher the ladies before him.

The other rooms were strangely quiet. Gone were the roisterers
of a while before. The greyhound bitch still rested with her litter
and the monkey sat on its perch. Only two men waited by the fire.
One was Pembroke . . . the other was a stout lord of some age who
was a stranger to Alice.

Edward looked enquiringly around the empty room. "What's amiss
here?"

The older man stepped forward quickly. "There is nothing amiss,
Your Grace." He went to his knees before the King, helped by
Aymer de Valence.

"Rise, my Lord of Lincoln, you have no need to bend your knee
to me. But is this not rather a late hour to seek me out?" He smiled
kindly.

Gaveston leaned forward with his arms upon the back of a chair,
his shrewd eyes wandering over the two who faced him. "It is never
too late for business, is it my Lords?" His voice was soft, as if he
had some notion of what they were going to say.

Lincoln did not look at him but addressed himself only to
Edward. "Your Grace, as a servant of your father, a trusted servant,
and now as your own true man, may I speak openly to you?"

The King shurgged. "You know already that to be my father's
true servant is no commendation to me! I hated my father, his
methods and most of what he stood for. But if you also be *my* own
true man, then speak your piece." He smiled shamedly at Margaret
for speaking in so forthright a manner of her dead husband. She
lowered her eyes.

Pembroke helped Lincoln to his feet. "Your Grace, firstly I would speak of the abandonment of the war with Scotland . . . "

Edward was irritated. "I have said before and I say again. I had no choice. My father left me an empty exchequer. I could not finance another war."

Lincoln plodded on with his unsavoury task. His age and experience had made him the reluctant spokesman for the Earls of England. "Very well, let us put aside the matter of the Scottish war . . . "

"Oh yes indeed, *let* us!" Gaveston's soft voice was even softer, and his eyes were glittering.

The plump Earl reddened a little. "There is another problem, smaller, but nevertheless which needs attention. It is the dismissal of your father's servants and councillors . . . "

"At *this* hour?" Edward gaped in amazement. "In the middle of the night you choose to waffle about my father's servants?"

Gaveston straightened, his long fingers wandering over the carved back of the chair. "Yes, my Lords, it is late for so trivial a subject. Let us get to the meat of your visit. Let us have the *real* reason for your visiting here tonight!" He raised his eyes to stare at Lincoln.

"Very well. The final matter." Lincoln's eyes unwillingly met Gaveston's. "Your father's dying wish was that this man be kept in banishment from England, and yet your father's body was not cool before you sent word for Gaveston to return!"

Edward's lips were a tight line of anger. "Lincoln, you have reached the line over which you may not step. I honour you as a man, I pray you do the same for me. I was brought up with Piers, we are as brothers. I will not desert my brother, and certainly not at the wish of a father who despised me and whom I despised." He turned to Gaveston suddenly, putting his hands to cup the other's face, and before their eyes he kissed him on the lips. "A man may kiss the lips of his true brother, and thus I kiss the lips of the man I love as my true brother."

Alice saw that Gaveston did not move away from the King, but neither did he raise his hands to touch him. He merely submitted to the caress.

Edward turned back to the disgusted faces of the Earls. "Besides, my *Lords*, I did not notice you to be absent from his investiture as Earl of Cornwall, nor from his marriage with my niece. It is a little late, is it not, to be remembering my father's death-bed. If you have no further business with me, then I bid you be gone!"

42

The dismissal was abrupt in the extreme and the Earls had no choice but to obey.

Lincoln bumped into a chair as he passed, and Gaveston said aside to Edward, " 'Burstbelly' is about to live up to his name!" Again, Alice noticed, he changed Edward's mood with a sentence.

The King laughed, lowering his face that the Earls could not see his amusement. Alice wanted to laugh too. Here was another nickname. First 'Joseph the Jew' for Pembroke, then the 'Black Dog of Arden' for Warwick . . . and now 'Burstbelly' for the stout Lincoln. Small wonder these men of little humour disliked the King's favourite so intensely.

Gaveston heard the sounds of a large craft arriving outside the Palace and he went to the window to peer out into the night. Torches lit the scene brightly, and his handsome face broke into a smile. "Behold, a bristling barge approaches, a-flutter with ragged staffs and bears . . . or is it ragged bears and staffs, one can never remember these things!" The flippancy was always there, close to the surface.

"*Bears* and staffs, Perrot! Warwick's badge is the ragged *bear* and staff!" Edward corrected him absentmindedly.

Piers continued, staring down from the window. "Ah yes, here comes our howling boarhound! Mother above, he looks thunderous! He is alternately as red and white as his badge! Beauchamp is about to bark, I think!"

Alice's lips parted in fear. The moment was here. Warwick had found her. The Queen made as if to leave, taking Alice with her, but Gaveston stopped her. "Nay, I think Your Grace that the Lady Alice deserves to witness this moment. It is her triumph."

Margaret glared at him, but Edward agreed with his favourite. And so Margaret and Alice remained. Gaveston took Alice's hand and drew her to a couch where he sat her down and then joined her, slouching easily with his legs stretched out before him. Margaret sat stiffly in a chair in a distant corner and tried to look as if she was not present. Edward smiled gleefully, his grief for Robert forgotten in this latest escapade with Perrot.

Alice could not help noticing how eagerly she allowed herself to be swept along in the wake of this fascinating, glittering man, this irresistible man who tweaked England by the nose and laughed as he did so. Every moment in his presence was almost an adventure. She heard footsteps approaching along the corridor and her hands began to shake.

His fingers closed over hers, tightening gently. She glanced up and he winked at her.

Then Warwick was there, a nightmare figure with his uncombed wiry beard and muddy clothes. The smell of horses entered with him. He looked at Edward, not seeing the favourite and Alice. But Alice's heart almost stopped within her, for there, in the small group of men with Warwick was Gareth.

He saw her at once, recognising her easily through the dainty veil. His glance fell upon Gaveston's fingers enclosing hers. He looked away coldly, the action insulting and disdainful. Her female pride overcame all else and she too looked away. Gaveston's sharp eyes missed nothing.

Edward's pleasure was immense as at last Gaveston decided to make Warwick aware of his presence. "My Lord of Warwick, I bid you good day, or rather night! What pleasure it gives me to see your face at court again. And you have hurried greatly to our company, how splendid!" He waved an elegant hand to indicate Warwick's untidy appearance.

A retort was blistering on Guy's lips when he saw Alice for the first time and his lips froze.

Gaveston rose, still holding Alice's hand and so she rose too. Her knees felt unsteady with the fear which even Piers Gaveston could not dispel.

Edward entered into the scene. "You are in time, Warwick, to greet the Lady Alice . . . whom I have just placed in the household of my beloved stepmother."

Warwick's mouth opened and closed and he looked at Gaveston with poison in his eyes. Alice could not bear to see such hatred.

Queen Margaret decided that at long last she could not stand any more of this play-acting. She stood, calling Alice to her. "Your Grace, my Lords, we will leave you to your business!" Resolutely she walked past them all to the doorway.

Alice's grey and black skirts brushed against Gareth's travel-stained cloak. Her pride was still wounded and so she flicked herself away from all contact with him. He noticed, he could not help but notice, and he did not even glance at her.

As the door closed behind them, Alice heard Warwick stammering out his excuses for his hurried appearance.

"Your Grace, I came in such haste to acquaint you with the unhappy news of my nephew's demise . . . "

44

SEVEN

THE open land before Wallingford Castle was a blaze of colour. The cold December breeze did not dampen the splendour of the gathering. Great tents and pavilions flapped brightly as everyone prepared for the tournament.

Wallingford was now the possession of the Earl of Cornwall, and Gaveston was determined to make his grand acquisition known to all the jealous barons who hated him so. Ostensibly the tournament was to celebrate his marriage, but in reality it was to make the English barons even more aware of his power. How they loathed him and how they hated to see the green and gold eagles of Gaveston flying from the turrets of Wallingford.

Alice sat excitedly in the Queen's enclosure, watching the colour and activity in front of her. For three weeks she had been at court and she had enjoyed each and every moment. The undercurrents passed her by.

She saw nothing of Gareth, and did not know if his absence brought relief or sorrow. She deliberately reminded herself of his insolent expression on seeing her with the Earl of Cornwall. How dared he look at her like that!

Warwick had kept well away from her, except when she had been forced to attend a mass for Robert at Longmore. They were the chief mourners and had to stand close together, but he had remained politely distant. She had not gone alone to Longmore, for the Earl of Cornwall had sent a company of his own men with her. She had been well protected. There had been a sweet moment of revenge too, for now the red and white of Warwick was no longer streaming from Longmore's towers. Instead the golden dragons of Longmore on their green background fluttered proudly over Gloucestershire once more. It had been a precious moment, an atonement for everything.

"Your Grace, the tourney is about to commence I believe!" Beatrice of Pembroke leaned forward to touch the Queen's shoulder.

"Why indeed you are right. Does your good Lord Aymer enter the lists today?"

"No, Your Grace, do you not remember? He has gone to France to make the final arrangements for the King's marriage to your niece, Princess Isabella."

"Ah yes." Margaret smiled, the smile fading a little as she looked at a very rich and ostentatious pavilion across the field. "A pity he did not take Thomas, Earl of Lancaster with him!" There was dislike in the Queen's voice when she spoke of the most important peer in the realm, the King's first cousin and her own brother-in-law. Thomas of Lancaster was of very high birth, second only to King Edward himself, and his sister was married to Margaret's brother, the King of France. Isabella, when she came to England, would call him her uncle. His marriage to Lincoln's only daughter would bring him, on Lincoln's death, two more earldoms. Margaret shuddered to think of the power which would fall into Thomas' incompetent hands on *that* day. She knew Thomas well enough, and she had known of the great affection her dead husband had had for him. Edward II's father had more than once expressed his private regret to her that Edward was his son and not Thomas. Thomas knew this, fed on it greedily, but had to swallow the bitter pill of the truth. Edward was now King, not Thomas.

Trumpets sounded a fanfare as the armour-clad knights urged their caparisoned mounts forwards to line up before the King's pavilion. The King himself came out to start the tournament.

Edward had seldom looked more handsome than he did this day. He was twenty-three and seemed everything a King should be. A small crown of jewelled gold lay against his brow, finding reflection in his curly golden hair.

Alice did not listen to his speech for his voice was quiet and did not carry to the ears of the multitude gathered around. She held in her hands a small green veil which she had worn as a child. It was one of the few things she had brought with her from Longmore. All the clothes she had worn as Robert's wife she had ordered to be burned, deciding to begin her new life completely afresh. She had sold some valuable pasture land to the Abbot of St. Peter's in Gloucester who had long coveted the acres. With the money she bought new clothing, ordered rich materials such as she had never worn before. Today she wore the first of her magnificent new gowns, discarding all pretence at grief for Robert.

The tight-fitting pale green velvet clung to her figure, widening into gentle folds only when it reached her hips. The neckline was high, with an embroidered collar of silver thread. The large, loose sleeves fell away from her elbows to reveal the sleeves of the silver undergown, buttoned from her wrist to her elbow. A loose cloak of dark green, trimmed with white fur lay over her shoulders, fastened across her throat by a silver buckle. A circlet of chased silver rested on her dark red hair, and looped through the circlet was a pale green veil, drawn tightly beneath her chin and over the silver above each ear. The trailing ends of the veil floated in the breeze. Her eyes blurred a little as she looked down at the small green veil twisting in her hands, the embroidered golden dragons shimmering in the watery sunlight.

She felt the atmosphere grow tense around her and glanced up from her lap. A breeze had carried the King's soft voice across the open field. "Well, Perrot, will you not carry your lady's token this day?"

Her eyes picked out Gaveston immediately, for the emerald green plumes which streamed from his helmet were longer than most, and the crest of a golden eagle glittered as his horse moved. He bowed stiffly, for the armour would not allow much movement.

He turned his great white destrier and approached the Queen's dais, and everyone assumed he would pass by to the next enclosure where his new wife sat with her ladies. But he stopped altogether in front of Alice.

"Your little veil, sweet lady! T'will make the finest token I might carry to victory upon this day."

She could not see his face which was hidden behind the visor of his helmet, but the Queen leaned forward angrily. "Piers! You make matters worse by this!" He glanced up at the Queen and Alice knew that he was smiling. His attention returned to the veil in Alice's lap.

The hum of conversation died away and a silence settled upon the crowd. What should she do? She looked up desperately at the hidden face. "Would you shame me, Sir?"

Another knight approached, his chestnut horse led by a page who struggled to control the animal's tossing head. Alice recognised the red and white of Warwick. "What manner of insult do you intend my nephew's widow, my Lord of Cornwall?" Guy's voice sounded oddly muffled by his helmet, but his edginess was apparent.

Alice felt a sudden desire to protect Gaveston from Warwick's spite. A foolish desire which would not be smothered. She stood, holding out the veil to the King's favourite. "My Lord of Warwick, do not hurry to my aid, although I thank you most kindly for your thoughts. The mistake was honestly made. My Lord of Cornwall mistook the colours of Longmore for his own. Now he dares not incur my wrath by admitting the error he has made." She smiled bravely, although her stomach churned.

Gaveston's mailed fingers closed over the veil and he urged his mount closer. Warwick's chestnut took an immediate dislike to the white destrier, and snapped its yellow teeth. The white horse laid its ears back, its mouth curling back to show its own teeth. "Warwick, I suggest you remove your savage brute from my vicinity, else the tournament will be ended before it has begun!" Gaveston's voice was smoothly reasonable.

Warwick snorted angrily, turning his horse away roughly, snatching the reins from the frightened hands of his page. The harness jingled as he returned across the field.

Gaveston leaned down to Alice. "So that I know I am completely forgiven for my 'mistake', will the mistress of Longmore tie her token about my arm with her own hand?"

Alice stretched up to him, taking the veil. His voice was quiet, that no-one else could hear. "What a strange little dragon from Gloucestershire, a dragon which leaps to the defence of so odious an eagle as myself!"

"Odious indeed! Twice you have caused me much embarrassment, I pray you do not cause a third occasion to arise!" She wished the armour was not there to protect his arm as she tugged roughly at the veil, tightening the knot. He was laughing as he rode away from her.

The moment of interest having passed, the noise and chatter broke out again. As Alice sat down, the Queen's hand was gentle on her shoulder. "Take no blame upon yourself, Lady Alice, the fault was entirely Piers'."

Beatrice leaned forward again. "What I cannot understand is how he can so insult his wife. She is the King's niece. Has he no sense?"

"Beatrice! Aymer would despair of you! The Countess of Cornwall cares nothing for her husband, and he nothing for her. He accepted the match for the prestige such a bride would bring him, and also to please my stepson. She has given her heart — and everything else from the tittle-tattle I hear — elsewhere. To Sir Hugh d'Audley to be precise."

Beatrice sat back, deflated. "D'Audley? A mere knight? And she the niece of the King of England! She shook her head at such behaviour. She turned to look sideways at the Countess of Cornwall.

Gaveston's wife was pretty enough, with her Plantagenet colouring, but she was spoiled by a continuous sulk which hardly ever left her mouth.

As they craned their necks to watch, a man in Warwick's colours bowed low before her. He was about Alice's age, with auburn hair, and not ill-looking. The sullen expression softened on the face of the King's niece and she smiled lovingly at him.

"There he is now!" Beatrice threatened to fall off her seat with excitement.

The Queen glanced quickly and then away, not wishing to be seen staring. "Aye, and see how the good Sir Hugh fair eats her hand! They have no discretion at all if even *I* can see what they are about."

Beatrice sat back suddenly as d'Audley turned in their direction. "Does she not fear her husband's reprisals?"

Silence fell upon them as d'Audley passed in front of them. Alice could not take her eyes from the man who was apparently making a cuckold of Gaveston. He crossed the field and entered Warwick's pavilion. Through the draped doorway she could see him quickly putting on armour, as he was to ride in the tournament.

"Reprisals? Piers?" The Queen stifled a laugh. "If he saw them abed together I doubt if he would care. I have no doubt that he treats her as she treats him!"

A jealous finger touched Alice's heart. She did not like to think of any woman enjoying Gaveston's embrace . . . Hot colour spread over her face at her own thoughts.

A lady curtsied before the Queen, making apologies for her late arrival. Alice knew her to be Arundel's young wife. She sat beside Alice, inclining her head briefly in acknowledgement of Alice's murmured greeting.

The herald was calling out the names of the knights and the opponents they had drawn. Alice's neighbour stiffened as her husband's name was called against that of Gaveston. Already Alice had heard that the King's favourite was renowned for his prowess on the field of tournament. His skill was well known, and he had yet to be bettered. It was yet one more reason why the English nobility hated him so; the Gascon squire could better them in the lists!

She looked at Arundel who was a blaze of scarlet and gold lions. He sat with apparent steadiness upon his mount, his handsome face hidden by his helmet.

Warwick's name was called against one of Gaveston's lesser knights, and the outcome of that struggle was known before the outset. On either side of Warwick sat two of his own knights. D'Audley was one, and Gareth was the other. Alice knew that it was Gareth, even though he was hidden from view, but there was only one man in England who rode as if he were part of his horse. The young Earl of Gloucester was one of Gaveston's associates today, and he apparently bore no grudge for the insult offered to his sister for he was close to his brother-in-law, talking animatedly, his arm waving around.

Trumpets sounded again and the opponents took up their places. The tournament seemed to start suddenly; one moment silence, then a fanfare and the thundering of hooves upon the hard earth. The harness and armour jingled exhilaratingly and Alice caught her breath as the two sides came together.

There came a gasp of dismay from Alice's side, for only one knight lay upon the ground as the sides drew away from one another. Edmund Fitzalan suffered the immense disgrace of being the lone casualty. To be the only one defeated was bad enough, but to have been unseated by the King's favourite was supremely galling. Never would Arundel forgive Piers Gaveston for this day's work. His wife glared fiercely at Alice, and Alice remembered then that it was the colours of Longmore which had helped unseat the Earl.

The sides were lining up again as the names were reshuffled. The Queen's cool voice came down to Alice. "This will prove mightily interesting for I hear that Sir Hugh d'Audley is drawn to face Cornwall. Now we shall see if Piers cares aught!"

Gloucester was still beside Gaveston, and Alice soon saw that *his* opponent was Gareth.

Before the fanfare for the second onslaught was sounded, the Earl of Cornwall suddenly urged his mount forward and slowly rode across the field towards the opposing line. The trumpeters put down their instruments and everyone watched, the knights controlling their impatient, excited mounts with difficulty. It was not to Sir Hugh d'Audley that Gaveston rode, but to Gareth. He called him forward and as they came close together, the Earl leaned over to hold the bridle of Gareth's horse. Their conversation was short and whispered, and everyone sat forward to try to hear, but to no avail. Gareth bowed stiffly as the conversation finished, turning in the saddle to call for a page who came running swiftly over the grass.

As the page took a message and then hurried to the King's dais, Gareth turned his horse's head and rode back to his position. Gaveston remained where he was for a moment, watching the young Welshman.

The herald rode out into the centre of the field and announced a change in the draw; now the Earl of Cornwall would ride against Sir Gareth ap Llewellyn, and the Earl of Gloucester against Sir Hugh d'Audley. Gareth moved his excitable mount around d'Audley's, and took up his new position opposite the King's favourite.

A ripple spread around the crowd. Why was this? Why did Cornwall decline to ride against d'Audley? Beatrice of Pembroke turned her head slyly to look at Gaveston's wife, who sat unmoving in her place, her pretty face a mask of embarrassment.

The Queen sniffed in disappointment. "How frustrating, I wonder why Piers was so intent upon avoiding d'Audley?"

The trumpets sounded yet again, and Alice had eyes for only two combatants as the two sides came together. The horses thundered towards one another, meeting with a tremendous clatter and crash. This time there were more casualties, one of whom was d'Audley, plucked from the saddle in a most ignominious fashion by his love's brother. Gaveston and Gareth both survived the joust. The Earl had the greater skill and experience, but Gareth's supreme horsemanship saved him from defeat.

The injuries sustained by those who rode for the barons were far greater than those upon the side of the King's favourite, and Alice saw how the barons rode close together, talking amongst themselves as they returned to take up their positions yet again.

The Queen turned in her seat to call a page to bring some wine, then she looked out over the lists again. "Piers is very foolhardy to thus rub in his superiority, for they will hate him all the more. But I must admit to finding his behaviour a little strange. He directs all his attention to this Sir Gareth ap Llewellyn and cares nothing for the rest of the tourney! I wonder what lies between those two to draw Piers so much?"

Alice wondered too, but she wondered also why the Queen did not seem to hate Gaveston. Why was it, when her late husband's wishes had been so flagrantly set aside in favour of the favourite, and when her niece was shortly to come to an English court reigned over by this handsome Gascon? "Why do you not hate him as the English barons do?" The question slipped out before discretion bade her keep silent.

The calm eyes rested on the upturned face before her and then Margaret waved her hand to dismiss her attendants to some distance away. Beatrice complained under her breath as she heaved herself up from her low seat, but she was soon chattering with the young

Countess of Arundel who had returned from seeing that her husband was not injured.

Margaret stared at Alice as if deciding how far to confide in her. "I find it most refreshing to speak with someone new, Lady Alice, someone with little knowledge or prejudice concerning the situation here. No, I do not hate Piers, because I understand him. At least, I think I understand him. My husband, whom I loved, was a hard, unbending man, and was wrong to seek to separate Edward from Piers. They were foolish young men, true, but not vicious or sadistic . . . words which could, I fear, have been applied to my lord." She paused. "With your unhappy experience of marriage with Warwick's nephew, you will suspect, I feel, that Piers does not share the unhappy aberration which touches my unfortunate stepson. I cannot be sure, of course, but I think that Edward has much to thank Piers for, for Piers protects him far more than we realise. I speak only of suspicions, you understand, but my instinct tells me that Piers Gaveston is a true man, a man who enjoys only the love of women. For the sake of my niece Isabella, I pray that my intuition tells me the truth."

Alice felt confused. "How can it make any difference to her? You say that the King has this . . . deviation . . . " Alice's face was hot with embarrassment at the trail this conversation was leading her on.

The Queen twisted a huge sapphire ring on her finger. "Lady Alice, my niece is a very beautiful young girl, very beautiful indeed, and her charm and innocence would surely win Edward's heart; if not entirely, then at least a little, for he is a kind man and would not hurt her. But if she must look to Piers Gaveston for her rival then I fear she will be unhappy . . . and alone. Look at him, Alice, look at him. If *he* be the King's lover then no woman on earth could steal Edward's heart from him."

Alice looked back at the armoured figure on its white horse. Gaveston had removed his helmet and was wiping his face. The black hair was damp with perspiration and his skin was streaked with dirt, but even so his enormous attraction could be seen. He saw her looking and raised his arm in salute. The tiny green veil fluttered in the breeze.

The herald called out the draw yet again, and Gareth's name was against that of the favourite for a second time. Alice knew instinctively that this was no accident, and that if Gareth should survive this next joust, then his

52

name would be drawn against Gaveston's time and time again.

The trumpets sounded and the two sides rode together. Once more Gareth held his balance as Gaveston's blunt jousting lance struck him squarely in the chest. He swayed dramatically to one side, but saved himself from the fall which would have meant defeat. Alice watched him miserably. Why was the Earl of Cornwall doing this? Gareth was so obviously less skilled, and was only a worthy opponent by virtue of his horsemanship.

The herald rode into the lists yet again, and this time his announcement brought hissing from the crowd, for the barons had elected to discontinue the tournament. It was obvious that they had no wish to be further humiliated by the hated favourite. The King's face was pink with pleasure at seeing them so uncomfortable, and all because of his Perrot.

Gareth turned his tired mount away, obeying Warwick's signal to retire, but Gaveston's voice cut loudly across the field. "*Our* business is unfinished, Llewellyn!"

A hush settled, even the King stood to watch Gareth's reaction. He halted his horse and turned awkwardly towards the green and gold figure on its white mount. "Dearly as I would wish to continue, my Lord of Cornwall, there is another whom I must obey before you!" Warwick was walking across the field towards him.

"Aye!" came Gaveston's sneering voice, "Aye, whom you must obey to the detriment and neglect of all else!" There was a curious anger in that voice, a world away from the soft, disciplined tones he normally used.

Everyone gasped, such a rude challenge must surely goad the Welshman into retaliation. Gareth's gauntlets stiffened visibly on his reins and he quite obviously asked Warwick's permission to continue. Warwick was reluctant, for he knew that to the world he, Warwick, would be personally bettered if Gareth was defeated. At length he agreed.

"What *is* all this?" The Queen was irritated for she so dearly wished to know what lay behind Gaveston's conduct.

Alice shook her head. "I do not know, Your Grace. As far as I knew Gareth had no dealings with the Earl of Cornwall."

"*Gareth?* Ah, so *you* know him do you?" The Queen's eyes gleamed as if she saw some secret revelation now.

"I have known him since I was a child, and was once betrothed to him."

The trumpets sounded, and Margaret was forced to leave the

tantalizing subject of Gareth and Alice. The two lone horses pounded towards one another, their hooves drumming on the earth. They met with a terrible ferocity, Gareth's fury having at last been aroused by the taunts. So very nearly he fell, and his arm was struck sharply by Gaveston's lance, but he held his seat. The King raised his hand to call a halt to the proceedings, for he began to fear that his Perrot was about to virtually murder one of Warwick's knights before the entire court. But his gentle voice went unheard by the Earl of Cornwall who was already wheeling his foaming mount around on its haunches to return towards the adversary. The speed of his attack left Gareth unguarded for that mere second in time, and the Earl's lance pushed him from his saddle and deposited him upon the ground.

Alice stood, her hands to her mouth as she saw Gareth lie there, winded. Gaveston turned his mount yet again and approached his defeated foe, his lance pointing down towards Gareth's heart. The chink of the blunt end upon the armour was plainly heard as he made a show of ending the fight completely, but he merely rode past and on to the King's dais.

In a frenzy Alice turned to the Queen. "I must go to him, Your Grace, he is wounded."

"Indeed you cannot, my Lady! Yours was the token which won the day and so you must remain here to receive the crown of flowers from the hands of the knight who carried it. Not to do so would be a dreadful breach of etiquette. Be seated!"

Slowly Alice sat down, watching Gareth being helped to his feet. His horse was already being led away. Hugh d'Audley had hurried out to his companion, and now removed Gareth's helmet. Gareth's face was white, but he smiled his thanks at d'Audley who helped him from the field. Briefly Gareth turned his head to where Alice sat.

Gaveston had removed his gauntlets and helmet and was reaching up to the King's dais to take the crown of flowers from Edward's hands. He rode across the field to the Queen's enclosure, bowing his head to Margaret before looking down at Alice.

His face was grimy and the beads of perspiration gleamed on his forehead, only to be brushed aside into a streaky black stain by his hand. The long dark hair was wet and clung to his face and neck. He held out the crown to her.

It was fashioned of fresh yew and the flowers were made of silver. She took it from his hands and placed it upon her head, and a cheer rose from around the field. He untied the green veil and pressed it to his lips before handing it to her. She took it with trembling fingers but could not meet his gaze. His action disturbed her.

She looked across the field to where a group of nobles gathered. There they were, the highest in the land, together united in their hatred: Lincoln, Warwick, Arundel and his insignificant brother-in-law Surrey. Even Gloucester was with them. Only the mighty Lancaster was absent, conspicuously so. Their surly resentment reached across the vacant field.

Seeing that she was not going to speak with him, Gaveston made to ride away, but she called him. "My Lord of Cornwall!" He returned, his face still. "As the lady whose token you wore this day, I take advantage of my position to bid you take care, take great care." Her fearful eyes wandered to the group of barons again.

"You offer me advice?" He was smiling.

"Aye, and 'tis good advice, Piers!" Queen Margaret stood. "Look at them, gathering like storm clouds over a mountain."

He turned his head. "Pah, it is merely the Black Dog howling in the pack! I make no note of them!"

"Then you are a fool, Sirrah!" The Queen turned and swept away, leaving Alice behind.

"Do you share that view, sweet Alice?" He was serious as he looked down at her.

"I have no view, my Lord, I know little of court affairs and cannot presume to state an opinion." She was unaccountably disturbed by him, and by the menacing threat those disgruntled barons presented to him.

"You are no ordinary woman, my Lady of Longmore. You stand apart, and this day I have saluted you." He put his hand across his chest, against his heart, and then rode away.

EIGHT

NOW she must go to Gareth. Alice hurried from the enclosure and across the muddy field, pausing only to

55

send a page scurrying to find Morvina and her casket of herbs.

Gareth shared Hugh d'Audley's pavilion, and d'Audley himself was attending to the unsightly bruise which blossomed brightly on the white skin of Gareth's arm near the shoulder.

D'Audley was older than Gareth, a thin man with sharp pale blue eyes. His complexion was ruddy, reaching to spots of red upon his high cheek bones, and his hair was auburn and straight. A soft brown beard curled from his chin, and a thick moustache hid his upper lip. He was dipping a cloth into a bowl of cold water as Alice entered, and now his hands stopped as he saw her.

Gareth turned his head, opening his eyes as he heard the rustling of her skirts. He looked at the crown of flowers on her head. "Alice, what are you doing *here?*"

"What indeed! Have you mistaken the pavilion, Madam?" Hugh's eyes were unwelcoming.

She ignored him and leaned over Gareth. "You knew that I would come, Gareth. I have sent for Morvina. She will not be long." Hugh leaned back, a smile on his lips, but his eyes were hard. She took the cloth from his hand, dipping it once more into the bowl of water. "Sir Hugh, have you no business of your own to attend to?"

He raised his eyebrows. "Would you have me forsake the proprieties and leave you alone?"

She disliked him, and made no attempt to conceal the fact. "From all accounts, Sir Hugh, you forsook the proprieties long ago!"

Gareth frowned. "Alice, guard your tongue."

"Sir Hugh has not sought to guard his since I came here, I see no reason to afford him the politeness he denies me!"

D'Audley stood, swallowing his anger as best he could. "Very well, Gareth, I shall take myself elsewhere." In a friendly fashion he pretended to push his fist into Gareth's cheek, before sauntering from the pavilion.

Alice glared after him. "What a very rude man."

Gareth sighed and leaned back. "You were rude yourself, Alice, and cannot fairly point an accusing finger at Hugh!"

Silently she pressed the cold cloth to the angry bruise, dabbing at it gently to take out the sting of pain. His eyes were closed again and she looked closely at him. Was it possible that she felt nothing for him now? She had dreamed of him for so long and yet now she realised that she had rushed to him now only out of a sense of duty. She had come as a loving sister would come to her brother.

His eyelids flickered and the green eyes stared up at her. "Alice, 'cariad', what a nest of hornets you have stirred up by your pretty presence at court."

"What do you mean?" Her hand stopped its dabbing.

"Don't you know? It was for *you* that the mighty Gaveston drove himself to such efforts today. He challenged me for *you*, my lovely, *you!* I bid you enjoy his caresses, no doubt he is as skilled with women as he is with men!"

She dabbed her hand sharply at the bruise and he winced. "I enjoy no man's caresses, Gareth ap Llewellyn, and you do me wrong to insinuate otherwise! You mistook his meaning, surely, for I doubt if he knew that you and I are acquainted."

He moved away from her hand, rubbing the bruise. "I can do without your ministrations, Alice!" He took a deep breath and reached for her other hand, holding it tightly. "Listen, 'cariad', he has made it his business to delve into your background, and he knows most of what there is to know. He disapproves of my past conduct where you are concerned, and today's events were a revelation of that disapproval. He singled me out for personal combat, and what he did had nothing to do with Hugh's attachment for the Countess of Cornwall. You under-estimate your charms, Alice, for it seems that you have ensnared the King's favourite no less. I must congratulate you."

Morvina hurried into the pavilion, her casket clutched under her arm, and Gareth lapsed into silence. Alice could not bear the heavy atmosphere of his hurt and unfavourable opinions any more, and handed the cloth to Morvina.

He saw that she was leaving and tightened his grip on her fingers. "Beware how you tread, Alice, for his days are surely numbered." His voice was not unkind now, and his deep love for her shone out from his tired eyes.

"Why? What do you know?" Her anxiety for Gaveston was sharp and intense.

"Only the murmurings of those who lost today. They are mighty men, made to look foolish and to feel small. Gaveston was the cause of their loss of face and they mean to be rid of him."

Her eyes showed the depth of her concern and Gareth's hand loosened upon her fingers. He turned his head away with the unhappy knowledge that she would once have shown such feeling for him.

She left the red and white pavilion, deep in thought. Dully she saw ahead of her, across the field, the green and gold of the Earl of

Cornwall's tent. Her steps took her close, drawn as if by a magnet, but then she stopped as common sense prevailed.

"Lady Alice?"

She started as a voice spoke next to her. "My Lord of Cornwall . . . " A blush stole over her face because she knew that he must have watched her progress towards his tent.

He was smiling. "You have been tardy in thanking me for carrying your token to victory today, but I will forgive you if you take a cup of wine with me." He did not wait for her to reply, but took her hand and led her into the green and gold depths of his pavilion.

The cool light inside was gentle and soothing as he led her to a rich couch. She sat and watched him as he loosened the drape which was pulled back across the entrance to the tent. As he did so, the drape swung across and hid the world outside from view. He turned back and went to pour two cups of wine.

He was transformed from the dirty, tired knight of an hour before into the brilliant courtier known to all. His hair was combed and shone in the moving light as the breeze took hold of the tent. The coat he wore was parti-coloured, being wine-red on the one side and indigo on the other, and the collar, cuffs and hem-line were embellished with silver embroidery. His black velvet shoes were very long and pointed, and his legs were encased in parti-coloured hose to match his coat.

He brought the wine to her. "Do you love him?" The question was abrupt, direct.

She shook her head. "Once I would have said 'yes'."

He put his hand to her cheek, and the touch of his fingers upon her skin seemed to burn her. She pulled away. "Why do you bother yourself with me, my Lord? Is it merely to re-assert your ascendancy over the rest of England's nobility? To show your wife that you care not a fig for her royal blood or her feelings? To prod Warwick in particular? Why choose me as your tool?"

"I am not using you, Alice, never that. Please do not think that of me."

"What else am I to believe?" She looked at his long fingers clasping the goblet of wine.

"Believe what you see in my eyes when I look at you. Believe that I want you more than I would wish to admit, and that today I fought a man I deemed unworthy even to breathe your name."

She put her goblet to her lips, but her hand was shaking too much.

He took the goblet from her and replaced it upon the table. "Will you admit to nothing, Alice?"

"Admit?" Her pulses were racing.

"Yes. You are concerned for me, you sought to warn me today." The dark brown eyes were warm as he looked. "You would deny me the comfort of knowing you love me?"

She blinked. "I do not love you!"

"Ah, but you will, Alice, you will." He put his hand to her chin and raised her face towards his own, kissing her lips gently. She had imagined herself to be in love with Gareth, but that small emotion was as nothing compared with the tumult of her feelings now. Her fingers crept up to his wrist, holding him tightly.

He took the crown of flowers from her head, and unwound the pale green scarf which was twisted around the chased silver headdress, and then took out the pins which secured the dark red hair in two bunches over her ears. The hair tumbled down, loose and free. He put his hands to her temples and ran his fingers through the hair, caressing it as if it were spun gold and priceless. Her whole body was stirring to him and she shivered as he put his lips to hers.

She leaned back on the couch as he pressed against her, putting her arms around him. There was no resistance she wished to offer as she drew him closer. Briefly she thought that the lips which kissed her now had been kissed so lovingly by the King himself . . . but the thought did not linger. Now he wanted *her*, he was *hers*; Alice gave her love completely.

When he lay beside her afterwards, he smiled up at the roof of the tent. Rain was falling outside and the pattering was loud upon the canvas. "I told you that you would love me, Alice."

"Are you always so sure?"

He leaned on one elbow over her. "It has not happened before that I have wanted a woman's love — her body, yes, but not her love. I have known many women, and possessed those I have wanted, but never before have I needed to know that I was loved." Her golden eyes studied his face, and he pushed her hair along the outlined pattern embroidered on the couch, arranging it precisely. "Is that not an admission from the Earl of Cornwall, Alice?"

She slipped her arms around his neck and pulled him close again. Was this gentle, loving Piers the same as that other with the sharp, cruel tongue who reigned over the King? He was so powerful in the land, so high and important, and yet he seemed so vulnerable.

His voice was muffled as he buried his face against her neck. "I can give you only my love, Alice, for I have a wife already . . . "

She closed her eyes. "Your love is all I want," she whispered.

"Will you be there when I need you? I do not mean merely to satisfy my lust for you, although as God is my Witness I have lust enough . . . " He smiled and then was serious, "I mean that you be there when I need you for yourself, your company, your presence. Do not go back to Longmore."

She shook her head. "I will be wherever you wish me to be."

They lay there quietly together for a while, until an unpleasant thought crossed Alice's mind. "What will the King say?"

He sat up. "Ned? He will be pleased for me." The smile faded from his face as he read her thoughts. "Sweetheart, I am not and never have been the King's lover. I have shared his bed for nought else but sleep." He stood, picking up his belt from where he had discarded it and drawing it around his waist.

She regretted that she had asked the question, for now he was a little withdrawn and angered. "Will I not remind him of Robert?"

The gentleness returned. "Robert is dead — the King has seen you many a time since he learned."

"But will he like me to be so close?" To *you*, my love, will he like me to be so close to *you?* The doubts were endless, nagging. Alice was torn by the wretchedness of her uncertainty. That kiss . . . the King had kissed him . . . She glanced at his finely drawn lips.

He did not seem to notice her quietness for he held out his hand to her. "Come, my love, you must tidy yourself. And do not worry about the King, he will be pleased for me. Shall I send a page for Morvina — that is your maid's name is it not?"

"Yes."

"Where may she be found?"

She swallowed. "She is in the pavilion of Sir Gareth ap Llewellyn — attending to his wound."

He raised an eyebrow, snapping his fingers to call the page.

NINE

IT was Christmas Eve and the excitement of the season was upon the court. The first Christmas of a new reign, and the festivities were to be grand.

Alice was in the Queen's chambers with the other ladies, attending to Margaret's robing for the banquet to be held in the great hall at Windsor. Her special task was to brush the Queen's hair, and it was almost the final part of the Queen's preparation, leaving only the small golden band to be placed over a loose flowing headdress of black. Margaret was in good spirits, humming as the ladies slipped the heavy black brocade gown over her shoulders. She laughed as Beatrice of Pembroke struggled in with a large oak log.

"Heaven forbid, Beatrice, you are not seeking to burn a yule log are you? It is a heathen superstition and not truly to be smiled upon at a Christian festival!"

Pembroke's wife pushed the log on to the glowing fire, and sparks shone red and bright, extinguishing on the hearth. "It may be a heathen superstition, Your Grace, but my mother always burned an oak log upon Christmas Eve, and I have always followed in a like fashion. It is a tradition, no more."

Alone in the corner, Alice sat waiting, the silver hairbrush in her hands. She stared down at the brush, turning it slowly so that the metal flashed in the light of the torch on the wall above her. On her shoulder a brooch glittered with fiery, blood-red rubies. Piers had given it to her as a Christmas gift, a circle of rubies to wear. It had been his mother's he had said. How she was filled with pride at being the owner of such a gift, not only because it was so valuable, but because he had given her something so dear to him.

Morvina had seen the brooch and her eyes had become strangely thoughtful. "Where did you come by such a . . . jewel . . . my Lady?" she had asked as she prepared Alice for her duties and for the evening's banquet.

"Piers gave it to me." His name slipped so easily from her lips now.

Morvina continued to button the tight sleeves of Alice's sapphire blue gown. "But it was not his."

Alice had looked sharply at the maid. "What makes you say that? Of course it was his to give!"

"That is not what I said, my Lady, I said that it was not his."

61

"Oh Morvina, you are so odd at times. No, he said that it had been his mother's."

A smile had crossed the maid's lips, a knowing smile. What thoughts lay behind it could only be guessed at.

The Queen spoke sharply to Alice, rousing her from her dreaming. "Lady Alice, am I to miss the banquet because you have not brushed my hair?"

Hastily, almost dropping the brush, Alice hurried across the room. The Countess of Arundel, holding the black headdress in her hands, smiled, pleased to see Alice's confusion. The Arundels had not forgiven or forgotten their humiliation at Wallingford at the beginning of the month.

She began to brush the Queen's hair, and Beatrice leaned forward to the table and picked up the polished metal mirror. "Your Grace, you are looking so much more well today, see?"

Alice could see her own reflection behind that of the Queen. With an exclamation, Margaret turned suddenly, standing so abruptly that Beatrice dropped the mirror. Margaret's eyes were on the ruby brooch. "Where did you get that?"

Alice's hand went immediately to hide the precious gift. "It . . . it was a gift, Your Grace, a Christmas gift."

"From whom?" Margaret was cold.

So silent had become the room that the fluttering of the flames of the torches could be heard, and the rich crackle of the yule log upon the fire. The Countess of Arundel waited eagerly, for it had soon become known that Alice was Gaveston's mistress.

There was no choice. "From the Earl of Cornwall, Your Grace."

The Countess of Arundel sucked in her breath with barely suppressed pleasure at this disclosure. Beatrice looked from the brooch, to Alice and then to the Queen. "Give it to me, Lady Alice," said the Queen, holding out her hand.

Alice shook her head, stepping back, and then Margaret's anger erupted. Without warning she reached out and ripped the brooch from Alice's shoulder. The blue velvet tore and the pin of the brooch snapped, but it was now in the Queen's tight grip. "Get you from my sight, my Lady, and do not return. The day has not yet come when *you* may wear the jewels of the royal family of France! Be gone!"

Alice turned and ran from the room. The French royal jewels? Surely not, Piers would not lie to her. He would not give her a gift which would be recognised by the Queen.

She ran to her own small rooms, closing the door behind her and leaning back against the wood. Morvina sat inside with her casket open before her. The herbs were tenderly laid out before her on a table, and strange little bottles accompanied them upon the rough surface. She looked up in surprise, seeing Alice's distraught face and the tear upon her shoulder.

"What has happened?" She stood, for once forgetting the herbs, some of which tumbled to the floor. A cat also fell to the floor from its resting place on her lap.

"The brooch . . . the Queen has taken it from me and said that it belongs to the royal family of France."

Morvina pushed Alice into a chair close to the brazier. "Indeed?"

Alice was almost weeping. "You were right when you said the brooch was not his. Oh, how could he lie to me, how could he put me in such a position!"

"Well, my Lady, either he lied to you . . . or the royal family of France are of the Old Religion." The words fell quietly into the room.

"The Old Religion?"

"Yes. That brooch was once worn by a High Priestess of my faith. The design is known to me, and apart from that I knew what it was when I touched it. If Queen Margaret thinks it belongs to her family, then she is mistaken. A resemblance to some other jewel maybe, but it is not what she believes it to be, most certainly not."

Alice stood, going to the small room where her wardrobe hung and staring blankly at the array of gowns which faced her. Morvina followed her, watching which one Alice touched to indicate her choice. "Morvina, is Piers . . . "

"One of us? I am not sure, I have spent but little time in his company." She took down the dull green gown which Alice's fingers lingered over, putting it down and beginning to take off her mistress' torn clothes. "I know one thing, however . . ." the dress slipped to the floor, " . . . his heart is not in your Christian masses, pomp and ceremony. I have watched and seen. He has a certain . . . disregard."

Alice did not want to believe this. "But he has a rosary and kneels to pray, he takes his Confession . . . "

"So could I, my Lady, the deception would be relatively simple. The Old Religion is not acceptable to you Christians, its ways are frowned upon . . . feared even. His intelligence is great, it must be

63

else he could not maintain his power over the King. Edward may love him deeply, but I doubt if his love would be so deep if the Earl of Cornwall were a fool."

The new gown felt cold, and Alice drew closer to the brazier, holding out her hands. She saw the small oak log lying on the top of the fire, and on the top of the log rested a charred, cold fragment of another log. "What is this?" She pointed to the tiny cold piece of wood.

"It is a yule log."

"I know that, I am referring to this old piece of wood." Her finger nudged the small sliver of oak from its place.

Morvina retrieved it immediately and replaced it upon the fresh log. "It is a piece of the yule log of last year, my Lady. We believe that to burn the old with the new is a good thing, a thing which brings luck and happiness. Your Church took our winter festival and called it Christmas, but your Jesus was not born in December. To us the action taken by the Church is an admission that it needs to keep to the festivals of the Old Religion, because my faith has such deep roots that the Church cannot shake free." Morvina smiled at the winking, flashing log, sniffing with pleasure at the wood-smoke. "The yule log is to help the sun re-kindle his light, for it is now the middle of winter and the sun is being re-born for the coming year. He needs all the help we can give him for such a great flame to burn anew . . . and so we burn yule logs to aid him."

Alice was unimpressed. "Surely a vain attempt at something which nature will perform for you. How can you believe such nonsense?"

The maid returned to the table and touched the bunches of dried herbs. "How can *you* believe that when you drink wine at your Christian ceremonies you are drinking the blood of your Jesus? To me, *that* is revolting. It is a matter of which faith you follow, is it not?"

Smiling, Alice reached out and touched the Welsh girl's hand. "Forgive me, I did not intend to sneer. It was unworthy of me."

Morvina returned the smile readily. "Are you going to him now?"

"Yes — well at least I shall go to him after the banquet. But he will want to know why I do not wear his gift."

"Tell him what happened. You are not to blame and he cannot be angry with you."

Alice went to the doorway, shivering as she left the warmth of the brazier behind. A thought took her. "Does Malcolm share your faith?"

The maid shook her head. "No, he disapproves greatly, but he does not interfere in any way, just as I do not interfere with his worship. We have an unspoken agreement not to speak of such things, for if we do then we argue. But if it worries you to think that the Earl of Cornwall may not be a Christian, then see what log is burning upon the fire in his rooms tonight. Many Christians burn yule logs, I know, but they will not burn a piece of the old log as well. Look and see."

Opening the door, Alice turned back to the maid. "I do not know if I wish to look, perhaps I would rather not know."

Morvina's slender fingers stroked the cat which leapt on to her lap again. "But if you love him, then you *must* know. You must know all about each other, for that is the essence of love."

The door closed behind Alice, and as she walked towards the great hall where the banquet was to be held she thought of Piers . . . and the King. If to know all about one another was the essence of love, then she had not sipped that essence as yet, for the doubts and unhappiness lingered.

TEN

THIS was not a happy evening for Alice. The banquet had been grand and everyone had celebrated to the full, but the festivities had turned sour for the heiress of Longmore.

Again and again Edward had shown to the world his great and deep love for Piers. They had sat together on a couch, the King's arm continuously about his favourite's shoulders, leaning closely, familiarly. Alice's heart had twisted with jealousy and uncertainty, but she dared show nothing. The Queen had manifestly shown her anger at Alice, by refusing to allow her to sit close, forcing the unhappy girl to sit well down the table. The Countess of Arundel was aglow with pleasure at Alice's plight.

But now she was slipping away from the hall to her lover. The King had left a long time since, as had Piers, and she had awaited an opportunity to leave unseen. She turned into the wide passageway which led past the King's apartments to Piers' beyond. There was surprisingly little noise, so little that the castle was eery in its silence. The great hall seemed a whole world away.

The torches were few and far between, casting unpleasant shadows upon the stone walls. Ahead of her a figure approached in the wavering light, and she was sure that it was Piers. Was that not the cloth-of-silver coat he had worn? She was about to call out to him when he turned abruptly into the King's apartments. She hurried forward, but her heart fell within her; if he was going to Edward . . .

She was upon the entrance to the royal apartments almost before she realised and inevitably she peeped around the curtains which were drawn back. There were no guards to be seen.

Inside the first of the rooms sat Walter Reynolds, Bishop of Worcester and Treasurer of England. He had been in Edward's employ for many years now and had been close to the King for longer even than Piers. Alice disliked the man intensely. Jesu, if the barons laid blame for Edward's weakness upon Piers, then they must surely be blind! This Reynolds was evil.

But it was Piers who held her attention now. He had walked across the otherwise empty room directly to the Bishop, reaching across the table and plucking the man almost over the top towards him.

"What evil are you up to, little fox? Eh, Reynard? I managed to get rid of Robert Beauchamp, but more's the pity I could not get rid of you too! Have you been procuring 'amusements' for him yet again? Answer me, you miserable wretch!" He shook Reynolds and she could hear the man's teeth rattle in his head. She was shocked that Piers could so lay hands upon a Bishop of Holy Church. Fascinated, and silent, she watched.

Piers' strong hands twisted the man's collar until it bit into his neck. "What have you been up to, sly fox?" His voice hissed.

Still Reynolds did not answer and was flung backwards across the table, knocking over everything which lay upon it. He sat there upon the floor, a vessel of ink dripping over his vestments, staring up his dislike and spite at the King's favourite.

Piers leaned forward, his voice dangerously quiet. "You know who has the real ascendancy over the King, the real power . . . it is not the fox but the eagle. If I find that you have been procuring again, undoing all my work, then you shall pay dearly little man."

Reynolds scrambled to his feet, his hands sliding on the pool of ink, and he ran past Piers and out into the passageway. He was so frightened that he did not see Alice.

Piers strode towards the inner rooms, throwing open the narrow door of Edward's bedchamber. Then he stood there, motionless, his hands upon his hips. Alice, unable to bear not to see, bowed to her womanly curiosity and moved to where she could peep into the King's private room.

Edward sat upon the richly-draped bed, his beautiful hair ruffled and his face flushed. His arm was around the slender figure of a youth who lay upon the bed, and the youth was naked.

Piers moved on into the room then, picking up the clothes which lay upon the rushes and flinging them contemptuously at the youth who grabbed at them and fled. Alice pressed back into the shadows as he hurried past, and again she was not seen.

When he had gone she looked again. Now, she thought, now I shall know. Piers was alone with Edward, and now she must surely see if her persistent doubts had any foundation.

Edward's flush had paled a little and he stood. He wore only a loose robe, tied at the waist, and she saw that his chest was covered with fine, fair hairs which curled softly against the white skin.

"Perrot?" His voice was hesitant.

"You imbecile! I have warned you endlessly about Reynolds, but still you persist in keeping him in your household! You deviate, Ned, but the deviation could so easily be conquered were you not that fox's tool! He feeds you these boys and you so willingly enter into these . . . these . . . " He broke off, taking a deep breath to calm his rage.

Edward was a little indignant. "They are not boys, Perrot, they . . . "

"Does it matter what they are? I had thought that Robert's death would bring an end to all this. You are King of England, Ned, and you must act thus! Be rid of Reynolds, that is my counsel, for by all the gods you employed him originally more because of his ability to produce plays than because of his Christian beliefs! He has led you into his foul ways and stinking sodomy! Be the man you really are!"

The King's hand rested upon the carved post of the bed, and his fingers nervously followed the outline of the carving. "Perrot, I regard you as my brother, my dear and most beloved brother, but do not deny me this pleasure. It is harmless."

"*Harmless?*" Piers rounded on him like a tiger, astounded that he could not see the way his path was taking him. As he turned he saw Alice for the first time, but he dared not let the moment slip

67

away from him, he must hold Edward's attention completely now. "Ned, the world may smile and turn a sightless eye towards a man who fornicates with many women. They will laugh and clap you on the back for the stallion you are! But a man who lecherously fawns upon other men is another matter! The world will not smile upon you then. Do you realise that it is believed you and I have such a relationship?"

"Perrot, I . . . " Edward was bemused. "Perrot, you are my brother . . . my brother . . . "

Piers put his hands on the broad shoulders. "In a few weeks, Ned, you are to marry a Princess of France. Put aside your low desires and take pleasure in so beautiful a wife, for I hear tell that her loveliness astounds all who see her."

Edward hung his head miserably. "I cannot love her, it was Robert I loved . . . "

The hands on his shoulders tightened their fierce grip. "A pox on Robert! You were persuaded into believing yourself in love with him by Reynolds . . . and by Robert himself. I tell you this, Ned, if you continue upon your present course then I shall leave you, I shall leave England and never return! You will be alone, Ned, alone but for Reynolds. Can you exist without my hand to stay you? Can you?" Briefly his eyes met Alice's and she saw how much he was hurting himself by this threat.

Edward clutched at him. "Do not leave me, Perrot, I beg of you! I will do anything you ask of me, but do not leave me."

"Then be rid of Reynolds."

The magnificent blue eyes winced a little. "I cannot throw him out, Perrot, for he is my friend. No, listen to me! He does this only because he believes I wish him to. He has been with me ever since I was little more than a child, and he is loyal to me. I return his loyalty with my own."

Piers nodded. "Very well, but be deaf to him. Do not listen to his wheedling! I shall know if you deceive me, Ned, for I always know."

Alice melted behind the doorway as the King turned towards her for the first time. "Perrot, I shall do as you say. I must have you beside me, you are everything. Oh Holy Mother, today has been surely my most miserable Christmas. Not only have I angered you, but my stepmother accuses me of giving the jewels of her dowry to you. Many jewels have I given you, but nothing which was hers!"

Piers waved his hand to dismiss the subject of Margaret's jewels.

"It is perhaps only her grief at such a happy time, being without your father at this festive season. But you, Ned, are celebrating your *last* Christmas alone. Think on that and be thankful for so lovely a bride."

"But I shall still need you. Promise me that you will not leave me." Edward slowly turned back.

Closing his eyes, Piers drew the King close, holding the golden head against his shoulder as if he held a child. "Uphold your promise to me and I shall never desert you! You know that I speak the truth."

He opened his eyes and stared over Edward's head to where Alice stood. Without a sound she turned and left the apartments.

In Piers' apartments she waited. His attendants knew her and admitted her without question. Her hands twisted and twisted in her lap as she sat there waiting for him. She knew that he was angry with her for what she had done. Her doubts had been dispelled by her eavesdropping, but instead she knew that she had placed herself in jeopardy with him.

Soon his light footsteps approached and he was there, angrily dismissing all his attendants and standing before her, his hands on his hips. "Well, my Lady of Longmore? Did you hear all you wished to hear?" There was a hardness in his voice which struck her like a blow.

"I . . . " she hesitated, floundered.

"You could have left your station before you eavesdropped upon so private a meeting. You listened to words which were for the ears of none but myself and the King! You slide downwards in my estimation, my Lady! Have you an excuse to offer me?"

And you have risen in mine, oh Piers, Piers . . . She shook her head miserably. "I did wrong. I eavesdropped as you say. There is nothing to be said in my defence. I offer no excuse." The tears were close. He was right, she had no right whatsoever to do what she had done. She had trespassed most deeply and his anger was justified. She turned her face to the wall, trying to hide the tears which poured down her stricken face as her misery overwhelmed her.

Such wretchedness confused him. He could not bear to see her thus and his hand reached out to brush away the tears. "Do not weep, my anger with you can only ever be a momentary thing, already it is fading."

"Forgive me . . . forgive me . . . "

He knelt beside her, his perplexed fingers wandering over her hair, and he tried to change the subject. "Come, sweetheart, why do you not wear the pin I gave you?"

She took a deep breath and stared at a huge boarhound which stretched and yawned on the hearth, its legs twitching as if in some deep dream. She told him of the Queen, and the brooch.

"So that is what Ned was speaking of. There must be some trinket which bears a resemblance. The Queen is mistaken my love, that brooch was my mother's. I will retrieve it, for it is all that I have which was hers."

He stood, going to the hearth and tossing fresh logs upon the fire. The hound stood, its tail wagging with pleasure at seeing its master. Alice's view of the fire was obscured.

There was something agitated about the manner with which he fussed around the fire. Alice went to him, sensing his concealed distress. "What was she like? Your mother?"

The dark brown eyes turned to her, steady and unwavering. "She was burned at the stake as a witch!"

ELEVEN

WITH the new year came the new Queen. Isabella of France stepped ashore at Dover into a realm where the nobility was now stirred up beyond endurance by the Earl of Cornwall.

The magnificent ship which bore the King and his new bride back to English soil was painted gold, and its sails were scarlet and blue. Long pennons streamed from the masts, the lion of England fluttering proudly in the stiff sea breeze. Seagulls screamed and wheeled overhead, their noise obliterating the fanfares which greeted the bride.

Edward had gone to France to wed, and in his absence had appointed the Earl of Cornwall as Regent. It was not to his powerful, discontented cousin, Thomas of Lancaster, that he granted this honour, but to his Gascon favourite. No other action could have brought about so speedy a turbulence in the hearts of those jealous barons. Piers had performed his duties with ease, managing the affairs of England with a facility which irritated the nobility still further. If only he could fail at something, then perhaps he could be borne; but it seemed that nothing was beyond his ability, and so their jealousy was intense. They despised him.

Isabella was worthy of her reputation. She was only sixteen and already her beauty had earned her the name 'the fairest of the fair'. Her eyes were a soft brown and her hair black. Her white skin was flawless, and enhanced by the magnificence of her ermine-trimmed robes. She was unmistakably a princess.

Alice smiled as she watched Isabella greet her aunt, Queen Margaret. The two embraced affectionately. Margaret's anger at Alice had evaporated. Piers had persuaded the King to bring out the real French brooch from the royal coffers, and Margaret had seen her mistake. Margaret was a kind-hearted woman, and had welcomed Alice back into her household readily.

All the nobility of England came to pay homage to the new Queen. The pomp and ceremony which Piers had arranged was splendid, and naturally impressed Isabella and her French entourage. There was one notable absentee from the welcoming multitude. Thomas Plantagenet, Earl of Lancaster, had not yet arrived.

The glittering procession moved slowly up towards Dover castle, encountering as it did so another procession approaching from the opposite direction. Thomas of Lancaster took his moment of glory in a gaudy fashion. He rode with his friend and constant companion, the Earl of Hereford, but Hereford's colours were completely swamped by the green and silver of Lancaster. Thomas himself was an insignificant man, being short and a little plump, with yellow hair and watery blue eyes. He took great care to greet Isabella as his niece, and Edward as his cousin, and he enquired loudly of his sister, the Queen of France. Edward's face did not reveal his feelings but Alice could guess at his anger. Piers' smile did not falter.

There was not room enough for the royal procession to pass Lancaster's. Piers smiled sweetly, his handsome face bearing a benign expression. "My Lords of Lancaster and Hereford, I pray that you turn yourselves around that we may all proceed. Do, pray, enter the castle first." The sarcasm was heavy.

Hereford's dark face stained with a dull embarrassment and his thick, bushy eyebrows almost met at a point over his nose as he frowned and lowered his glance to his horse's ears. Lancaster's pink face became even more pink, and he turned in the saddle to signal to his men to turn their mounts. And so it was that the green and silver of Thomas Plantagenet came into Dover Castle ahead of the royal banners of the King himself. Lancaster's grand arrival had been irretrievably spoilt by the sharp wit of the hated Gascon.

Edward sat with his new wife at the head of the great hall. He smiled at her, nodding and speaking often, but this revealed to Alice and Piers the truth of his dilemma. He found it hard to converse with Isabella, and virtually impossible to hide his true feelings. His glance strayed miserably to his Perrot.

Piers was anxious, he felt that Edward was about to act rashly or say something foolish which might reveal the truth. Again and again he drew the attention of the court to himself, showing his brilliant wit and amusing conversation. Isabella laughed with him, clapping her hands with pleasure at the entertainments he had arranged. The English nobles sat sullenly around until even she noticed their considerable lack of enthusiasm. She looked around the hall, and then more especially at her aunt Margaret. Margaret could not meet her niece's innocent eyes and looked away.

For the first time Alice saw a wariness creep into the bride's pretty face.

At last the banquet was done with, and the minstrels' playing took the onus away from Piers. Alice could sense his relief. He had worked desperately hard for Edward that evening.

From her place at the side of the hall, Alice watched him. She still did not know the truth about his faith. He would not speak further about his mother. She glanced down at the apricot-coloured folds of her velvet gown, and at the golden brocade of the tight-sleeved undergown. She had dressed finely today, for she wished to be as beautiful as was possible, because Piers' wife was with him. The Countess of Cornwall had to be present with her lord for all official occasions, and there were few more official than the welcoming of a new Queen to England.

"Your lover sparkles does he not, 'cariad'?"

She gasped. "Gareth!"

"Yes, *Gareth!* Had you forgotten my existence then?" He smiled mirthlessly.

"No." It was a lie and they both knew it. She had hardly given him a thought since Wallingford, and had not even sent to enquire if his arm was well.

Some dancing was beginning, with the King leading Isabella out to commence the measure. Piers led his wife out, noticing as he did so the glowering face of Sir Hugh d'Audley watching from the side of the Earl of Warwick.

"He cannot lead *you* out, can he Alice? He cannot acknowledge *you!*" Gareth's voice showed his own resentment.

"Do not be so crude, Gareth! If you cannot be pleasant I would rather not speak with you at all."

He bit his lip. "Very well, I will be pleasant. I know that you like to dance, and so I ask you to accompany me."

She did like to dance, but she did not wish to dance with Gareth when Piers was watching.

"Come on, 'cariad', it is only a dance. Let us put aside our differences in a measure together." He was dragging her unwilling figure forward.

She allowed him to lead her at last, knowing immediately that Piers' sharp glance had seen them. "I am *not* your 'sweetheart', Gareth, so please do not call me so."

He did not answer, for he too had seen the Earl of Cornwall's displeasure. He took a vast delight in taunting Piers who for once could do nothing. But his delight gave way to the pangs of jealousy once more as he came close to Alice in the dance. "Is he worth it, my love? Is he worth the torment?" They drew apart immediately, following the pattern of the dance.

Alice glanced quickly at Piers, so splendid in his black velvet coat. A golden belt studded with diamonds flashed at his waist as he moved. Oh yes, he was worth everything . . . everything, and more. "He is." She was so intent on saying her words as she came close to Gareth again, that she almost missed her steps.

"Have a care, Alice, such vehemence is not necessary — I believe you."

The dance took Alice past the Queen, and she felt Isabella's eyes upon her. So already the bride had been apprised of Alice's situation had she? The Countess of Cornwall looked stonily past Alice as they crossed one another's path — to her, Alice did not exist.

The dance was at an end and Gareth led Alice from the floor. Guy Beauchamp's figure barred their path for a moment. His wiry grey hair shone in the light of a nearby torch, and his dark grey eyes gleamed maliciously. His glance wandered insolently over Alice's body, and it was some time before he bowed with seeming grace.

"Lady Alice."

"My Lord of Warwick," Her voice was quiet, for he still frightened her.

Again his eyes wandered suggestively over her, lingering upon her breasts. "How good it is to see the colours of the House of Beauchamp so close to those of the House of Longmore — I pray the Gascon squire appreciates the piquancy of the situation."

Her face flamed with anger, but Gareth's fingers stole around her elbow, pressing a gentle warning. She had forgotten for a while that he was still in Warwick's service and that he wore Warwick's badge. Warwick stared at her, a nerve flickering over his temple, then he bowed again and moved away.

Gareth led her into the shadowy corner of the hall, slipping his arm about her waist to steady her. "Careful, my love, you must not let him see how he' affects you." She leaned against him, grateful for his strength.

He pushed her away softly, unable to bear her so close. His pulses were quickening as always they did when he was with her. He saw the flash of the diamonds around the Earl of Cornwall's waist. "I am thankful that he makes you happy, 'cariad', for I perceive that there is far more to Piers Gaveston than meets the eye. It was my own fault that I lost you, I have none to blame but myself. Let there be a friendship still between us, that is all I ask."

She smiled. "That is what I wish too, Gareth." He lifted her hand to his lips.

Morvina appeared suddenly, looking embarrassed. "My Lady, I am sent to fetch you from here."

Gareth scowled at his kinswoman. "Morvina, who dares to send you with such an order?"

The maid glanced at Alice, and she knew that it was Piers. Gareth realised in the same instant and turned sharply to where Piers was standing, watching. The two men eyed one another, but then Gareth turned back, already Alice had gone.

In her small room, Alice sat disconsolately. Outside the high sea wind howled around the castle, and vaguely she could hear the crash of the surf upon the distant beach. The seagulls were silent in the darkness of the night.

Morvina smiled. "You are better up here, my Lady, believe me."

"Why do you say that?"

"Because I have not been idly watching the festivities, I have moved around, listening, taking note. Queen Isabella is being made fully aware of the true situation in her husband's court. There are many only too willing to tell her, poor child. Her heart is hardened already towards your Piers, it took only a few words and the damage was done. She will believe anything of him now, the Countesses of Arundel and Lancaster have seen to that. Arundel's wife is making herself vastly sweet and gentle towards the bride, and has already asked Queen Margaret if she may enter Isabella's household. I saw too how kindly Isabella received the Countess of Cornwall, whom she now believes to be a kindred spirit, suffering at the hands of a perverted husband. The web is spinning fast, and you, my Lady, will most certainly be the object of much of Isabella's hatred."

Alice did not want to listen. It was so complicated, so horribly complicated and she knew only that it all spelled more danger for her reckless lover. Piers. "Did you see him tonight, Morvina? Was he not fine?" she murmured softly.

"I saw him. His task is growing with greater speed than he can handle, I fear."

Once again Alice's spirits plunged. Could Morvina speak of nothing but misery and foreboding? She changed the subject abruptly. "What of your Malcolm? Have you seen anything of him?"

"Oh, he has come to me from time to time. You have seen him yourself and not recognised him."

"Have I indeed? His impudence is immense."

"His impudence saved you . . . and me . . . from Warwick."

"So it did, Morvina, and I am grateful. Perhaps there is some way in which I may show my gratitude, for it is difficult to know how."

Morvina pursed her lips with pleasure, this was what she had been waiting for. "You could make him your steward at Longmore Castle, my Lady."

Alice stared. "Ask Malcolm Musard, the outlaw, to be my steward? You jest!"

"I do not, for there are many other names by which you could appoint him. Malcolm Musard is only one of many."

"Give me one then and I shall do as you wish, no doubt he will be a splendid steward. The table will not lack for provisions if *he* is in charge, although no doubt my neighbours will find their game strangely depleted suddenly."

Morvina ignored the taunt. "Call him Stephen Dunheved."

Alice sighed. "No doubt you have the parchment already penned and awaiting only my seal." She knew her maid well.

The Welsh girl smiled and nodded, hurrying to a chest and taking out a yellow document.

Alice took the parchment and placed it on the table where a

quill and ink rested. "Stephen Dunheved! Whatever made him choose that name?"

"It is his real name, my Lady."

"Then what decided him on Malcolm Musard?"

"That I do *not* know, my Lady."

TWELVE

THERE had been much anger and argument between the King and the nobility over the new Coronation oath. Edward had no desire to adopt the new clause which they pressed so. It would give them powers which they had no right to. The nobility were most anxious that he say this clause, for they knew that it would trap him in their power. If Edward should utter those words at his Coronation, then they would be in command and not he; for if they were united in their disapproval of his actions, he must by his own oath bow to their wishes.

Edward held out against them, seeing the danger presented, He saw the risk to Piers. But the decision was taken from him by an unexpected twist. Queen Isabella wasted no time in making her unhappiness known to her father, the King of France; and in retaliation the French King made known his intentions of signing an alliance with the Scots! He knew well enough that Edward would not be able to withstand such a union of two powerful enemies.

In March 1308, Edward acquiesced in the matter of the oath, and granted many gifts to his aggrieved young wife in order to silence her complaining for a while.

Piers was exposed at last to the vengeance of the English Earls. As one they made known their disapproval of the presence of the Earl of Cornwall. They shouted aloud that the King's father had banished him as an evil influence; they screamed that he was waxing fat on the backs of the English people and sending vast sums of money to his native Gascony. Their spite knew no end.

Edward shrank before them, refusing still to do their bidding in this one thing. He would not banish Piers Gaveston. No-one could see that the Earl of Cornwall was essential in upholding Edward Plantagenet.

The April sunshine shone warmly on a Westminster spinning with activity. Alice was uneasy. Piers had been absent since the early morning, attending a meeting of the Council. The events surrounding the Coronation oath had left Alice with this uneasiness whenever she was apart from him.

Beatrice of Pembroke was anxious as she stood before her. "Queen Margaret has sent me to bring you to her, Lady Alice." Beatrice kept her eyes downcast before Gaveston's mistress. Alice followed her.

Margaret was kind as she greeted her. "Well, my Lady, Westminster is in a fine state is it not?"

"Yes, I can hear that something is happening, but I do not know what, Your Grace."

Margaret dismissed all her attendants except for Beatrice of Pembroke. "I shall acquaint you then. Be seated I pray you, for I think you are to have a shock."

Fearfully Alice took a seat, her golden eyes wide as she stared at the French Queen.

"The nobles of England came to the King's Council today fully armed and demanding their way. They told the King that he must do as they wish because his Coronation oath binds him. My poor Edward can withstand them no more, and he has agreed that the Earl of Cornwall must be gone by the end of June. Two months, my Lady."

"No." Alice felt faint. Piers.

"Yes, Lady Alice, and what is more *your* name was brought into the matter. The Earl of Warwick publicly demanded that his nephew's widow be restrained from her immoral existence with the King's favourite; he claims that your actions are a continued and unbearable slight upon the name of his family! He also claimed that the King's niece, the Countess of Cornwall, was being treated with contempt. The other lords upheld him. You are not to go with Piers."

The Queen motioned to Beatrice to fetch a cup of wine, seeing Alice's distress. "Do not weep, for I have no doubt that Piers' banishment will be of short duration. Edward will not rest until he has his Perrot with him again."

The bowed red head was raised then. "And the Earls will not rest until they have rid the earth of Piers Gaveston."

Margaret's eyes slid away from the unhappy face. "The remedy lies in Piers' own hands. If he would only act with moderation, and restrain his tongue . . . "

"He does not act immoderately, Your Grace. He does not seek to manipulate the King to his own ends, he holds no position in the Council, and indeed has never wished to. The Earls are jealous of him because when he is there, Edward takes note of no-one else. Therein lies their true complaint. They feel ousted by one whose birth although noble is not so high as their own."

Margaret walked to a window which overlooked the wide courtyard of the rambling old palace. Westminster bristled with banners and badges today. The horsemen and foot-soldiers filled the courtyard, above them the colours of Lancaster, Warwick, Lincoln, Pembroke, Hereford, Arundel and Surrey. They were all there. United. One.

Beatrice was angered by Alice's words, perceiving a slur upon Aymer de Valence. "My Lady of Longmore, Gaveston is an upstart, and he weans the King away from his people and country. He has even accepted Queen Isabella's jewels as a gift from the King!"

Alice was horrified. "Is this true?"

Margaret nodded stiffly. "In this I am united with the Earls, my Lady. Such an insult to my niece cannot be accepted. For once Piers' greed has completely overcome his common sense. He has even worn a jewel or two in Isabella's presence."

It could not be so simple. Alice's brows drew together. She knew and loved Piers, and she knew that whatever he did was done with good reason. Her loyalty was not shaken.

Margaret waved Beatrice away. "Lady Alice, on an occasion last Christmas I caused you some considerable pain and embarrassment before your detractors by my accusations concerning yet another jewel. The jewel was not mine, but belonged to Piers and was his to give. I apologise to you, and now make amends as best I can. The Earl of Warwick demanded that you be returned to his keeping and protection, and the others would have agreed to this had I not interceded on your behalf. I pointed out that you had come to court to join my household and that I was pleased enough with you to wish to retain you in my service. Warwick was foiled because the others bowed to my request. You may not go with Piers into exile, but you are saved from Guy Beauchamp. Your place with me awaits you still."

Alice knelt gratefully before Margaret, taking up the ermine-

78

trimmed hemline of her gown and pressing it to her mouth. Not only was *she* saved from Warwick, but Longmore survived yet again.

"Piers, may I not at least come with you to Bristol?" Alice leaned her head against his shoulder as he lay on the bed. She pushed her toes against his foot and ran her fingers over the dark hairs on his bare chest. Tomorrow he would be gone.

The room was warm. The June weather was humid. His skin was damp.

He turned his head to look at her, and his dark hair dragged on the mattress. "You are saved from Warwick because of Queen Margaret. Her household remains here, and so you must remain with her." He touched her face with his finger.

"But I shall not see you again . . . "

"I go only to Ireland, sweetheart, it is not the end of the earth." His attempt to lighten her heart failed.

"It might as well be for the sea will separate us."

"Not for long."

She sat up eagerly. "You have discovered a way for me to join you?"

"No, I mean that I shall soon come back." He pulled her head down and kissed her lips.

She shivered, even in the summer night, and he drew her closer to his warmth. She stared unhappily at the single candle which burned upon a table. "But you will risk excommunication if you return, the Archbishop of Canterbury has said as much and has received the Pope's communication to prove so." Her eyes grew large in the half-light. Excommunication. There were few darker fates.

He raised his eyebrows, almost laughing. "That holds no fear for me." As she turned sharply towards him he added hastily: "What the Pope says today may just as easily be reversed tomorrow."

He reached out to prod a large spider which clung to the velvet drapes around the bed, drapes which were drawn back to allow some cool air to enter the bed. The huge emerald ring on his finger flashed like green fire and drew her attention. The ring had been part of Isabella's dowry.

She had never asked him about his strange acceptance of these gifts. "Piers, why did you take the Queen's jewels?"

"What do you believe, Alice?" His question caught her unawares.

"Me? I do not think it was merely a greed for more wealth, which is what the vast majority of people choose to believe."

79

The green fire sprang to life again as he moved his hand from the drapes to her breast, stroking the soft tender skin. Her pulses tingled. He leaned over and put his lips against her breast, kissing it, then he raised his head to look at her. "Isabella's father was in some way responsible for my mother's death. I know it but I cannot prove it. Isabella has proved herself in a short time to be her father's daughter in every respect. I accepted the gifts from Edward because of that."

She closed her eyes as he continued to stroke her. Her senses were reeling at his touch. She loved him so much, so very very much . . .

His hand paused for a moment. "Isabella condemns me unheard and whines to her father about the injustices done to her and about my evil influence. Sweet Heaven, if she only knew how I have striven to make matters easier for her, how I have pleaded and reasoned with the King . . . but no, I am condemned out of hand. Just as my mother was condemned."

She leaned over him, pressing her lips upon his to stifle his words. Soon he would be gone, but now . . . now . . .

He laughed as his arms slipped around her. "Sweet, sweet Alice, I think that when you have done I shall be too weary to sit my horse for a journey to Bristol."

THIRTEEN

A YEAR passed by. A whole year without Piers. Alice did not think she could have withstood the dragging of the hours for much longer, but now he was coming back. As he had said, so he was coming back.

No more would she have to travel with the knowledge that Warwick's men were following, no more would she have to walk the palaces and castles of Edward's court knowing that the Countess of Arundel watched her every move. How eagerly they had all awaited her first false move, one step towards Ireland and Warwick would have swooped upon her.

Edward had worked ceaselessly for his favourite's return. Just as Piers had said he would, the Pope had been persuaded to reverse the excommunication upon the Earl of Cornwall. Piers' absence had dimmed the memory of his sharp tongue, and one by one the Earls capitulated to Edward's promises and gifts. Only Warwick remained adamant that Gaveston should not come back. But now the coronation oath worked in reverse; the vast majority of the Earls were in agreement to the King's request. Word was at last sent to Ireland that the Earl of Cornwall could once again set foot in England.

The Earls were smug. They felt certain that Edward and Piers had learned their lesson and would tread carefully from now on. The King was doing their bidding meekly and the return of Perrot could not vastly alter this state of affairs.

Alice had seen how Reynolds had endeavoured to reassert himself over the King, but Edward had remained true to his promise. He turned Reynolds away time and time again when he came with his soft words, and tried desperately to live happily with Isabella. The little Queen was very pleased at Cornwall's absence, for she still believed that it was to Piers Gaveston that she had forfeited her husband's love.

But now he was coming back.

Alice travelled to Longmore in a warm, hot June a year after Piers had first gone to Ireland. How pleasant to be mistress of the castle, completely and undeniably. She was recognised as she travelled through the villages close to the castle, and the people had cheered loudly for her as her cavalcade rode through.

At the foot of Longmore's hill she passed through a small wood and then steadily rode up the long incline towards the castle itself. From the turrets streamed the green and gold of her family, and she reined her sweating palfrey in to gaze up with pleasure at her home.

From the left another party approached, a small party of horsemen. She turned her head to look at them, feeling a little shudder as she recognised Guy Beauchamp. He rode swiftly along the road from Berkeley, and had chosen the less used route across the marshes to Gloucester. He glanced up at Longmore, but rode past the winding track which led to the castle he coveted. Then he saw Alice.

The dust swirled in a cloud as he halted his party. She waved her hand before her face to clear away the dust. "My Lord of Warwick, your haste causes other users of the highway a little discomfort."

He smiled, steadying his shifting horse. She recognised it as the same bay charger he had ridden at Wallingford over a year before. "Do you return to Longmore then?"

"Do not pretend that you have no knowledge as to my activities, my Lord Earl, or could it be that somewhere your men have lost track of me?"

The dark eyes were bland. "I cannot imagine what you mean, Lady Alice."

Meticulously she brushed away the dust which settled on her blue cloak. "Well I shall inform you of my movements from this moment onwards. I ride now to Longmore, as you can see with your own two eyes, and tonight I entertain the Abbot of St. Peter's and Sir Thomas Berkeley. At the end of next month I shall return to Queen Margaret's household."

He took off his black velvet hat, slowly unwinding the long scarlet scarf which lay around his throat. He passed his fingers through the wiry grey hair and grinned at her. "What possible interest could I have in your movements now, Lady Alice? The Gascon returns, and so we shall all know then where to find you."

She gathered up the reins, feeling a hot colour staining her cheeks. "Indeed you will, my Lord, for I doubt if your fellow Earls will agree to your demands that I be kept away from him now. They have taken the King's gifts, their greed more than matches anything they could ever have accused the Earl of Cornwall of. But your hands are clean of accepting such gifts, are they not? Perhaps I will allow that you have at least the courage to follow your convictions to their conclusion."

"Oh I have, Lady Alice . . . to their absolute conclusion. Have no fear of that." He replaced his hat, and bowed his head politely as she rode on up the hill.

He watched her until her party had ridden into the confines of Longmore.

Sir Thomas Berkeley bit into the juicy, hot piece of mutton, laughing as he watched the antics of the Fool on the floor before him. He leaned towards Alice. "My Lady, your father often entertained me here at Longmore, and he was renowned for the variety of his table and the lavishness of his hospitality. Today I think you have awakened his memory."

"Thank you Sir Thomas, how very kind of you to say so." She smiled at him.

Sir Thomas' hair was receding at a rapid rate now, she thought, her eyes wandering over his thin, stooping figure. He even seemed to stoop over his food when he sat down.

From the minstrels' gallery came the sound of music, and the air was heavy with the smell of food. The evening was humid in the way which only the Severn valley seemed to have. No breath of a breeze stirred the leaves on the trees outside the castle, and inside even the thick stone walls did not bring a cool touch. It was as if the river had sapped the strength from the earth, drinking greedily and leaving a lifeless corpse behind. She picked up a feathered fan by its carved handle and tried to cool her face.

Her lilac brocade gown was the lightest she possessed, but even so the neckline was high, and the waist tightly-fitting. The wide sleeves were bordered with chestnut-coloured fur and the undergown was rust coloured. Her wrists felt damp at the closeness of the long sleeves, and as she rested her arm upon the table she felt the many buttons pressing upon her flesh.

Alice's lovely hair was held in two bunches on either side of her head by a golden net, and she wore no other headdress. The weather was too stifling to consider a veil or cap, and the good Sir Thomas and the Abbot could think as they wished, but she refused to bow her head beneath such fashions today. She looked very beautiful and drew the admiring glances of most of the men present. Even the plump Abbot smiled graciously at her.

Sir Thomas tossed the bone of the mutton to the rushes, and two hounds fell upon it savagely. They snapped and snarled over the bone until two of Alice's servants pulled them apart. Alice took another piece of meat from the platter and threw it a little way away. One of the hounds was released, and when it had taken the bone in its mouth the other was led to the second piece of meat. Contentedly they chewed and crunched.

Alice wanted to laugh, for she was reminded of Guy Beauchamp's savage greed for Longmore castle.

"I was visited yet again by your late husband's uncle today." Sir Thomas spoke as if he had heard her thoughts.

"I met the Earl myself as I returned to Longmore." She raised the fan again.

"He worries me immensely with his frequent journeys across my lands. Sometimes he stops at Berkeley, on other occasions he merely lets me become aware of his presence. I wish he would cease his pestering."

The Abbot held out his goblet to a page who lifted a jug of wine

83

to it. "The Earl of Warwick torments me in the same manner, Sir Thomas. I fear that Guy Beauchamp is at war with the world in general. He is an uneasy soul."

Berkeley snorted. "And so am I when I learn that he has been close to me yet again! He may be at war with the world, but it is a singularly unpleasant type of war which he wages. He plays upon the taut nerve and agitated hand. I know that what he wishes is for one of my men to overstep a line which only Beauchamp can see. Once that happens, then he has his excuse for riding into my territory and picking an open quarrel."

The Abbot's head bobbed up and down in agreement. "My sympathy goes out to you, Sir Thomas, for I realise that that is his game. He dares not harry the Church to the same extent, but even so his interference in my affairs is most displeasing. I dare not complain though, for he could make my existence miserable."

Alice smiled at her guests. "It seems, my Lords, that we are all three in some way united, for you both know only too well what *my* quarrel with the Earl of Warwick has become. He will not cease his work to regain Longmore."

Sir Thomas looked sideways at her. "But you are blessed with important friends, indeed *royal* friends, whereas we . . . " He threw down another bone.

"I promise you, Sir Thomas, and my Lord Abbot, that if at any time the Earl of Warwick does encroach too fiercely, then I will endeavour to influence my royal friends to aid you. I cannot give an assurance that they will act, but I will surely plead for you."

The Abbot beamed at her. "I thank you most heartily Lady Alice, for I know that you are a lady of your word, and as honest as your father was before you." A frown crossed his face. "But I could wish that you were a little more firm with the peasants upon your estates."

"My Lord?"

"Yes indeed. As I rode through the village of Longmore today I was displeased to see that they were busy cleaning out their houses and hanging green boughs and flowers from every nook."

Alice stared. "What grievance can you have at that?"

Sir Thomas grinned. "He complains because tonight is St. John's Eve, and he knows that cleansing houses and hanging garlands are heathen practices. Am I right, my Lord Abbot?"

"Quite so, Sir Thomas, quite so. Heathenish." Piously he touched the heavy gold cross which hung against his chest.

Alice found her glance straying to Morvina who sat demurely at the trestle. The maid looked up and met her mistress' gaze. Alice put down the fan. "My Lord Abbot, I do not see that I can command my people not to clean their homes."

"Nor I, Lady Alice." Sir Thomas turned to the Abbot. "The Church will forever be beating its head upon a rock by attempting to stifle the remnants of the Old Religion. I allow my people to continue as they wish . . . the old faith lingers, but each year I feel that more and more turn away from it."

The Abbot was cross. "I still say that if all the landowners and nobility were united in their work of stamping out these unholy celebrations, then we would shortly have a completely Christian realm."

Sir Thomas rolled his eyes at the smoky ceiling. "Then I suggest you begin your work in Gloucester, my Lord Abbot, for I have seen much activity in that fair city . . . some of it even in the shadow of St. Peter's itself!"

The Abbot crossed himself in horror, his eyes wide.

Malcolm Musard stood before Alice suddenly. She still found it difficult to remember that he was now known as Stephen Dunheved. "Master . . . Dunheved, I wish to thank you for the thought and consideration you put into this evening's banquet." She smiled.

He bowed, his laughing eyes glancing quickly at Morvina who could hardly conceal the mirth from her face. Would Alice and her guests have been so pleased had they known that Sir Thomas' woods had provided the venison and the Abbot's Cotswold lands the mutton for the feast? Stephen Dunheved had not forsaken his former activities.

The mention of the banquet brought back a pleasant expression on the face of the Abbot. "Indeed, indeed, Master Steward, I too must thank you. The venison and mutton were superb." He nodded benignly, stretching forward to take a venison joint from the table.

Stephen felt that he would burst with laughter, but he contained himself admirably. "Lady Alice, you have another guest. Sir Gareth ap Llewellyn awaits you."

"Llewellyn? Warwick's familiar!" Sir Thomas scowled.

Alice stood. "Pray bring him to us, Master Dunheved. Sir Thomas, I would remind you that Sir Gareth is not only Warwick's man but also my friend."

Berkeley nodded. "I take note of your gentle reminder, Lady Alice, but can only be suspicious when Warwick's creatures are presenting themselves close by." His pale eyes hardened as Gareth walked into the noisy hall.

Gareth strode up to the dais, bowing low over Alice's hand. "Alice, forgive my uninvited presence."

She smiled. "You are always welcome, Gareth, you know that. Please sit with me, for it is long since last we met." Long indeed, not since Isabella's arrival at Dover.

Gareth sat down, his green eyes surveying the hall. His eye fell upon Morvina who was sitting with Alice's new steward. He had recognised Stephen Dunheved as the outlaw who had rescued Alice from Warwick, but he was true to his word and remained silent. Now he looked at Alice. She was radiant, more lovely than he could imagine. He bit his lip, for he knew that it was Gaveston who wrought this change in her. It was Gaveston who was returning to this warm, loving Alice.

"What brings you here, Gareth?" She put a goblet into his hand.

"Warwick has decided to spend the night in Gloucester. I took the opportunity of visiting you."

The Abbot overheard. "Warwick stays on in Gloucester? God save us, what does *this* mean?"

Gareth smiled wickedly. "You may rest easy, my Lord Abbot, for the Earl seeks only to pleasure himself with some wench he has discovered. There are no devious plans afoot."

Sir Thomas hid a smile. He too enjoyed the chances which presented themselves of shocking the round Abbot.

Gareth drained his goblet, refusing more refreshment. "No Alice. Listen how well your minstrels play. Could it be that I may dance with you again, without being watched by jealous eyes?"

She blushed quickly at the oblique reference to Piers. "If you wish to dance Gareth, then I will be pleased to accompany you."

He took her hand and led her down from the dais. In the centre of the great hall was a space where others were already dancing. Gareth's heart twisted within him for love of Alice. She was so graceful, so infinitely precious to him . . . His love pricked him savagely and he was filled with an urge to hurt her suddenly. "You are eager for his return then? Are you so certain that he will want you back again?"

The smile became unhappy on Alice's lips. She looked at him reproachfully, "Why so sour, Gareth?"

"Perhaps the enforced exile has taught him moderation and

wariness. Perhaps he will not wish to renew so dangerous a relationship."

Her steps faltered, her doubts aroused, her uncertainty redoubling itself. What if he was right? What if Piers had changed?

Gareth despised himself for hurting her, but he could not help himself. She had hurt *him*, Jesu, she hurt him with every emotion which passed across her face, with every movement of her hands . . .

Now she stopped. "I think Gareth that I have no desire to dance. The pleasure is gone."

He still held her hand. "I think perhaps that I had best be gone too, Alice. My visit was ill-advised was it not?"

Her golden eyes met his gaze for a moment before she looked away. He bowed to her and then left the hall, passing Stephen as he did so.

The roguish Stephen turned to watch Gareth's hasty departure with surprise, then hurried to Alice. "My Lady, you have yet another visitor." He grinned broadly.

What on earth was he beaming so stupidly for? Alice sighed. "And who is it this time?"

"He gave no name but Peter, my Lady." Still the grin.

"Peter?" She repeated the name. It meant nothing to her. Peter. *Piers!* "Where is he?" Her eyes were bright with excitement as she realised.

Stephen's visits to London to see Morvina had left him in no doubt as to the identity of Longmore's latest visitor. "I took the liberty of taking him to your private apartments, my Lady. He had no wish to meet your guests."

Her flying feet took her from the hall. She had no thought of her guests, leaving the smiling Stephen to take over her duties. He took a deal of pleasure in sitting so openly with Sir Thomas Berkeley and the Abbot. If only they had known who he really was!

She could not walk sedately, she could not halt her flying feet. Nothing could keep her from him now. She pushed aside the curtains at the entrance to her rooms and her eager eyes sought him out.

He stood by the black, empty fireplace, and turned to look at her as she entered. "Alice." He murmured her name softly, the sound a caress.

"You did not forget me then?" The space between them was so small and yet she could not cross the room to him.

"Would I be here now if I had forgotten you . . . or if I sought

87

ever to forget you?" He held out his hands and the chasm vanished. She was in his arms.

The kiss was sweet, all the sweeter for the passing of a year in time. She felt weak with love for him.

"Easy, my love, another hour cannot hurt. You have guests to attend to." He stepped back from her, gazing at her. She knew well how to choose her colours, that lilac with her so beautiful hair . . . He put his hand to her cheek gently.

She put her fingers against his. "My guests have entertainment enough for them not to notice my absence. Another hour is more than I can bear now that I see you before me again."

He moved his hand to the nape of her neck, pulling her closer.

FOURTEEN

THE sun had long since set and the guests gone their separate ways. The castle was in silence.

Alice lay in Piers' embrace in the huge bed, and she gazed at the narrow window. A tiny breeze crept through that slit, but even so it was not enough to cool the air. The Severn valley was still tight in the grip of that breathlessness.

Morvina had been strangely eager to finish her duties that evening. Alice pondered on the maid's behaviour. Perhaps it was that she had some tryst with Stephen . . . Outside a strange light wavered in the darkness, casting a glow on the dull stone of the window. Alice sat up, staring at the hesitant glow.

She was about to slip from the bed to look more closely, when a movement by the doorway froze her where she was. A dark cloaked figure slid over the rushes to the bed. She recognised Morvina.

The maid reached out and shook Piers' shoulder. His eyes opened.

"It is time, my Lord." Morvina's voice was calm.

Alice looked at him. "What is all this?"

"Be calm, sweetheart." He took her hand and squeezed it.

"But why . . ."

He swung himself off the bed, standing naked in the tiny light of the single candle before stooping to pick up his clothes. He accepted Morvina's presence without comment.

"It is St. John's Eve, my Lady." Morvina smiled shyly at her mistress, bending to pick up Piers' belt and hand it to him. A flash of white was revealed beneath her dark cloak.

"You are of Morvina's faith then, Piers." It was a statement of fact, not a question.

He paused to fasten the belt around his narrow waist, then came to her. "I am my mother's son, Alice. Forgive me my deception, but I cannot deny my beliefs. Shall you come with us?" His eyes were warm as he looked down at her.

She did not know what to do. She wanted to be with him, to share everything with him. But could she forsake the Church for him?

He kissed her gently. "Just *be* there, my love. I ask no more of you than that. Watch, but you do not have to take part. I would like you to share a little of my faith, for if you never see then how can you judge?"

"Hurry, it will soon be midnight, we have not long." Morvina's voice was urgent.

Alice slipped from the bed. She must go with him. She must.

Morvina helped her into a gown. There was no time to prepare the long red hair. "Tonight is very special to us, my Lady, for St. John's Eve is our festival of water, and this time there will be a bore. What power can that mean? A bore on St. John's Eve." The excitement quivered in the soft voice.

Close to the river's edge, not far upstream from the hill of Longmore, there was a great gathering. The rowing boats at Stonebench had been dragged up on to the banks, and the cottages were in darkness. Alice shivered as she thought of Robert's coffin lying in the murky depths, so close, and yet so very far away.

Faces she had known all her life were revealed to her in the moonlight, and in the light of the St. John's Fires which burned around. People she had believed to be of the Christian faith, gathered here to worship the old gods, the old faith of centuries before Christ.

She stood alone amongst some small willows, and her fingers held her rosary tightly. The wavering light of the fires cast a weird aura upon the whole scene. Morvina was obviously of great

89

importance to everyone here, even Piers bowed before her. The Earl of Cornwall on his knees to Alice's maid!

The smoke from the fires fled upwards, straight and true, for there was not breeze enough to drive it in any other direction. The heat from the fires seemed trapped by Longmore's hill. Perspiration dampened Alice's hot forehead.

Strange music filled the heavy air, music played upon the pipes by Bedith, the cobbler who had rowed them across the river on the night when Robert's coffin had slid over the edge of the stone bench. Bedith, whose nimble old fingers had made the very slippers she now wore. She pushed her foot forward and looked down at the dainty, embroidered slipper. All this was not possible, it was a dream. Her fingers moved over the rosary.

Morvina took off her dark cloak and Alice saw that she wore beneath a robe of white, long and flowing, and on her shoulder was pinned a ruby brooch so very like that other which Piers had given her. Could Morvina then claim to be a high priestess of her faith? Had Piers' mother been like this?

All those present were seated upon the ground now, in a huge circle, and Morvina took her place in the centre. Alice stared at Piers. He sat facing her, with his eyes closed, and his lips moved to the unfamiliar words which they all murmured.

The pipes played faster now, and Morvina began to dance to the rhythm. The white robe floated around her, and she moved with such beauty and intricacy that Alice was held spellbound. The weird music was intoxicating. Alice, who so loved to dance, found herself wanting to dance with the twisting, turning figure in white.

So suddenly the music stopped. Morvina stood on the very edge of the bank and a silence fell upon them all. Only the vague rustling of the willows disturbed the deep silence, and the crackling of the fires. Far away, on May Hill above the Forest of Dean, Alice could see fires burning. St. John's Fires. She glanced behind and saw the line of the Cotswolds alight with flames as those of the Old Religion gathered in their numbers to celebrate.

But the silence was deafening as she turned back to look at the circle before her. Then she heard it. Distant at first but growing ever stronger with each passing second. A gurgling, splashing, hurrying noise as the bore approached. She could see nothing but the silently moving black waters, but by straining her eyes she saw at last the white, frothing wave as it crashed upstream towards them. The moon settled its silver light upon the Severn.

Alice had seen larger bores than this, but at night, and in such circumstances, she became aware of the strength and power of nature as she had never before been aware. The bore was almost upon them, sliding up the bank as the river swung around the bend towards Stonebench. The banks closed in, narrowing the path of the wave, and with a great noise it hit the ledge of stone, tossing up spray and foam high into the air. Alice felt small droplets of water fall upon her face as she sheltered amongst the trees.

A sound almost like a groan escaped from the lips of those seated in the circle. Morvina still stood on the lip of the river. Her white robes were soaked and clung to her small figure, but she had not moved.

The bore was gone on its way, rushing upstream towards Gloucester. The level of the river had risen steeply and now it flowed back upon itself in an uncanny way.

Alice wanted to run then. She was afraid. She could feel the unseen power of the Old Religion reaching out to her, calling her from the past.

The moment was broken by the pipes of Bedith as he began to play once more. She closed her eyes, counting her rosary over and over again.

"You are all right, sweetheart?" Piers stood by her.

He was a stranger. She could not shake off her dread and nameless fear. He understood. "What you can accept for Morvina you cannot accept for me?"

His voice was so normal, so well remembered and utterly loved. "I *want* to, oh how I want to!" Her thoughts were jumbled, scattered.

He slipped his arm around her waist, lying his cheek against her hair. "My faith need not touch yours, nor yours mine, Alice. Here, in this part of England, the Old Religion flourishes and is recognised. Here I have no need to pretend for I am with others who share my belief. We do no evil, sweetheart, we do not practise the black arts. Is that what you fear?" He smiled.

She shook her head, still hiding her face against his chest. "No, I am afraid because of the effect this has all had upon me. My own faith has been shaken a little and I am afraid."

He tightened his arm around her. "Poor Alice, I had not expected that."

She looked up at him. "When Morvina danced, I wanted to be with her, I was excited by the music, and overwhelmed by the

91

atmosphere which pervades everything. Oh Piers, what a weapon this would be in the hands of your enemies. What if Warwick should discover . . . "

Unexpectedly he laughed. "Warwick? Alice, the noble Sir Guy shares my religion. Why else do you imagine he seeks to be in Gloucester tonight? It is not as he has told Gareth. Like me, Beauchamp knows that he is safe here, safe to follow his beliefs. I am secure from Warwick's attention in this respect, Alice, believe me."

He bent his head and kissed her, and she returned the kiss. Even tonight's events could not alienate her. Her love was as firm and strong as ever, and she recognised the fact.

FIFTEEN

ALICE sat down in her rooms at Westminster and sighed with relief. "Ah, Morvina, my first days back at court have wearied me immensely." She pulled off her slippers and wriggled her cramped toes. Jesu, but the Queen had been demanding today; Alice had hurried all over the palace on this and that errand, and now that her duties were over for the day she looked forward to a rest.

Morvina raised her eyebrows. "It is not the Queen's demands which have wearied you, but weeks spent in reunion with the Earl of Cornwall!"

Alice glared at her. "You are impudent!"

Morvina's lips closed, but her eyes showed her ill-concealed amusement.

Alice tried to continue her frown but could not. She laughed. "You are right, Morvina, you are right! I have slept but little of late." No shadow of her disquiet at discovering Piers to be of the Old Religion crossed her mind now. She could think only of her love for him and her great joy at being with him again. Nothing else mattered.

The curtains were dragged roughly aside and Alice stood in fear. "My Lord of Warwick, how dare you enter here!"

"Be done with such words, my Lady, for your presence is

required elsewhere!" He moved his head to indicate that she should follow him.

"Where do you take me?" A small note of fear crept into her voice.

"Do not worry, Lady Alice, your presence is needed at a meeting. Nothing more." He stood back further and she saw that he was accompanied by some of his retainers. She had no choice. As she walked past him, Morvina's lithe figure slid back silently into the shadows, melting from sight.

She followed Warwick's men through the lesser frequented passageways of the palace, down steps and across rooms, until they came to a closed door. It was opened and inside she saw a long table around which sat many of England's Earls. Lancaster, Pembroke, Arundel and Lincoln, as well as other noblemen she did not know so well. She seated herself in a chair which Aymer de Valence drew for her. Her heart was thundering in her breast.

Warwick began to speak, and it was upon her association with Piers that he dwelt. Again and again he referred to the insult she caused his family. The Earls shuffled their feet occasionally, but they heard him out. When he finished the plump Earl of Lincoln stood. "I will not remain here for such foolishness! Warwick, if you call me again for such a contemptuous reason, I swear I will lay my hands around your neck!" He stamped from the room, stiff with fury.

Warwick crashed his fist down upon the table and Alice flinched. "I say, my Lords, that my nephew's widow shall not be permitted to cohabit with the Earl of Cornwall!" He almost spat out Piers' name, so deep was his hatred.

She felt her face suffusing a bright red with embarrassment that her affairs should be so bruited before these men. What right had they . . .

"Guy, why are you so set upon this? I cannot see that we must be dragged here for a meeting merely to discuss Gaveston's mistress." Thomas Plantagenet stretched his arms above his head, yawning. He did not like matters to be brought down on to such a level. They had the King where they wanted him, why bother about who graced the Gascon's bed at nights?

Beauchamp's lips curled back. They were all weak! Spineless! He was so enmeshed in his desire to regain Longmore and defeat Alice, that reason was blotted out. They had all eagerly accepted the King's gifts and promises, they had all gone back on their word. He ignored the warning which picked at his common sense. "My nephew's honour . . ."

"By the Rood, Warwick, you begin to vex me!" Lancaster stood suddenly, frowning. "Your nephew *had* no honour! Robert Beauchamp's name does not come into this at all. You merely use him as an excuse. Now, let this meeting be closed before more is said which will later be regretted."

Warwick worried at the subject, like the boarhounds at Longmore. Indeed, he almost growled. "Gaveston should not have been allowed to return, he should have remained in Ireland — further if possible!"

"We cannot agree entirely with you as yet. Cornwall has only been back a short while. If he behaves himself then we can have no grievance against him. You know that well enough. Your personal affairs enter too greatly into this, Guy." Lancaster used Warwick's forename gently, striving again to maintain a balance of calm in the rising temperature of the room.

"He will not have changed, the Gascon squire will be as grasping as ever he was! Then what will come about, eh? Answer me that!"

Pembroke eased his angular frame from his chair. "That is yet another matter, a bridge to cross over when the road arrives there — not before! Now we digress from the original reason, as I understood it, for your calling us to this meeting. I fail to see that the Lady Alice's affairs have any connection whatsoever with us. She is a widow, entitled to conduct her life as she sees fit. What is more, she is in the household of Queen Margaret and therefore answerable only to the Queen. I begin to suspect, Warwick, that your interest in the lady shows in rather an unsavoury light."

"What do you mean by that?" Warwick's grey eyes were hard.

Pembroke sighed, flicking the oversleeve of his coat against the back of his chair. "I will put it as plainly as you like, Warwick! I think you are jealous! You would like the lady to adorn *your* couch and not Gaveston's."

Silence fell upon the room, and Alice looked from one angry face to another. Warwick straightened. "Retract those words, Pembroke!" His voice was a hiss, like a snake.

"I will not!" Pembroke's own anger was roused now. "I speak only what *must* be in the mind of every man here!" A murmur of agreement greeted these words, and Lancaster picked up his cloak and began to fasten it.

Even the handsome face of Arundel showed a disapproval of Warwick's conduct. He regretted that he could not thwart Gaveston's life, and at the same time thwart Alice, for he had not yet forgotten Wallingford, but even he could not openly support Warwick in this — it was too obvious.

"My Lords, you have finished with me?" Alice stood, the fear of earlier evaporating as she saw Warwick's position deteriorating.

Lancaster nodded abruptly. "I think you may assume so, Madam." His contempt for the woman who loved the King's favourite showed plainly on his rotund pink face.

The door opened and Piers stood there. He gazed around the room slowly, his hands on his hips, then he stepped up to the table, his crimson velvet coat a bright splash of colour in the sombre room. What goes on here, my Lords?" His voice was dangerously quiet.

Pembroke's breath escaped between his lips in an unhappy sigh. Warwick's foolish behaviour would bring Cornwall's wrath down upon them all. "Merely a misunderstanding, my Lord of Cornwall, a misunderstanding."

"I think not, my good Aymer. I do not like to think that my affairs and the affairs of the Lady Alice are being discussed without my knowledge or consent. Who called this meeting?" His dark brown eyes wandered slowly over each face before him, coming to rest finally upon Warwick. "Ah . . . Earl Guy! I need look no further, I think!"

Lancaster stepped hastily between them. "The matter is ended, Gaveston, leave it be!" He was worried as he saw the hardness in Piers' stare.

"I think not, Lancaster, I think not!" Piers turned to Alice, holding out his hand, then he glanced again at Warwick. "Matters will never be ended between us, Warwick, our differences are too great save in one respect."

"Such talk does no good." Pembroke spoke up quickly, fearing that a challenge was about to be issued.

Piers smiled unexpectedly, his great charm exerting its influence upon all but Warwick. "Do not fear *my* hasty tongue, my Lords. Beauchamp understands my meaning well enough, but even if he does not I doubt greatly if he will ask me to explain further."

Alice saw from the corner of her eye that Morvina had slipped into the room and was standing next to Warwick's cloak. Something puzzled her about her maid's attitude, but she could see nothing untoward. Warwick walked slowly to his cloak, putting his hand out. His face was white at Piers' words, at the subtle implication that he had something to hide. There was only one thing which he concealed so carefully, and that was his faith. His eyes were haunted by the shock of discovering his secret to be known, and he glanced at Morvina's motionless figure. The ruby pin gleamed on her shoulder. The ancient gods reached out towards him suddenly.

He grasped his cloak, crying out as something unpleasant ran over his fingers. The cloak dropped to the floor and he stepped back from it, terror exuding from every pore. Morvina's foot moved quickly, so quickly that the movement must not have been seen. Alice saw the exchange of looks between her maid and Piers.

"What is it?" Lancaster was startled.

"A spider, a huge black spider . . ."

Lancaster was thoroughly exasperated then. "I'faith Beauchamp, you call yourself a man and yet cry out like a child when a spider is in your cloak. I see no great beast running about the floor." All eyes were on the floor then, but there was nothing to be seen.

The Earls left, murmuring amongst themselves. Warwick hesitated only a second before following them, leaving his cloak behind. At the door he turned, looking not at Piers, or Alice, but at the silent, menacing Morvina. The door closed behind him and they heard his footsteps hurrying away.

A nervous laugh welled up in Alice's throat. "What was all that about?" She licked her dry lips.

Piers was looking at Morvina. "That was a great risk to take before non-believers."

"Warwick believes, and that is what matters. There was no spider to see."

Alice leaned forward. "What have you done?"

Morvina bent down and took off her slipper, turning it over so that Alice could see the squashed form of an enormous black spider. She shuddered as the maid went to the empty brazier and scraped the remains off against the blackened iron. "Warwick was warned tonight, in the manner of our religion. The spider is a symbol he recognises as meaning danger to himself. If he chooses to ignore it, then he must take the eventual consequences."

Alice contained the urge to cross herself. "What consequences?"

"You need not concern yourself with that, my Lady, suffice it that just as your Church deals with its heretics, then we too have ways of dealing with those who displease us." Morvina's eyes were fathomless.

Alice pulled Piers around to face her. "Be done with all this, my dearest love." She was afraid for him.

He smiled, lifting her fingers to his mouth. "I cannot, sweetheart, any more than you could have done with your God."

She bowed her head.

SIXTEEN

ALICE'S fears for Piers were justified, but it had nothing to do with religion when the time came. It was the King himself who escalated matters, for his unhappy deviation was threatening to come to the fore again. Reynolds' persuasive tongue was eating away at Edward's resolve. Isabella's anger at Gaveston's return had shattered the delicate web of friendship she had begun to enjoy with her husband. As Edward struggled with himself, so Piers was forced to assume his previous place. He dominated everyone and Edward openly leaned upon him. Whispers about the King and his favourite were resumed as Edward constantly took Piers with him in public. The Earls were affronted again, and the downward spiral began to twist.

It took only a few more months for matters to reach a dangerous point. Piers drew attention away from Edward as often as possible, succeeding grandly in bringing about exactly the same situation as had preceded his exile to Ireland. The Earls directed all their hatred and spite towards the Earl of Cornwall. So offended were they that many refused to attend Council meetings called by the King because Piers was present. But Edward refused to dismiss Piers . . . and Piers refused to go anyway.

Edward sat miserably staring at the slow flames which licked around the logs of the fire. It was only early September but the autumn chill had come early this year. Fourteen months had passed since Piers had returned from Ireland, fourteen months of constant struggle with his discontented nobility.

Alice and Piers were the only other occupants of the room. Piers poured some wine, forcing a cheerfulness he did not feel. "Come, Ned, drink up and let us have a smile."

Edward took the cup, his fingers touching Piers' for a moment.

He must always be able to touch the man he loved so much, needed so desperately. Alice watched silently. She should hate this weakling King, for he was destroying Piers. Each caress meant more spite for the favourite. But Alice could not hate Edward. He was kind, soft-hearted, and friendly, and his gentleness towards Alice was constant, Edward Plantagenet might be weak and perverted, but he was steadfast in his friendships and in return earned the devotion of many. She could understand only too well why Piers strove so endlessly to help him.

The King gulped the wine without savouring its flavour. "If I do not do something to'please them then they will surely invoke that accursed coronation oath once more and I will be forced into banishing you, Perrot. What can I do?" The blue eyes gazed up at Piers.

The dark brown eyes smiled down at him reassuringly, but Alice knew the disquiet which filled Piers. He could see that soon he would no longer be able to protect Edward. His task was impossible and he was being forced to acknowledge to himself that even he could not carry Edward's weaknesses for much longer.

Alice put down the book which lay unopened in her hands. Something which she had heard Piers say came to her. "Your Grace, there is one thing which would perhaps mollify them. A resumption of the war with Scotland."

Edward smiled at her, holding out his hand and pulling her close. "Sweet Lady Alice, your common sense defeats us all!" He kissed her forehead, squeezing her fingers in a most unregal fashion. He was, she thought suddenly, more suited as a country gentleman than as a King of England. Fate had cast him in a miserably wrong role for his nature.

She returned the handclasp, bowing her head to hide the easy tears which came to her eyes. For Edward Plantagenet she would have risked her life, just as Piers Gaveston was surely risking his.

The expedition against Scotland was arranged speedily, and Edward marched north leaving the trustworthy Earl of Lincoln to look after matters in England. But the discontented nobility still argued and became more and more surly. Many of them did not accompany the King, choosing instead to remain on their estates in a state of unarmed rebellion.

The winter passed uneventfully, with Edward conducting many attacks upon the border lands of Scotland. Early in the new year came a disastrous setback for the King. Lincoln died. The capable 'Burstbelly', with his calming influence and moderate views, left behind him a son-in-law who inherited the greatest fortune and most extensive estates ever possessed by a nobleman. Thomas Plantagenet, Earl of Lancaster, became immediately the focal point of the barons' activities, they looked inevitably to him for leadership. The incompetent, unscrupulous Thomas saw at last his chance of greatness, and his closest friend and ally was the ruthless, calculating Earl of Warwick.

Edward must some time come face to face with his cousin, and the time came when Lancaster did homage for his father-in-law's earldoms. Thomas rode northwards in July, inflated with his own sense of importance, and installed himself at Haggerston Castle, just south of the Scottish border. There he stubbornly remained, refusing to cross into Scotland to meet Edward. Edward was at Berwick, on Scottish soil, and he too refused to cross the border to meet his cousin.

Thomas waited, confident that Edward must capitulate, for the King must tread carefully with this new, influential Lancaster. Eventually Edward gave in, and with a small group of friends he rode southwards towards Haggerston to meet his cousin and to receive his homage.

Haggerston seemed to teem with green and silver banners, and Lancaster's men were at every corner of the town. The castle itself was a rough, strong tower, built to withstand raids from the Scots. Thomas Plantagenet took over the town completely.

Alice had followed him to Haggerston. She had been released from her duties by Queen Margaret, who now found her a little of an embarrassment. Alice knew that if she followed Lancaster, she would eventually find Edward, and to find Edward was to find Piers. She was accompanied by Stephen Dunheved and many of his men from Gloucestershire, and they took the smaller tracks towards the border country, leaving a single scout to follow the Earl closely and report his position. Two days after Thomas' magnificent arrival in the town, his friend Warwick joined him.

Stephen decided to hide in the woodlands south of the town and await the outcome of events. Daily he and Alice rode into Haggerston, wearing heavy winter cloaks and riding poor ponies, for neither wished to be recognised by the two English Earls. It was easy enough to gain entry into the castle, and their presence was not questioned at all. Once Alice came face to face with Guy Beauchamp, but he did not glance at her as he passed by.

Then at last, early on the morning of the fifth day, one of Lancaster's men rode swiftly into the town bringing the news that the King was approaching. Alice and Stephen hid at the rear of the hall, unnoticed, and awaited Edward's arrival.

Thomas prepared himself grandly for this occasion. He dressed himself finely, bedecking his short figure with jewels, including a pin of the fleur-de-lis of France — just to gently remind Edward of his connection with the royal family of France.

The weary party which rode in from Berwick bore little resemblance to the King of England's former splendour. Edward had ridden overnight through foul weather, he was tired, irritable, and in no mood to bandy words with his pompous cousin.

Edward went immediately into the great hall, sitting abruptly in a chair close to the roaring fire and snapping his fingers at a page to bring ale. Piers was with him, and Alice saw that his face was pale and drawn. Edward's foot tapped the floor impatiently. Lancaster was taking his time.

Into the hall swept Thomas of Lancaster, glittering and brilliant in a coat of blue velvet. He marched elegantly towards Edward, bowing low and with needless extravagance.

Edward was provoked. "My Lord Earl, do you think perhaps that we should exchange places, for I vow that your splendour is royal indeed!"

Lancaster had not expected Edward to attack so swiftly, and he glanced nervously at the impassive face of Guy Beauchamp. Beauchamp could stare only at Piers, hating and despising. Piers perceived the stony gaze and raised his eyebrows, lifting his cup of wine in salute and then drinking. Warwick's face twisted with anger, and Piers smiled at the success of his silent taunting. Thomas regained his equilibrium. "I came dressed in a manner which I deem correct for such an occasion, Your Grace."

"And I come fresh from battle against the Scots and so am dressed likewise in a manner to suit the occasion!" Edward was scathing.

Thomas gritted his teeth at the ungentle reminder that he and his rebel Earls had refused to join the King's army. No, he would *not* be placed in the wrong, he was Thomas Plantagenet, the greatest magnate in the land . . . Edward had only himself . . . and Gaveston . . . to blame for the present state of affairs. Lancaster's immense pride reasserted itself firmly and he scornfully glanced at Piers.

Edward could not bear such impertinence. Piers was not to be treated so disdainfully! "My Lord of Lancaster, you show a sad lack of manners in failing to acknowledge the presence of the Earl of Cornwall."

Thomas' overweening pride carried him resolutely onwards. "I will not salute a man who has no right to such an earldom!"

A gasp went around the room and Alice's hand went to her mouth. Piers did not flinch, or react in any way. He made no movement at all.

Edward stood, tossing the dregs of his cup into the flames. "Indeed? Then you are sadly at fault, *cousin*. The Earldom of Cornwall was mine to give as I saw fit, or do you now challenge my right to do even that?"

Lancaster hesitated. There was danger in this simmering rage of Edward's. "Nay, Your Grace, I do not challenge . . . "

"Then acknowledge the Earl of Cornwall!"

"No." The answer was clipped, immovable.

Piers' lips parted slightly and he stared down at his cup. Alice could see that he struggled to know what action to take, but Edward took all chance away from him. "Then you may be gone from my presence, my Lord. Rudeness begets rudeness." He held out his cup for more ale and a trembling page carried the heavy jug to him.

Lancaster felt the strength of his position, felt the silent support of Guy Beauchamp, and all the other Earls still in the south of England. He felt the same surge of self-importance that had consumed him when Edward's father had professed a wish that Thomas had been his heir instead of Edward . . . "But I think not, Your Grace, for I am come northwards on affairs other than my own. I am come to beg you to return to London to attend a council meeting."

"Beg? Your attitude smacks not of begging!" Edward's hands shook with the force of his Plantagenet rage. His angry eye fell upon the silent, smug Warwick. "So, you have brought the black dog with you!"

Nothing could have provoked Lancaster more than hearing one of Piers' expressions upon the King's lips. "Yes, the Earl of Warwick is with me, Your Grace. You are asked to ride south . . . alone!"

"Why alone?" Piers spoke for the first time, and his gentle tone was a marked contrast to the quick-tempered voices of the others.

Lancaster looked at him coolly. "Because otherwise there can be no meeting, Gaveston! Your presence is a considerable stumbling-block."

Edward shrugged. "Then there can be no council meeting. If you wish me to do your bidding in this, then I shall do so on my own terms." He prepared to be a true, stubborn Plantagenet, and Thomas, although he bore the same name, was no match for him.

Piers touched the King's arm. "Ned," he said softly, "This will achieve nothing. Go with them."

Edward stared at him. "But who is King, Perrot — the barons or I?"

"You are King, Ned, the anointed ruler of this land. Know this and act accordingly."

Edward continued to stare at him. The moments passed and then he wheeled about to face Lancaster. "Very well! I shall go south and the Earl of Cornwall shall remain here. But he shall hold Bamburgh Castle for me." Bamburgh was a vast and mighty fortress by the sea, and Edward knew that Piers would be safe there.

Lancaster raised his shoulders briefly to show his indifference. It did not matter to him where Gaveston was, so long as he was not with the King. Warwick, however, was displeased. He could have rid the world of the Gascon squire, given a chance here in these wild desolated acres of the border . . . but not if the walls of Bamburgh protected him.

For once Edward read Warwick's thoughts precisely. "Perrot, you will ride now for Bamburgh. I will leave with my Lords of Lancaster *and* Warwick in the morning!"

A nerve twitched at Warwick's temple, but he said nothing.

Piers bowed and prepared to leave straight away. He called for fresh horses, and food and drink for the few men who accompanied him. So small a force to protect him on the miles between Haggerston and Bamburgh. Alice's heart dropped when she saw how very few they were. She held Stephen's arm. "I think it is time to disturb our camp in the woods, Stephen. I shall wait on the road to Bamburgh, but I want you and all your men to be at the very edge of the town on the same road. As soon as Piers leaves the castle. I want you to position yourself with him. Do not show your face to anyone but Piers himself, he will recognise you for certain, but there is no need to acquaint anyone else with your identity."

Stephen nodded and slipped away, hurrying out through the

narrow doorway and into the cold air outside. Shortly afterwards Alice followed him, and her heart almost halted within her as she saw Gareth and Hugh d'Audley coming towards her. They both stood aside for her to pass, and neither one recognised her. Once outside she hurried to where her pony awaited, mounting with difficulty in her cumbersome skirts, and turning the animal's head towards the south.

An hour later Stephen approached the outskirts of the town with his large force. The noise of their arrival inevitably drew attention, and Edward came outside with Piers who was now ready to depart. Lancaster and Warwick came too, and Warwick's face changed absurdly as he saw the many horsemen who awaited. Who were they?

The wind blew gustily through the town, bringing the summer rain of Scotland's mountains. Stephen put up his hand to hold his hood over his face, but the wind was swifter. It seized the hood playfully, puffing it backwards to reveal his face to all who looked. Warwick recognised Alice's steward. If his heart had dwelled upon a plan to murder Piers Gaveston, then that plan was now cast aside. There would be far too many obstacles.

Piers mounted and with his few friends rode towards Stephen, raising his hand in salute. "Well, Master Dunheved, you are welcome indeed. Alice . . . "

"Awaits you further on, my Lord."

And wait she did, shivering with cold and fear for Piers. She smiled with relief at seeing him ride beside Stephen.

He leaned over from his large horse to touch her hand as she held it out to him.

"Well," he murmured, "The dragon rescues the eagle yet again." His fingers closed tightly over hers.

SEVENTEEN

THE gale blew in fiercely from the North Sea, howling around the rocks of the Farne Islands and beating gustily upon the high stone walls of Bamburgh. The low outline of Hoiy Island was barely visible through the spray-filled air which whirled and spun across the

103

sands at low tide. The seagulls screamed their excitement to the heavens as the waves crashed upon the lonely shore where none stirred. The fishing boats were beached, and the people of that wild coastline waited for nature to calm the storm.

Inside the castle, the torches flickered brightly upon the warm room, casting a soft glow upon the colourful tapestries which bedecked the walls. A fire crackled in the brazier and a greyhound stretched in its sleep as close to the warmth as possible. It was hard to remember that outside the storm raged on. A draught of air sucked through the castle, sharply reminding Alice and Morvina as the torches flared and the brazier suddenly shone with a red brightness.

Morvina was pleased to be with her mistress again, and she smiled as she brushed the lustrous red hair until it seemed almost to match the firelight. The brush hissed richly through the beautiful tresses, a satisfying, soothing sound.

But Alice was not soothed. Her hands twisted in her lap, fingering a golden chain and lingering over the pendant of brilliant enamel. She gazed at the beautiful ornament. "Morvina, I am not certain that . . ." Her voice died away as quickly as it had come, and she bit her lip.

The maid's busy hands paused in their work. "My Lady, if your Christian heart is too fearful . . ."

"No!" Alice spoke almost too quickly. No, she was not fearful . . . not exactly fearful . . . She *wanted* to be there, she *wanted* to celebrate the new year of his religion with Piers. Hallowe'en, Morvina called it. The thirty-first of October, which to Alice was the Eve of All Saint's Day. The enamel pendant was warm now from her touch.

It had been five months since Edward and Piers had parted company at Haggerston. She had been with Piers at Bamburgh for five happy months; happy for herself, enjoying his company, his love, his closeness, seeing Piers as he truly was. There was nothing false about him, nothing untrustworthy or cynical. Her love for him deepened, grew warmer, and seemed to engulf her entirely. Now, away from court life, she could know finally that it was not Gaveston the King's favourite, the brilliant Earl of Cornwall, whom she loved, but Gaveston the man.

But danger seemed to cleave ever closer. Throughout the five months they had received intermittent word of events in London. Time and again Piers had requested Edward to send for him, but on each occasion Edward refused. He feared greatly for his friend's safety, and knew that Bamburgh offered greater security than London. The Earls had grown strong and their demands were great. They formed themselves into one large group and called themselves the Lords Ordainers, but what they wished to ordain wrankled bitterly with Edward. His coronation oath, that unhappy oath, now weighed heavily against him once more, and he was forced eventually to agree to their demands; all that is, except one, the final one. He refused to exile Piers yet again.

The enamel pendant caught the torchlight, flashing a brilliant azure shaft across her white fingers and vanishing swiftly into oblivion in the dull blue velvet of her gown. Alice glanced at a table where a parchment letter lay where Piers had tossed it. Edward's seal moved slightly in the heat from the brazier close by. That very day they had heard from the King that the Earls were threatening to resort to force in their efforts to be rid of Piers. They promised civil war if he did not capitulate in this one thing. He had refused yet again, and so matters stood at the moment.

The gale outside moved the drape which had been drawn across the narrow window and Alice glanced at the rippling cloth, seeming to hear the sound of the sea outside. The draught sucked through the fortress again, extinguishing a taper which stood upon the table where Edward's letter lay. The scent of wax hung in the air, heavy and acrid. The sea offered safety. Oh Piers, take my advice, my heartfelt advice, and flee the land. Leave England behind. But she knew he would not, for he had given Edward his word that he would always remain with him, and so he would abide by that word.

Unhappiness settled over her in a solemn cloak, her spirits low. Morvina sensed the thoughts which wandered through her mistress' bowed head and she tried to bring a lighter vein. "Tonight is very special to us, I think that it will interest you, my Lady." The soothing brush renewed its industry.

Alice seized at the offered change of mood. "Why do you celebrate the new year now instead of on the first of January?"

"To us the old year is now dead. The harvest has been gathered, the leaves have fallen from the trees, and all waits in readiness for spring. If the old year is dead then so the new year must begin, and tonight we celebrate with a great bonfire."

Alice laughed suddenly. "In this weather?"

Morvina turned her head towards the moving curtain over the window. "The storm will quieten within the half hour, my Lady. I feel it. The bonfire will kindle well enough. Tonight also we welcome into our midst the souls of our dead who wish to shelter by the warmth of the fire for one night. And we must protect them as they shelter from the evils of witches and sorcerers who fly the skies on Hallowe'en seeking to capture those long-dead souls. Fire warms, and fire protects."

Alice turned over the pendant, a smile touching her lips. "You speak so eloquently of your faith, Morvina, so eloquently indeed that I find my interest waxing again."

The maid put down the silver brush and picked up the circular padded headdress. A chain of gold was wound around the padded brocade, and the tiny links winked in the warm light trembling as Morvina placed the circlet upon Alice's head. She took a long mustard-coloured scarf and looped it over the circlet above Alice's ear, passing it tightly beneath her chin and then looping it once more above the other ear. Now the headdress was held firmly in place, and the wispy scarf was free to move. fluttering and streaming behind Alice as she stood.

Morvina reached out and plucked at the scarf so that it fell correctly. "We of the Old Religion are as old as time itself. We survive your Christianity, and we shall always survive. Who is to say which are the true beliefs?"

Alice crouched down to stroke the sleeping greyhound, her heavy skirts disturbing the grey ashes by the brazier. "Yes, who is to say . . . " She stood, her eyes bright with excitement as the forthcoming celebrations were remembered. "Shall we go now?"

Morvina and Alice slipped through the quiet castle. They were not leaving by the main entrance, but by the postern gate which was on the north-west side. Piers was waiting for them there.

The maid looked disappointed for he was alone. "Stephen?"

Piers' dark brown eyes were gentle. "He would not come, Morvina, and nothing I could say would change his mind. He is more than a little angry with us, I fear."

"He always is. I think it is because he is afraid." The maid slowly opened the small, heavy door, and the gale rushed wildly in at them. The steps which led down from the postern were steep, and Alice held tightly on to Piers' hand.

They slipped away from the castle, out into the stormy night where the salt spray already tasted upon Alice's parted lips. The mustard scarf streamed from her head, flapping audibly. She was glad that her winter gown was warm. The castle upon its rocky cliff was soon behind them, a vague black shadow filling the skies to the south. The path wound its way past the cottages of the town of Bamburgh and on over the sand dunes towards Budle Bay. The wiry seagrass was bent almost flat by the gale which streamed in over the sea. The distant waves crashed upon the wet endless shore.

A small rowing boat was drawn up at the edge of Budle Bay, and Piers rowed them across the narrow strip of water. The gale lessened dramatically as they slowly crossed the shallow water to the other side. When they reached the opposite shore the storm had diminished to no more than a strong breeze. The seagulls were silent, gone for the night to their unseen resting places, and the vast expanse of Ross Back sands awaited them.

Bamburgh was invisible in the night as their feet sank into the pliable sand. The scent of seaweed was strong and heady, and they seemed so alone in the immense emptiness of that shoreline, that Alice gasped as the sand suddenly sloped away into a hollow. There, in the hollow, a huge crowd waited.

The knowledge of Morvina's presence had spread far and wide, and those of the old faith had gathered to celebrate Hallowe'en at the side of so high a priestess.

Morvina took off her cloak and Alice saw again the long white robes, grey-pearl in the darkness. A great unlit bonfire stood in the hollow, quickly built since daylight had gone. Daylight meant prying eyes, and perhaps telltale lips to speak of what the prying eyes had seen.

Alice held Piers' hand still. Now she felt a guilt creep over her, a guilt at so nearly participating in the strange rites which were about to commence. May God forgive me . . .

Two sticks of dry oak were brought and given into Morvina's hands. All torches were extinguished now and complete darkness engulfed them all. Low clouds scudded across the heavens, parting occasionally to allow a watery moonlight to struggle into being. Morvina began to rub the oak twigs together, and Alice could hear the sound above the noise of wind and sea.

It seemed a long time before the fire was kindled and a small finger of smoke was snatched away by the breeze. Oiled torches were brought swiftly and lighted from the precious oak fire. Soon the bonfire was ablaze, crackling loudly and shifting occasionally in the swift stream of air from the unseen sea. The smoke poured inland, sweet and perfumed to the nostrils of those who believed. The bonfire was not unwilling to burn, even after the dampening it had received from the storm.

There was no dancing around this fire, for tonight the dead were to be welcomed and the occasion was solemn. After a while Morvina called to some men who hurried forward and picked up burning sticks from the fire and tossed them high into the air. They whined in the darkness, sparks showering on the upturned faces of those who stood close.

"Why do they do this?" Alice's fingers tightened around Piers'.

He smiled in the darkness and kissed her forehead. "To fend off sorcerers who fly the night skies. The flames of the oak are death to them. Our faith is akin to yours in this, my love, for we too fear and despise witches who follow the black arts and worship only the Devil."

Now everyone was throwing small pebbles into the heart of the fire. Piers took one from his purse, turning to Alice as he threw it. "Come, throw a pebble."

"What does it mean?" She was doubtful.

"By looking in the ashes of the fire in the morning, Morvina will be able to see who will die within the next year. If a pebble is cracked or harmed in any way, then the owner of that pebble will come to grief."

"How can you tell whose pebble it is?"

"They are all marked." He bent to the sand and picked up a small white pebble which lay close to her feet. "Here, take this one. We shall know it is yours because it is not marked."

Alice had taken the pebble and thrown it almost before she realised that she had entered into the Hallowe'en rites. She closed her eyes tightly as the pebble struck the glowing heart of the fire. Sparks rose, gyrating in the breeze, and the pebble sank into the depths of the bonfire.

Shortly afterwards the gathering broke up. The bonfire was almost spent and now glinted redly upon the burnt sand.

They returned through the night to Bamburgh, slipping quietly into the castle through the postern as the drawbridge was lowered noisily to allow entry to a messenger from the King.

Morvina had changed from her white robes and wore a simple grey gown when Piers entered Alice's rooms. His face was white, his eyes worried.

"What is it?" Alice stood quickly, her fear rising sharply.

"We have come full circle, Alice, and once more I am banished from England. The Earls have forced Edward into agreeing to their final ordinance by coming to him fully armed and speaking loudly of civil war. He dare not allow war to break out."

She watched his face, seeing the tired lines which marked his handsomeness. His dark hair curled tightly after the salt air of the shore, and she wanted, nay longed, to touch the springy curls. He smiled at her. "I am expected to be out of the country by sunset tomorrow! Do they think I have sprouted wings? To be at Dover within the day is impossible."

"And what of me?" Alice's voice was small, frightened.

He walked over to her, taking her hands and pulling her close. "Edward warns in the letter that Warwick has once again demanded that you be separated from me. The Earls have agreed — I suspect to silence him rather than to uphold their belief in his reasons. However, Warwick is sending his men northwards to detain you."

"I will not give myself into Guy Beauchamp's keeping!"

Piers stood back from her, glancing at Morvina. "You have friends hereabouts, Morvina, will they not keep her in safety until Warwick's men have gone?"

The maid nodded. "That will present no problem."

Alice pulled his arm. "But what of you? What shall you do?"

"Alice, I must do as Edward says. I will ride south and leave from Dover as soon as possible."

She swayed. "Why? In the name of God, why? Why run so many risks? Hide with me and then we can escape together. To Brabant maybe."

He bent his head and kissed her shaking lips. "No. If I go, then I go with the dignity my rank demands. I shall not scurry like a frightened rabbit before the so-called Lords Ordainers. Such satisfaction I would not give them."

Stephen pushed open the door and hurried in. "I fancy that Warwick is almost upon us. There is a large party of horsemen approaching the town."

"So soon?" Piers drew Alice into his arms. "You must go now, sweetheart, for once you are in Beauchamp's clutch you will not escape easily." He kissed her once more and then pushed her gently towards Morvina. "Hurry now."

"Without you? What if Beauchamp forgets that he comes merely to escort you? He hates you sufficiently to risk a great deal . . ."

The dark brown eyes softened at seeing her distress. "Alice, go with Morvina." He was firm, but still she hesitated.

109

Morvina stretched forward and touched her. "Come, my Lady, there is precious little time. We can leave by the postern gate."

"No. Piers?" Tears started to her eyes. Why, oh why would he not come with her?

Stephen caught her hand and dragged her from the room. Piers turned his head away to hide his own feelings at parting with her. Morvina gathered up two cloaks and quickly closed the door behind her.

Piers walked to the table and lifted the flagon of wine which stood there. He slowly poured out a goblet of the sweet red liquid, and then sat down by the brazier. The goblet turned between his nervous fingers, the wine gleaming blood-red in the half-light.

He heard Warwick's party arrive at the drawbridge.

EIGHTEEN

THE sea breeze had dwindled to a mere whisper now, the wavelets lapping gently against the shoreline.

"Keep to the very edge of the water, my Lady."

Alice's slippers were soaked, and caked with wet sand. "Can we not keep a little further from the sea?" Her heart was thundering as if it would burst at any moment. Her gown was damp and trailed wetly against her cold ankles.

"No, for our footprints would be seen. Keep by the water itself and the waves will obliterate all signs of our passing."

She was right, of course she was right. Alice bit her lip to hold back the tears which were so close. Piers. She turned her head but could see nothing. Bamburgh Castle was a grey blur against the vaguely lightening skies. A pearl-like stain to the east foretold of the approaching dawn.

Her foot caught in a twisted piece of driftwood and she tumbled to the ground. Salt water lapped against her face and sand stuck to her. Her mouth was filled with its grittiness. The blue velvet soaked up the water and now hung heavily against her chill body. The tears spilled over and joined the saltiness of the sea.

Her breath came in gulps as she struggled to her feet and

hurried onwards. The dull glowing embers of the bonfire were passed almost unseen as they hurtled over Ross Back towards the distant spit called the Law. Here nestled a few shabby huts, sheltering as best they could against the sandy shoreline. Ahead Alice saw suddenly the dim, low outline of Holy Island, caught in the ghostly light of the eastern sky. She stopped, her eyes wide as she gazed at the wonderful sight, the spectacular eeriness of Lindisfarne.

"There is little time!" Morvina grabbed her mistress' arm roughly. There was no time for the niceties of mannerly behaviour either.

The huts were apparently bereft of life. No candle burned to shed its small light between the ill-fitting boards.

Alice's chest ached with weariness, the back of her throat sore with her sobbing breaths. She leaned against the nearest hut, her face damp and sticky, her mouth still filled with sand.

Morvina glanced behind in the direction of Bamburgh but there was no sign of Warwick's men. It could be that they would not search at all . . .

Her small hand hammered on the poor door. The smell of rotten fish was strong. Alice moved away from a pail which reaked unbearably. The door creaked slightly and a frightened face peered out.

The old man smiled as he recognised Morvina, and the door opened finally to afford them entry. Alice recognised him as one of the men who had been at the Hallowe'en bonfire. Even now he showed a great deference towards the Welsh girl. He stared at Alice as she came into the tiny circle of light thrown by a solitary candle.

I must look like some sea monster, she thought, staring down at her sand-caked gown. The blue velvet was lost beneath a coating of dull grey sand. Her leg was grazed from her encounter with the driftwood, and her scarf was ripped. She put her hand up to her face and felt the drying sand particles spring away from the salty skin. Where now the proud mistress of Longmore? The leman of the Earl of Cornwall?

Morvina took the old man's hand. "Hide this lady, conceal her well from the men in red and white who will come to seek her out. She is important to me and I wish that she remains undetected." He nodded.

His wife rubbed her hands nervously upon the skirt of her rough dress. "We shall do all we can, be sure of that."

The maid squeezed Alice's trembling hands and then left the

111

fisherman's hut. They could not hear her footsteps in the silent sand. She hurried back towards Bamburgh. Dawn brightened steadily, casting the pearly light of the rising sun upon the desolate coast.

Morvina paused as she reached the dead bonfire. Her sharp eyes picked out a single pebble which was shattered by the heat. It lay in a myriad of pieces amongst its fellows.

Hoofbeats splashed along the ebbing waves and Morvina spun around in time to see the red and white banners fluttering above a column of horsemen riding fast towards her. She scrambled over the slippery sand and behind a dry clump of seagrass, pressing her body into the ground. She kept her face down as they passed.

Alice's frightened ears heard the hoofbeats first, and her golden eyes widened. Her breath caught fearfully in her throat as she looked at the fisherman and his wife. Calmly they moved a pile of stinking, half-rotten nets from a corner of the single room, beckoning to her to crouch down in the vacant space. As she bent down they tossed the foul nets over her. Her stomach heaved at the stench as the slimy twine moved against her face.

The hoofbeats thudded loudly outside, and she could hear the snorting and stamping of the horses. Harness jingled and voices spoke in undertones. Then there was shouting as Warwick's men dismounted and began to systematically search the poor dwellings. She heard the crunch of boots and someone entered the very hut where she hid. The sound of searching was close now.

Her eyes were closed as she began to pray. Surely the man who searched could hear her wildly beating heart . . .

The footsteps were almost upon her, and the wicker basket next to the nets was moved. It clattered to the dusty floor and rolled backwards and forwards on its side. Holy Mother, save me, save me . . . The nets were lifted and she opened her eyes to stare up into the startled face of Sir Gareth ap Llewellyn!

She held her breath, her eyes pleading silently with him. He exclaimed in surprise, unable to prevent the sound escaping from his lips.

Outside she heard the sound of Hugh d'Audley's lazy voice. "You have found her?"

"Er . . . no, Hugh, I merely trod upon a rat, I swear that they have the largest rodents in Christendom hereabouts!"

D'Audley grunted with disappointment, but came no nearer to

the hut. "Think you that maybe she has crossed to Holy Island itself? Perhaps she would seek sanctuary there."

Gareth put his hand against Alice's cold cheek, smiling gently, but he called again to Hugh. "It is low tide still, perhaps we could cross the shallows to search the Island. I saw the path marked by stakes."

Hugh's grumbling undertones could plainly be heard as he remounted. Alice's fingers closed over Gareth's, but he drew his hand away, pulling the dreadful nets over her again. She heard him leave the hut.

He called the men together. "It is obviously a fruitless search, the lady is long since gone as the Earl of Cornwall tells us."

Hugh was contemptuous. "Gaveston would tell us anything to save his mistress! I think she has fled to Holy Island and that is where I intend searching. Llewellyn you grow soft in the head if you choose to believe the Gascon squire. I know that she is somewhere close by. I dare not leave any possibility unsearched, for Warwick is a savage man. If he thought we had been less than thorough . . . "

Gareth laughed. "Very well, Hugh, by all means let us search Holy Island." The hoofbeats sounded again as the column moved away towards the shining sands where the sea had ebbed. Holy Island was close as the pink and gold fingers of daylight crept across the heavens.

Beneath the fishing nets, Alice wept silently.

NINETEEN

AYMER de Valence scowled at Guy Beauchamp. "Warwick, it is as the lady says! You have no jurisdiction to seize her and take her off to your own estates! Be done with all this. The power vested in you was limited only to allowing you to separate her from Gaveston. That has obviously been done. She was wise in sending word to me of her whereabouts, I think, for I have no doubt that you would have considerably overstepped your authority had I not been present."

Alice sat meekly before the fireplace in the great hall at

Longmore. Home. Safety. Morvina and Stephen had urged her to write to Pembroke, and how well advised she had been. Aymer had come swiftly to her and now stoutly defended her against a furious Warwick.

Guy Beauchamp's intelligent grey eyes flashed with rage, and his thin face was pink beneath its ruddy tan. He smiled suddenly. "Very well, Pembroke, there is no more to be said. In this I am wrong, the ordinances do not extend to this. I bid you good day." He bowed stiffly, snatching up his cloak and swinging it around his broad shoulders and striding quickly from the hall.

In silence they listened to the sound of his party's departure, not speaking until they heard the thundering sound hollow as the horses crossed over the drawbridge.

Pembroke pursed his lips. "Such a sudden capitulation is somewhat unnerving."

"It does not matter, my Lord Aymer." Alice stood and took Pembroke's hand, pressing it to her lips. "I cannot thank you sufficiently for your presence here today."

He grunted. "I am a law-abiding man, Lady Alice, and cannot allow one of my fellow Ordainers to step outside the law for his own purposes. You were fortunate not to have been at Bamburgh when Warwick got there, for I have no doubt that if you had been you would by now have been a prisoner in one of his eyries in Warwickshire."

"As you say, I was truly fortunate." She glanced at the rushes on the floor and then met Pembroke's gaze again. "What has happened to him?"

Aymer raised his eyebrows briefly. "Gaveston? He sailed from Dover on the fourth of November. England has seen the last of him, I think. You are best without him, Lady Alice, believe me."

Her fingers twisted in the folds of her gown. "I love him as I love life itself, my Lord."

He was silent, watching her lovely face. "To love so much, Lady Alice, is to love inordinately."

She smiled. "Then I love him inordinately."

He turned to pick up his cloak from the chest where it rested. "He does not deserve one such as you, Lady Alice."

She put her hand on his arm. "Why do you say that? Whatever else may be said of him, he is unwavering in his loyalty."

He patted her fingers, smiling. "Maybe, maybe, but he is still not worthy of you." He left the hall.

114

One morning at the beginning of December, Morvina came into Alice's apartments and found her mistress alone at her embroidery frame. "My Lady, there is word from him at last."

Alice caught her breath, her golden eyes alight. "What do you know?"

"He is at Tintagel."

"Tintagel? But that is in Cornwall, surely you have the name wrong. He is abroad somewhere, in exile." Alice stood, skeins of cerise thread tumbling from her lap to the floor. A large tabby cat patted the colourful skeins with its paw, its ears pricking with interest.

"No, my Lady, I have the name correctly." Morvina bent to retrieve the threads from the eager claws of the cat, scratching its ears gently. "Stephen has seen him."

"Seen Piers?" Alice felt weak. "So that is why my steward has been conspicuously absent these past days."

Morvina picked up the cat, stroking the striped back lovingly. The cat purred loudly. "Stephen received information from his friends that the Earl of Cornwall was in Tintagel, and so he went there. The information proved true."

"Then I must go to him."

"Have a care, my Lady, for you know that Warwick has set his spies to watch Longmore. He waits for just such an opportunity. If you are seen to leave then you will be followed."

Alice smiled. "Then I must not be seen to leave! If Stephen Dunheved is my steward then surely I can be smuggled out. His ingenuity is boundless."

Morvina did not know whether to be pleased at this praise of her lover or worried at the danger into which Alice intended to step.

"We must be very careful, my Lady, for I suspect that Warwick has managed to infiltrate one of his toads into the castle somehow."

"Warwick's creature? Here?"

"I suspect so, my Lady, and if that is right then your escape is doubled in danger."

Alice paced up and down. "Bring Stephen to me, Morvina, and we will discuss it all. Perhaps some idea will present itself."

Morvina slipped away and Alice went to the window and peeped out. The pale December sunlight bathed the Severn valley with a primrose light. The river slid past the foot of Longmore's hill on its endless journey to the sea. Why was Piers back in England? He was banished forever by the Lords Ordainers and by the word of the King himself. If he was caught then he could legally be executed as a traitor. She leaned her face against the ice-cold stone. My love, my dearest love . . .

The early winter evening was almost upon the valley when the drawbridge was lowered to allow an oxen cart to rumble slowly out from Longmore's confines. It began its slow descent of the hill, with the drover chewing upon a straw and singing bawdy songs loudly to himself. The naked trees did not muffle the piercing tones of his voice, and the thin winter air seemed to echo to the sound. The cart rocked and swayed down the narrow track, the barrels which loaded it threatening to tumble to the ground with each bump.

Warwick's man sat with his back against the gnarled tree trunk, slowly swinging his horse's reins backwards and forwards. The bright bay mount hung its head with boredom, its ears twitching only as the oxen cart rumbled nearer. The man lifted his head to watch the cart's approach. A pox on watching the lady of Longmore. This past month she had not stirred once from within, but still he must wait and watch. He thought wistfully of a warm bed and some comely wench to brighten his nights. He stared at the oxen cart as it swayed past him, and still his thoughts were on the feminine charms of that wench . . .

Beneath the carefully arranged barrels, Alice crouched undetected, passing beneath the very nose of Warwick's man.

Two hours later the new blacksmith crept out of the postern gate and hurried to where his comrade waited in the darkness. Longmore's efficient blacksmith was Warwick's man and he gave the alarm of Alice's departure. There could only be one explanation. The oxen cart.

The new day was a few hours old when Stephen and Alice reined in their steaming mounts. Alice stared at the rocky cliffs where the castle of Tintagel stood. The castle showed no signs of life.

The fortress was perched high up on the Cornish cliffs above the sea. The rock-face was crumbling so that the narrow promontory which supported the castle itself was threatening at any moment to become an island. The keep would soon be on that island while the rest of the castle remained on the mainland.

She stared from the castle to Stephen. "He is not in *that* place?"

"I fear that he is, my Lady. There is a wooden bridge which

makes passage over the dangerous part of the cliff more safe. It is not so serious as mayhap it looks."

They urged their tired horses up towards the first part of the castle, passing unhindered over the lowered drawbridge and into the first courtyard. Everywhere seemed to be in a dreadful state of disrepair. King Arthur's castle was a sad and lonely place.

Stephen hid the horses in the deserted stables, and then took Alice through the cold, echoing halls and passages until they came at last to the bridge over the eroded cliff. She closed her eyes as they hurried over into the other part of the castle, hearing small stones and pieces of earth scattering away beneath towards the sea. Her scalp prickled with fear until the danger was past and they stood on the firm land beyond.

"Welcome to my castle of Tintagel, sweet Alice."

She spun round on hearing his voice again, a warm flame springing up within her. He leaned against the wall close to a window, his arms folded across his chest.

"Piers." Her lips moved but no sound came out. Her hungry eyes drank in every beloved feature of his face, dwelling lovingly upon the dark brown eyes.

Stephen left them alone as Piers held out his hand to her. She ran to him and he caught her, swinging her high into the air before kissing her. The touch of his lips upon her sent shivers of pleasure through her aching body. Her legs were weak as he pressed her closer, and she clung to him as he bore her roughly to the floor. Oh how tightly she held him as he made love to her, her very consciousness threatening to desert her. She closed her eyes as a warm lethargy stole over her; his love was a soporific, like the sweet essence of the poppy . . .

It was Stephen who disturbed their tranquillity a short while later. His footsteps grated upon the stone floor as he ran towards them, his sword in his hand.

"Warwick's men are upon us!"

Oh no! No! Alice struggled to her feet, her scattered senses reeling still. Piers grabbed at his belt which hung on the wall, buckling it quickly around his slender waist. He lifted the sword once to feel that it was loose and easy to unsheath.

She felt a clamminess between her shoulder blades. "How can we escape?" Her whisper was weak, frightened.

But he did not hear her for already he was with Stephen. "Where are they exactly?"

"They have reached the outer walls on the mainland and are apparently in some doubt as how to proceed. They do not know if we are well armed or not. Sir Hugh d'Audley leads them, and he was ever one to follow orders and not think for himself!"

Piers' irrepressible sense of humour rose quickly. "Aye, that is why my dear wife finds him so vastly to her liking! He follows his orders between the sheets to her satisfaction!" The smile faded as he thought again of their predicament. "However . . . There is only the cliff face then?"

"Aye, but you know what they told us in the village. The path is dangerous, even on so fine a day as this."

Piers grinned, his teeth white. "Which death would you prefer? A fall down a cliff face or a traitor's execution at Warwick's nimble hands?"

Stephen spat on the ground. "Give me the cliff face, each and every time! I shall follow our plan then and place a torch in the window we decided upon. Pray God we paid that scurvy fisherman sufficiently well for him to honour his side of the bargain."

He hurried away, snatching an unlighted torch from a bracket on the wall. Alice remained rooted to the spot, watching as Piers ran down the passageway to the open doorway which led on to the wooden bridge. "Bring a light from the fire, Alice. Hurry!" He looked back at her motionless figure.

She glanced around, seeing the small brazier in a sheltered corner, safe from the draughts and winds of the castle. A candlestick stood upon a trestle and she seized it, holding the wick to the fire.

Shielding the tiny unhappy flame with her hand, she hurried down the passage to where Piers waited.

The weather had been fine for some time in these parts, and the bridge was dry, tinder-dry. He had piled old rushes and driftwood around the bridge and now he held the candle to the bonfire-like structure. The flames leapt into eager life, spinning through the straw and rushes as if possessed. In a matter of moments the bridge was alight. Now it would be some time before Hugh d'Audley could pursue them.

Piers grasped Alice's wrist and the candlestick fell to the floor. They hurried back along the passageway and into the depths of the keep. Stephen waited for them by a dark, almost hidden staircase which led downwards towards the outer walls of the castle. A rat scurried away into the darkness and Alice stifled her cry of dismay.

Downwards curved the worn, ancient steps, downwards . . . and

118

outwards. Surely they must be under the walls themselves, almost out on to the cliff face! Alice could barely think as she flew along held firmly by Piers' hand. Stephen's footsteps were immediately behind her. A dank, stale smell filled the cold air now, and a frosty chill crept into their bones. The slimy steps were dangerous, and Alice fell forwards as her slippers slithered. Piers steadied her. "Have a care now, for the steps end shortly and we shall be out on the cliff face with only a small ledge between us and the sea far below."

The steps ended, sure enough, and they squeezed themselves out from the passage and on to the ledge. Alice's horrified eyes saw the glint of full sunlight upon the twinkling sea, a sea so blue and beautiful that the danger of Warwick seemed a lifetime away. The waves lapped softly against the rocks far below, as the ocean hissed gently to itself, waiting, watching.

Piers took a deep breath to steady himself now, his leg muscles still shaking from the effort of running down the steps. Now he must be sure, and calm, for a false step would mean a fall to death.

"Press yourself close to the cliff, Alice, and whatever you do, do not look down. And pray, to whatever God you wish, that our fisherman friend has seen the torch in the window and stands by his promise."

Alice could not look at all. Perspiration poured down her forehead, prickling in her hair. She moved step for step with Piers, her lips whimpering her fear in a sound so small that even Piers did not hear. Her palms were hot and wet, and dust stuck to her skin from the dry cliff face. Tiny stones were dislodged by their searching, nervous feet, and fell endlessly down to the water below, rattling and clattering. Downwards crept the unsafe ledge, downwards in barely discernible steps. The hiss and splash of the sea grew louder.

In the distance they could hear shouting.

"You can open your eyes now, sweetheart, we are almost there." Stephen's voice was weak with relief. "And here is our rescuer." There came the creaking sound of oars as a small boat nosed its way around the quiet rocks towards them. Seaweed swayed in the gentle movement of the sea, and a seagull perched upon a barnacle-encrusted rock, its head on one side as it stared at them. With a crisp flapping of its white wings it rose into the clear air, its voice loud and piercing as it shrieked and called. The noise was taken up by others and soon the air rang with their clamour.

The prow of the boat bumped gently against the rocks and the fisherman leaned towards them, his hand outstretched. In a short while they were all safely in the rowing boat and the oars creaked rhythmically as they were rowed swiftly away from danger.

The further away they went, the more clearly they could see Tintagel's promontory. The cliff slid away to reveal at last the roaring blaze of the wooden bridge, and the stationary figures in red and white who watched helplessly from the mainland. The bridge fell away suddenly, flaring brightly as it plunged to the sea. Warwick's men did not see the tiny rowing boat so far below them.

"Where shall I put thee ashore?" The fisherman's Cornish accent was heavy and somehow unreal to Alice.

Piers arm was around her shoulders, tight and protecting, and she leaned against him. A faint scent of perspiration pricked her nostrils as she slipped her hands about his waist and buried her face against his shoulder. She could feel the supple movement of his body as he held out his purse to the fisherman. "Take us to wherever horses may be safely procured."

The man nodded, his eyes wide as he saw the fortune in the purse. He turned the boat towards the shore some distance form the castle.

The seagulls wheeled in the air above them, but Alice heard nothing. Her ears were dead to all but the steady beating of Piers' heart.

TWENTY

"*STRIDE*, Alice — think like a man now!" Piers' distorted whisper spurred Alice into action. She bowed her head beneath the monk's cowl which concealed her face completely, and forced herself to take long masculine steps.

The three monks moved swiftly up the hill towards Longmore. Somehow they must gain entry without arousing the suspicion of Warwick's men who still clustered around like ants upon honey. She felt her pulses fluttering with fear as she strove to maintain the long, striding gait. But there need have been no fear for Guy Beauchamp's men were concerned still with searching carts and any other such traffic which could conceal the fugitives.

Stephen's tall figure was bowed like that of an old man and he leaned heavily upon a staff. Despite the situation Alice smiled to herself. Echoes of Malcolm Musard sounded faintly and she wondered upon how many raids he had used just this very disguise!

Stephen had sent word to Morvina that they were coming. The drawbridge would be lowered for three monks in white . . .

A distant sound came to their ears and Piers risked a glance behind, only to be afforded the sight of the red and white of Warwick approaching from the east. Alice saw too and her gasp of dismay came loudly in the still winter air. Her breath stood out in a silver cloud. They increased their pace, it was only a small distance now to the welcoming, protecting walls of Longmore. The drawbridge was lowering.

Guy Beauchamp himself rode at the head of his men. This time he meant to be sure that the matter was carried out to the best advantage. If Lady Alice de Longmore returned to her lair, then he, Guy Beauchamp, intended to capture her . . . *and* Gaveston! He turned slightly in the saddle to look at his two lieutenants.

Sir Hugh d'Audley stared steadfastly at his mount's ears, his dull eyes not flickering as he felt the Earl's cold glance on him. That Alice had twice escaped Hugh rankled greatly with Guy Beauchamp. First at Bamburgh, and now at Tintagel!

The Earl's clear grey eyes moved on to the upright figure of Gareth. Beauchamp was suspicious of the young Welsh knight. But suspicions were not enough, there must be more, something definite upon which he could act. Gareth met the stare of his master. His good-looking face broke into an innocuous smile and he inclined his head slightly.

Ahead the drawbridge rested upon the ground now. Warwick raised his eyebrows in surprise. "Longmore's lookouts are surprisingly alert! They lower the drawbridge already for us." His eyes narrowed, moving around the countryside on either side of the road. But there was nothing to see. Three white monks were crossing into the courtyard. Beauchamp spat on the ground and urged his mount up the hill.

Morvina's hands were outstretched to urge the three figures into the sheltering confines of the castle. They hurried through the passageways towards Alice's private apartments where already some trusted women were waiting. Morvina clutched Stephen's hand, and he stopped her for a moment to kiss her warmly upon the lips.

121

She held him tightly — he was safe, the gods be thanked, he was safe . . .

Inside the apartments she turned urgently towards Alice. "My Lady, you must dress with all speed, for in a short while you are to receive the Earl of Warwick. Stephen, you must change too, for the Lady Alice must have her steward. My Lord of Cornwall . . . " she turned her attention to Piers, " . . . you must remain here, although I think such advice is not necessary!"

Piers smiled, throwing back the hood of his monk's habit. "I am hardly likely to afford the black dog a view of *my* face!"

The women were virtually tearing the monk's habit from Alice's shivering figure. Her teeth chattered, but her skin was hot. The women were unhappy at undressing Alice in front of the two men. "Be quick, there is no time to worry about such things!" Alice shook one woman's arm frantically.

The undergown of apricot brocade felt cool against her fiery skin, but the heavy overgown of indigo velvet with dark brown fur trimmings was stifling. The women's fingers fumbled helplessly with the many buttons on the sleeve of the undergown.

Piers' voice was surprisingly calm as he held out the hairbrush to the older of the two women. "Leave the buttons, a mere man may attend to them. The Lady Alice must look as if she has been here all day and indeed for the past weeks. Concern yourselves with her hair for Guy of Warwick must be deceived into thinking his spies made a great mistake in reporting her missing."

He put his hand to Alice's taut face. "Have strength now, sweetest Alice, for the deception is almost complete." He bent his head to kiss her stiff lips, and then began to deftly fasten the buttons.

Her hair was just being plaited when they heard the Earl's party ride into the courtyard. A shudder took Alice and Piers embraced her. They watched Stephen hurry from the room, still tying the laces of his undershirt. Morvina was still gathering the monks' habits from the floor, pushing them away into a large chest.

It seemed a mere heartbeat before Stephen returned. "I have informed him that you will be with him presently, Lady Alice. He takes refreshment in the great hall. Sir Gareth and d'Audley are with him."

"What did he say when you informed him that I was in the castle?"

"He was hard put to conceal his surprise, my Lady. The sight of *my* face fair unbalanced him!" Stephen winked at her, and she drew strength from his jauntiness.

122

The plaits were coiled over her ears and a golden circlet placed on her head. The women threaded a fine apricot scarf through the circlet, and then she was ready.

She moved through the castle as if in a dream. Warwick's men were everywhere, their prying eyes searching into every corner as they sought out anything irregular in the activities of Longmore. Morvina and Stephen followed her, holding hands until the entrance of the great hall was reached.

At the entrance Alice paused, turning slowly to look around the three passages which converged. Warwick's red and white filled her vision. Anger surged through her. How *dared* he? How dared he take over *her* home in such a fashion! Her eyes flashed with fury.

She swept regally towards Warwick who stood by the blazing fire, a mug of ale in his hand.

"My Lord of Warwick! Your manners and the manners of your men are most certainly offensive!" She attacked him verbally, catching him well off guard.

He turned in surprise, startled to see her. He had not believed that she was in the castle at all. "Manners?" His voice was slow.

"Yes! Since when does a guest send his armies through his host's home as if they searched? I am most certainly deeply offended and shall convey my displeasure to the ears of the King himself!" Had she gone too far? Gareth watched her from the corner where he stood with d'Audley.

The admiration in his green eyes was immense. She was superb. Alice, my Alice . . . Gareth drank deeply of his ale, licking his lips nervously. D'Audley's knowing eyes watched him.

Warwick recovered. "My men are merely taking their ease, Lady Alice. I gave no orders that they were to remain in the courtyard. Maybe they remember that they were once permanently here and seek out their former lady-loves."

Her golden eyes were hard. "Then I suggest, my Lord, that you acquaint them immediately with the error of their ways. I will not have *your* men wandering over *my* domain! They are no longer billeted here and you trespass considerably upon what little goodwill I have left!"

Beauchamp grinned suddenly. "Very well, my dearest Lady Alice. D'Audley, see to it that the men return to their horses immediately. Llewellyn!" His voice sharpened noticeably as he spoke to Gareth. "Accompany Sir Hugh."

Morvina and Stephen left the hall with the two knights, intent

123

upon seeing that no-one entered Alice's private apartments where Piers was hidden.

Alice was left alone in the hall with the man she most hated in all England.

"Tell me, Alice, how did you accomplish your return?" He spoke quietly.

"Return? From where?" Her eyes were wide, innocent.

"From Tintagel, sweet lady, where you ran to your perverted Gaveston."

Her face became hot. "I do not know what you mean, I have been at Longmore this past month."

"You lie, beautiful Alice. D'Audley so nearly succeeded. Had it not been for that wooden bridge being set alight . . . "

Alice poured herself a cup of wine, her hands remarkably steady as she turned to look at him. "My Lord, I have no notion of what you can mean. Burning bridges, indeed, it sounds a vastly entertaining tale."

He watched her silently, then he drained his ale and walked towards her, standing so close that his legs brushed against her skirts. "You cannot fool me, I *know* that you have just returned."

"There is little point in continuing this conversation, my Lord of Warwick. I say that I have not left Longmore, and you say that I have. I suggest that we have reached an impasse."

"D'Audley recognised you in that boat. You wore no hood."

"D'Audley moons so over the Countess of Cornwall that I believe he romances considerably."

He licked his lips as if savouring some devilish secret, and then held out his empty cup. "You know that the Countess of Cornwall is with child, do you not?" He took a sharply different tack.

"I am not in the Countess' confidence." Alice was bored, her voice exuded that boredom.

"Maybe not, but you think yourself to be in her husband's confidence do you not? The child is his. Cornwall has got his wife with child."

A flush sprang to Alice's face. "The Countess is in exile with her husband then?" The effort of sounding unperturbed was great.

"No, Gaveston spent the night before his departure from Dover in his wife's fond embrace." Warwick enjoyed her dismay. "It is sad is it not, Alice, that a mistress must always take a second place to a wife."

Her hands shook very slightly as she began to slowly pour more ale into his cup. "I fail to see what this has to do with me. The affairs of the Earl and Countess of Cornwall are private."

"For shame! Did he not tell you then? Did he take you in his embrace after sleeping with his wife . . . and not tell you?" He mocked.

The jug crashed to the table and she turned sharply, holding out his cup. The ale slopped over the side and on to his fur-trimmed coat. "I suggest, my Lord of Warwick, that you speak your business with me and then take yourself away from my lands. At the same time take your cursed spies, for I will not answer for their lives if they remain past dawn tomorrow!"

He smiled, a nerve moving slightly at his temple. "Ah, Alice, so bravely do you try not to believe me. He has proved unworthy of your devotion, has he not? He is like some brilliantly-winged butterfly, dispensing his favours hither and thither . . . from the King, to you, to his wife, mayhap now back to the King! How vastly adaptable he is!"

She threw the wine into his grinning face. He exclaimed with anger and reached out to grab her. His grip was vicelike and he held her firmly. "You she-cat! I will not suffer you to act thus towards me!" He was breathing heavily, and the nerve twitched with increasing speed at his temple. She was afraid now, for he was hardly recognisable as he pulled her closer.

He could feel the softness of her body through the velvet. The fabric was so sensuous, so soft and so yielding when worn by one so beautiful. Her flesh was pliant beneath his fingers. He jerked her against him, pressing his lips down upon hers. With one arm he held her close to his body, while with the other he caressed her. She tried to struggle but his strength was by far the greater.

She tore her mouth away from his, her voice spitting in his ear. "And what if the great Earl of Warwick is discovered raping his nephew's widow?" It was a desperate attempt to bring him to reason, a desperate attempt to protect herself.

She could feel the effort with which he controlled himself then. His fingers cut into her arms as he forced a steadiness into his bearing. His lips curved into a cool smile; Warwick was himself once more. "You are saved this time, Alice, but beware, for there will come a time when I shall know there to be no danger of interruption. I shall have you yet."

Footsteps approached the great hall. She picked up his cup from where it had dropped and turned quickly back to the jug of ale.

Gareth and d'Audley entered, followed faithfully by Morvina and Stephen. D'Audley bowed, his surprised gaze perceiving Warwick's flushed face and Alice's trembling hands. "My Lord, the men are all in the courtyard now."

Warwick did not take his eyes from Alice. "Then we must depart, for I fear we have no hope of hospitality from the Lady of Longmore this day."

He gathered up his gauntlets from the table, leaning past Alice so that his leg touched her. She turned her face sharply away in revulsion.

He began to walk out of the hall when suddenly he halted. "But of course! The monks!"

Alice swallowed. "Monks?"

He returned. "Before we rode into Longmore, three monks came here." His eyes were glitter-bright then. He was sure that she was trapped at last.

Stephen bowed before the Earl. "They are at this moment awaiting your departure so that they might thank the Lady Alice for her hospitality in giving them food when they were sore hungry. Do you wish to speak with them?"

Warwick surveyed the steward with a penetrating eye. Was this a trick? Did Dunheved hope that by an audacious offer such as this, he, Warwick, would be fooled into believing such a tale? His teeth gleamed as he smiled. "Aye, I wish to speak with them."

Alice's eyes were haunted as Stephen walked from the room.

"Go with him d'Audley." Warwick was allowing for no trickery.

Gareth saw the misery in her face and he knew suddenly that Warwick's suspicions were well-founded. "My Lord, I myself saw three monks taking refreshment in the kitchens when I searched with d'Audley for the men." He lied with ease for Alice.

Warwick snarled. "If I need your interruptions, Sir Gareth, then I will ask for them!"

Footsteps came close again, and Stephen walked in followed by three monks in white habits. D'Audley hurried past them to Warwick. "They were waiting as the steward said, my Lord." There was disappointment in his voice.

Warwick's tongue passed slowly along his upper lip, his gauntlets tapping irritably against the table. He had been out-manoeuvred.

The monks stood quietly, waiting. Alice's dry mouth would barely allow her to speak. "You . . . you wished to speak with me before you departed?"

"We did, my Lady, May the Blessings of Our Lord be upon you and upon your house for the kindness you have afforded us this day." The tallest of the three spoke.

Warwick stepped forward suddenly and threw back the cowl which concealed the man's face. Then he did the same to the other two. Three unknown faces were revealed. Alice had not seen them before. The tall monk was vaguely puzzled. "Are our faces of interest to you, my Lord?" The voice was mild.

Warwick turned away furiously, leaving the hall without further ado. D'Audley followed him. Only Gareth paused for a moment. Alice smiled at him. "I must thank you yet again."

"It is not your thanks that I want, 'cariad'." Then he too was gone.

The clatter and noise was loud as the noble Earl of Warwick left the confines of the castle he coveted so greatly. There was anger in the hoofbeats which thundered away downhill.

Stephen let out a piercing whistle and tossed Warwick's discarded cup into the air. The ale splashed out over the floor and the cup bounced against the wall. He grinned broadly. "The day has yet to come when Guy Beauchamp can outwit me!" He swung Morvina up into the air and she joined her laughter to his. The three 'monks' sat down, beaming and looking well pleased with themselves.

Only Alice remained still and quiet.

TWENTY-ONE

THAT night she lay in Piers' embrace in the darkness of her bed-chamber. The winter gale swept unhindered up the Severn valley, blustering around the castle and moving the curtains and tapestries inside. The small wick floated in a sea of oil in a dish upon the table, and the steady flame moved from side to side as the wind bullied the air.

She could feel his heart beating as he slept. Warwick's taunting words came echoing out of the night to mock her again. *'For shame! Did he not tell you then? Did he take you into his embrace after sleeping with his wife . . . and not tell you?'* She sighed, her

127

tortured imagination conjuring the moving shadows into visions of Piers with his sulky but beautiful wife . . . *'He is like some brilliantly-winged butterfly, dispensing his favours hither and thither . . . from the King, to you, to his wife, mayhap now back to the King! How vastly adaptable he is!'* She swallowed, burying her face against the soft dark hairs of his chest. He began to stir, returning her embrace instinctively. Oh Piers, Piers, reassure me, tell me that he was lying . . . please . . .

She sat up, breaking the embrace abruptly. His eyes flickered and opened and he looked up at her. "What is it?"

"Your wife is with child." The words slipped out, bare, jealous and full of hurt.

He reached up to entwine his fingers in her hair. "And so?"

"The child is yours?" The pain in her voice swept over him.

His fingers paused. "It is possible." He spoke carefully.

"Oh." So small a sound.

"Alice, it means nothing. You know that." He was gentle.

"I know only that you lay with her, and that *she* carries your child . . . " She broke off, bowing her head.

He sat up beside her, putting his hand to her chin and turning her to face him. "I am not bound to explain myself to you, Alice, but I will. On the night before my departure from Dover the King gave a banquet. I was not to leave England quietly and unobtrusively. Throughout the evening I watched my wife fawning over d'Audley. She was laughing at me, at my defeat by the barons. There are times, Alice, when a man must take a stand. I determined that my dear wife was not going to enjoy her lover's embraces so that the court could laugh at me behind its hands. I commanded her to come to *me* that night. She is my wife, she could not refuse. I can assure you that I kept her immensely busy throughout the night, she will have cause to remember our encounter. I used her abominably."

"How she must hate you now then." She felt him move with laughter and blinked in surprise. "Why do you laugh?"

"Because, sweet Alice, she hates me supremely now . . . she enjoyed my attentions and could not hide the fact!"

"Do you feel differently towards her now? Will you acknowledge the child?"

He pulled her back down to the mattress and leaned over her. "I feel nothing for her, nor she for me. As to the child . . . yes, I will

128

acknowledge it. It is no fault of the child's that my wife and I so hate one another."

"D'Audley may be the sire."

He smiled, brushing his lips against her cheek. "I think not. She has been his mistress for long enough now to have borne him many a brat! No, the child will be mine."

Alice closed her eyes. "She has been his mistress . . . as I have been yours . . . and so she and I have that much in common. We neither of us can bear the child of the man we love."

He kissed her quickly to stifle her words.

Dawn was creeping over the sky when the sound of the seagulls flying inland awoke Alice from her slumber. The lonely cries of the birds sounded like wailing over the flat landscape.

She moved her fingers to clasp his. This could not last. Only fools would delude themselves into believing in this paradise . . . living here, at Longmore, with Piers . . .

She saw that he too was awake. "Why did you return to England, Piers? You are a traitor under the law here."

"Edward needs me, and I cannot desert him. We are as brothers."

"Brothers can part," she whispered.

"But not he and I. He made me, Alice. He loves me and he gives proof of his love with his every deed. He has not many friends, many true friends . . . what kind of man would I be if I deserted him now?"

Her fingers tightened. "What can your use be to him if you are dead? You can be no friend then."

He was silent, and she listened to the silence with growing fear. Something nagged, warned, scratched at her thoughts. She sat up as the knowledge of his intent came to her like the sting of an arrow. "You intend to give yourself for him." The statement lay uneasily upon the air.

He still said nothing. "Piers." She pulled him to face her, her hands lingering over his face. "You are not some beast to be sacrificed to the bloodlust and jealousy of England's barons, or to the vapidity of a weak monarch. You are more a man than any of them, than all of them together." Tears stung her eyes. Why could he not understand, why . . . ?

He spoke softly. "Alice, which is more important — a king or a Gascon squire?"

The tears welled from beneath her closed lids. "The Gascon squire . . . each time the Gascon squire." He brushed away the tears from her cheeks. "Any man may be as good or bad a king as

129

Edward Plantagenet. Oh I love Edward, for knowing him it is impossible not to; but *you* I love more, infinitely more." She kissed his fingers, her eyes closed still.

"But to England, sweetheart, to *England* the King is of the utmost importance. I am the cause of England's troubles, or so they all think. At my feet they lay the blame for the abandonment of the Scottish war, and for the continuing lack of monies in the Exchequer. It is because of me that the King and the barons are at odds with one another. Remove me completely and you remove their reason for uniting."

"I cannot believe that I am listening to this." She slipped from the bed, pulling on a robe and pacing up and down in the grey cold. "I cannot believe that you intend to do this, that you intend to lay your head upon the executioner's block so that the Earls may eat their food with quiet, self-satisfied hearts again. Besides . . . " she stopped and looked at him as he lay there on the bed, " . . . with you gone, Edward will lapse into his former ways again, and with a greater involvement than ever before."

He sat up, his skin glowing in the light of the oil wick. "My power to withhold him has diminished anyway. I cannot keep step with him. My use in that respect has gone forever. Reynolds will soon insinuate himself into Edward's complete confidence. I am useful now only by my presence with him."

"Your presence? Or your death?" Her voice was dull. "I hear *your* gods speaking now, Piers. Your faith bids you take this awful and final step does it not?" He stood and came to her, but she moved away. "Does the spilling of your blood slake the horrible thirst of some ancient god?"

"Such talk is foolishness, sweetheart. There are two people on this earth whom I love. You, my dearest love, are the first, the most cherished. The other is my poor Edward. By my presence I harm you both beyond redemption. Edward will lose his crown, maybe even his life, if the barons are stirred finally into civil war. He will not meet them amicably while I live in exile, and they will not meet with him amicably if I live in England. I shall be a shadow between them. And you . . . you Alice will be destroyed by me. How long can you exist like this? Unable to leave Longmore without being followed, wondering if Warwick or some other is awaiting around the next bend of the road, riding for your very life because I am pursued like a common felon. I *must* go, Alice, for your sake and for Edward's sake." He held her close. "I am not so low a creature that I would drag you into the mire to drown with me."

She leaned against him, her arms slipping around his waist feeling the warmth of his bare skin. There was nothing she could say, and she knew it now. Her heart was breaking within her.

There was a small tapping at the outer door and Morvina crept in. "My Lady, forgive me but I had to come. Gareth has returned."

"Whatever is *he* here for?" Alice began to fasten the cords of her robe. "Tell him to be gone and come again at a reasonable hour." She was angry at the interruption, angry at Piers for what he was doing, angry at the world; the suppressed anger centred itself upon the unseen Gareth.

Morvina stepped closer. "My Lady, I think you had best see him. He knows that the Earl of Cornwall is here and he seeks to aid you both."

Piers nodded. "Bring him here, Morvina."

"Not *here*." Alice did not want Gareth to see her in her bedchamber with Piers.

But the maid had gone, and soon returned with Gareth. He wore Warwick's colours still and the raw December air brought a ruddy glow to his cheeks.

Piers was slowly pulling a velvet coat about him and Gareth's unhappy eyes glanced briefly at the rumpled bed before he addressed himself to Piers. "My Lord, I come to warn you that unless you are gone from here within an hour or so then you run a serious risk of capture. The Earl of Warwick has secured the aid of Lancaster and Arundel, and rides at this moment at the head of a great force to surround Longmore."

Piers looked levelly at the Welshman. "And why do you, of all people, come to warn me?"

Gareth was not abashed. "I came because you mean so much to Alice. For her sake I would try to save you."

A smile touched Piers' fine lips. "You begin to learn at last, Sir Gareth, you begin to learn of her at last."

"Aye, but too late for my own ends!" Gareth was not resentful, and found himself returning the Gascon's smile.

Alice turned away from them both, standing by the table and watching the dancing flame of the oil wick.

Piers watched her as he dressed and then glanced at Gareth, his voice so low that Alice could not hear. "Never, Sir Gareth, believe that you are too late for so important a thing as a woman's heart, especially if that woman be Alice. It could be, Sir Welsh Knight, that

131

the most serious obstacle in your path to her love will soon be removed." He lifted his sword belt from the floor and fastened it around his waist. "What would you have me do now?"

"Warwick has removed his spies from Longmore, he took Alice's threats seriously. I have no plan save that you . . . we . . . ride away from Longmore immediately or else be taken."

"So — we ride, together I assume, for Warwick will find no pleasure in your presence here." He went to Alice. "You remain here now, sweetheart, I will not endanger you further."

"I shall come with you." She was fierce in her determination.

"You shall not! If I have to tie you to the bed then I will do so, make no mistake of it, my love!"

She was bitter suddenly. "Why not stay here and await their coming? Why not give your life now instead of waiting?" She bit her lip and stared at the flame.

He touched her profusion of hair gently. "Do not be angry with me, Alice, for you know that I must do as I say. To give myself to the three wolves who come now would be foolish beyond belief. The manner of my going is important; it must be truly within the law and I feel that Warwick will never be completely within the law, nor Lancaster or Arundel. I shall await Pembroke, into *his* hands I shall go willingly for he alone has honour. Tell me that you understand, sweetheart, for I must go with your blessing."

She turned to him, nodding. "Where shall you go?"

"I shall go to the King, wherever he is. Stephen . . . " he looked at the steward who stood in the doorway, " . . . maybe Guy Beauchamp cannot outwit you, but now *I* have a task for you which must serve to outwit him. Ride to Gloucester with all speed and bring, drag, or whatever, the Abbot of St. Peter's to Longmore and protect Alice. Warwick would have no compunction about offending Holy Church, but Lancaster and Arundel would refrain from such a deed, and Lancaster has the authority."

Stephen hurried away without a word. Piers bent to Alice and kissed her, a long, sweet kiss.

She could not look to see him go.

For a long while it seemed she stood there, unmoving. This was the end of her fool's paradise then, the end of her blissful happiness . . . Morvina watched her anxiously, but suddenly she spoke to the maid. "Morvina, send some of Stephen's men to ride with Piers and Gareth. Tell them to remain with Piers at all times and to send me word frequently of where he is and what is happening."

The day was well on when the lookouts called from the turrets that they could see the huge army approaching from the east. They called down as they identified the banners of the Earls. Warwick. Lancaster. Arundel. The vultures who called themselves Lords Ordainers were coming swiftly to devour their single small prey.

A voice called out from behind the raised drawbridge and Morvina recognised it as Stephen's. The drawbridge was lowered and he rode in with an indignant Abbot seated behind him. The abbot's fat face was scarlet with rage and he looked slightly ridiculous as he sat there with his arms around Stephen's waist.

"Lady Alice, I must protest at this high-handed treatment of my person." He was helped to dismount.

Alice sighed. "My Lord Abbot, you have my apologies, but your presence is sorely needed to protect Longmore. I shall not be slow to show my appreciation in some tangible form . . . you still cast your envious eyes over the meadows I own along the far banks of the Severn. They are yours if you give your aid now. The Earls of Warwick, Lancaster and Arundel are at this very moment riding towards us, intent upon gaining a forceful entry. They believe that the Earl of Cornwall is hiding here and intend to search for him."

The Abbot's mouth opened and closed. "Cornwall is in exile, so how can he be here."

Alice could not even smile. "He was here, my Lord Abbot, he *was* here. But now he has gone and I need your help."

The meadows were alluring, but three mighty Earls were a vastly dampening thought. "You have lived outside Holy Church for some time, Lady Alice. You have consorted with a proven traitor, an immoral and perverted foreigner who by evil means has weaned the King away from his people."

Now she did smile. "Good Sir, if you believe that of Piers Gaveston then you will believe anything of anyone. He is none of the things of which he is accused. But that is not the point. I am soon to be attacked and the castle laid to siege, and all for nothing because the Earl of Cornwall is gone. I intend to lower the drawbridge to my enemies for I have no wish to have the walls weakened by siege digging. When they enter the castle I shall be at their mercy, I shall allow them to search the castle at will. All I need you to do is stand by me and give me the Church's protection. For the sake of my father whom you knew and respected, I ask this of you now."

He gradually relaxed. He was powerful in these parts and he knew it well enough . . . and the thought of possessing at last those fertile meadows swayed him finally. "Very well, Lady Alice, I shall do all I can."

As the Earls rode up the long hill they found the castle unprotected. The drawbridge was lowered and they rode into the courtyard to find Alice waiting. With her stood Stephen and the Abbot.

Lancaster dismounted first and approached her, his intense personal dislike for her not concealed at all. He despised her. "My Lady of Longmore, we have reason to believe that the traitor Gaveston is hiding here."

"You have my permission to search all you wish, my Lord."

He was surprised, his eyes sweeping around the naked walls. "Have we indeed? That means either that you have him well concealed, or that he is not here now. I wonder which it is."

"Wonder all you wish, my Lord of Lancaster, the state of your mind matters little to me for I assure you that your contempt for me is well matched by mine for you. Search the castle and be damned!"

The Abbot's eyes widened. "Lady Alice, such words are not going to aid your present predicament."

Warwick came up to Lancaster. "What is all this? Why is the Abbot dancing attendance?"

Alice spoke before the Abbot could open his mouth. "The Abbot is my guest." The Abbot's half-parted lips closed again.

Lancaster looked spitefully at Alice. "Very well, we shall search this accursed stronghold inch by inch."

And so they did. All day long the castle echoed to the sound of their searching. The soldiers pried in every nook, every corner, they tapped walls and even dug beneath a flagstone in the dungeon which they believed to sound hollow. All to no avail.

Alice sat in her apartments with Morvina. She was pleased at the thoroughness of their search, for each hour spent in fruitless activity here meant another mile or so towards safety for Piers. She could not believe that the worst would happen to him.

Lancaster and Warwick busied themselves conducting the search. Warwick's frustration was immense, and Lancaster's cold anger was scarcely less intense. Only the handsome, golden-haired Arundel maintained a semblance of civility. He sat with her now, speaking frequently, trying vainly to lull her into an unwise word.

Edmund Fitzalan gained even more of her contempt than his two

134

accomplices. At least Lancaster and Warwick were open in their hatred, but Arundel hid behind a friendly charm more dangerous than all their raging. She remembered the first occasion on which she had seen him, so drunk that he could hardly stand. He smiled yet again as she glanced at him, and her stomach curdled. "Will you not take some wine with me, my Lord of Arundel — I shall send for a fresh tun to be brought for you. No doubt my steward's arm is as strong as the arm of Surrey!" The insult was driven home. Edmund's capacity, or lack of it, for wine was rather too touchy a subject for him to wish it bandied about in front of Alice's retainers and the boggling Abbot. His blue eyes revealed his true feelings for so brief a second, before he lapsed into a stony silence.

The sun was almost setting when at last Lancaster and Warwick satisfied themselves that their quarry was not here. They came into Alice's apartments where Arundel still kept silent watch upon her.

Lancaster stood before her, his hands upon his hips. "We have found nothing."

"No. You have found nothing because the Earl of Cornwall has long since gone."

Lancaster was exultant. "So! You admit to harbouring a traitor!" He would be able to punish her now, for hers was a great crime.

"I admit to having given shelter to the Earl of Cornwall — who is no traitor."

"By the law of this land, he *is* a traitor, my Lady, and you are guilty of aiding and abetting him."

"The law! *The law!* What law is it when wrung by force from an unwilling King? If Edward considers himself bound forever by such coercion then I shall be greatly surprised . . . and disappointed in my judgement of him!"

The Abbot gaped. How could he protect this goose of a woman if she openly admitted to the crime, and then proceeded to drive Lancaster to violence?

Morvina stepped forward, looking past them all at the shadowy far corner of the room. She addressed herself only to Warwick. "I think that the Earl of Warwick would not wish his nephew's widow to be arrested on such a charge." She smiled sweetly at him and then returned her gaze to the distant corner.

Beauchamp's eyes followed her glance, and so did Alice's. There, in the dust and cobwebs crawled an immense spider. No-one else in the room seemed aware of it. Warwick's face blanched and he swallowed with fear. Another warning. A second warning.

"I . . . " He paused, and Morvina immediately moved closer to him. She was small and dainty, but to Guy Beauchamp she was the ultimate in terror. He dragged his eyes away from the loathsome spider and spoke to Lancaster. "There is no point in pursuing this matter now. It is Gaveston we want, not this woman."

"By all the Saints, Warwick, you change your price more often than a whore! Very well, when the time comes we shall know where to find her." He walked to the window and looked out in the darkening evening. "Night draws on, there is little chance of giving pursuit tonight."

Alice's servants were moving through the apartments with torches, and the air was filled with the smoke and smell of fire. As Alice watched. Lancaster sat down; he obviously intended remaining at Longmore for the night.

"Oh no, my Lord of Lancaster. You and your fellow Earls are not welcome to sleep beneath my roof! My land you may sleep upon — outside the castle walls!"

Morvina's eyes were luminous in the changing light of the torches, and she stared on at the terrified Warwick. He had no intention whatsoever of spending a night under the same roof as Morvina.

"I shall depart from here, now!" He strode out, leaving a bemused Lancaster staring after him. Arundel's blue eyes narrowed a little and he awaited Lancaster's next move. Ever the follower and never the leader, Edmund Fitzalan would be a sheep for all his days.

Lancaster listened to the noise of Warwick's hurried departure. He stood suddenly. "I stay only with a gracious host, and such is not a description which could be readily given to you, Lady Alice."

She was ready for his spite. "And I give shelter only to men of honour, my *Lord!*"

They left Longmore then, even the Abbot taking a horse and riding back across the causeway over the marshes towards Gloucester, led by Stephen.

Above the silent castle, the seagulls called yet again as they flew back towards the open sea for the night.

TWENTY-TWO

ALICE reined her grey palfrey in and looked down at the swirling waters of the Severn. It was good to ride out in the spring sunshine, May was ever a beautiful month.

Large yellow pussy-willows dripped their pollen over her dark brown cloak as the soft breeze bent the branches towards her. This was how she loved to see the river, winking and shining in the full light of the sun.

There was no fear of capture now, for Piers was with the King, openly defying the Lords Ordainers. Where was he now? The last message she had received from Stephen's men had told her that the King and the Earl of Cornwall were in the north of England, moving from fortress to fortress ahead of the angry barons. Was this what England was now reduced to? A foolish pursuit across the hills and vales, a foolish but vindictive pursuit of one man?

The water gurgled unexpectedly and the nervous palfrey tossed its head, startled. Alice paid no heed. The river swallowed her thoughts. Tears sprang to her eyes. Where was Pembroke? Why had Piers not surrendered to Aymer de Valence as he had said? The names of all the Ordainers had reached her ears in one way or another, but of the trusty Pembroke she heard nothing . . . and he was the one and only noble to whom Piers was prepared to give himself.

Morvina and Stephen sat a little behind Alice, watching the lonely figure on the grey palfrey. Morvina's heart ached for her, but suddenly her sharp ears caught a new sound.

"My Lady, draw your mount back from the river, a bore approaches! Quickly!"

Alice's reactions were dull and slow. Her own ears were blunted somehow to the difference in the air around her. The splashing, rushing of the bore impressed itself upon her at last and she turned the palfrey's frightened head.

Already the bore was visible, a silver, shining strip of tumbling water rushing upstream against the current. The Severn seemed to be stopped, the force of the approaching tidal wave forcing the river to check in its endless passage. The wave hurled itself against the banks as if striving to be free of the confines of the river bed. Alice's palfrey panicked, its hooves cutting into the soft spring mud and slithering helplessly up a slight incline away from the terrifying spectacle of the bore. It cried out in its fear.

Stephen kicked his own reluctant horse forward and reached out to snatch Alice's slight figure from the swaying back of her palfrey. The bore crashed by, sending up spray and droplets of muddy water. The willow was dragged backwards in the sudden change of current, and the fresh spring leaves were torn cruelly in the fierce drift. Twigs and branches hurried upstream, twirling and bobbing in the sharply eddying water.

Alice clung weakly to Stephen as he urged his horse away from the river's edge. The unfortunate palfrey slipped and struggled on the evil mud, its panic taking it nearer to the waiting, watching river. Its hind quarters dropped suddenly as the bank was no more and with a scream of dread the creature was snapped into the boiling waters.

Stephen held Alice close, his fingers stroking her neck as she wept. Morvina watched silently as the palfrey was dragged finally beneath the surface, leaving no trace. The bore swept onwards, around the base of Longmore's hill towards the jetty and ledge of rock at Stonebench.

Slowly Stephen rode his quaking horse back towards the castle, and Alice did not lift her head from his chest until they were within the courtyard. She was lifted from his arms, and then he dismounted, picking her up again and carrying her to her rooms. Morvina followed.

Alice lay upon her bed and Stephen leaned over her, his face worried. "Lady Alice, the danger is past." He took her cold hands.

"Thank you for saving my life, Stephen. But for you I would have joined my poor mount beneath the river." She closed her eyes and turned her face away.

Morvina shook her head at him. "Be gone now, I will attend to her. This has proved too much to bear after all else that has happened. I know how to look after her."

With a deep sigh Stephen straightened and left the two women alone. Morvina brought her casket of herbs and medicines to the bedside and began to choose the ones she needed. The large tabby cat which doted upon the Welsh girl crept out from beneath the bed, purring loudly and beginning to rub itself around her legs.

Alice stared at the curtains which hung around the bed, green and gold, the colours of Longmore . . . green and gold, the colours of Cornwall. Piers. She had lain with him in this bed, she had held him close . . . A small cup was pressed to her lips. The draught tasted unpleasant but she could not refuse. A drowsiness began to slide over her, a warm drowsiness which could not be denied. Her eyes closed, and Morvina smiled. Sleep was the finest cure, sleep and rest.

The voices were distant, echoing around in her head. Alice turned her face towards the mattress to force the sounds away. But they persisted, growing ever more loud and insistent. Her eyelids flickered and opened, and she saw Morvina and Gareth standing close to the doorway. Gareth? Her fuddled brain struggled with this new circumstance.

"Gareth?" Her voice was scarcely more than a husky croak.

"See! Dolt! You have wakened her!" Morvina was angry.

"*I?* I came here quietly, it was you who shouted." Gareth scowled at his kinswoman.

"Gareth." Alice held out her hand to him.

He crossed the room quickly, taking the hand and pressing it to his lips. He did not release her fingers as he sat on the bed and looked at her. "Morvina has told me what happened."

She swallowed and bit her lip. The terrified screams of her palfrey seemed to ring in her ears again.

He squeezed her fingers gently. "I came to bring you good news."

"Of Piers?" The sparkle of hope in her eyes cut into Gareth's heart.

"Yes. He has surrendered himself to the Earl of Pembroke who has pledged on his honour to protect his prisoner and give him a safe journey southwards to London. The news is not entirely good, for Piers will have to stand trial, but at least you know now that he has not fallen into the hands of Warwick, Lancaster or Arundel. The King has revoked the charge of treason against him too."

Her fingernails dug into his hand as the relief flooded over her. "Tell me how it happened." Oh, Aymer de Valence, I bless you, I thank God for you . . . And the charge of treason was revoked! Piers would not die, *he would not die* . . .

"The King and Piers separated, and while Edward rode to York, Piers took refuge in Scarborough Castle. In less than two weeks the Earls of Pembroke and Surrey had arrived and began to lay siege. Piers sent word out that he would surrender to Pembroke only, and this was agreed to. Pembroke pledged his word that he would look after the safety of his prisoner."

"But how can one man speak for all the others?" Morvina's voice was doubtful of Pembroke's ability to control the activities of his fellows.

Gareth shrugged. "All the Lords Ordainers took oaths to uphold each other's decisions. If Pembroke swears to protect Piers then his oath is binding on the others. They took this measure to protect themselves, but now it serves to protect Piers too."

"And where is he now?" Alice sat up, her eyes shining.

Gareth gazed at her. Her hair was loose and tumbled about her shoulders, and the golden eyes were beautiful. He ached with love for her. But it was of Piers that she spoke; Piers, always, always . . . "Pembroke is bringing him south. I know that Pembroke intends to spend a little time at his manor of Bampton in Oxfordshire as his Countess is there at present."

Alice slipped from the bed. "And they will be there when?"

He leaned back against the post of the bed, watching Morvina lighting the candles upon the table. The spring evening was upon them already. "In about two weeks I should imagine – they are travelling very slowly as Piers I am afraid is wounded slightly. He cannot ride with any speed. Do not worry, it is not serious."

She smiled. "Then I shall have time to be there waiting for them. Beatrice of Pembroke will not mind my presence, she has always been kind to me."

He nodded. "I thought perhaps that that would be your plan. Beatrice already expects you, for I took myself to Bampton before spurring on for Longmore."

Alice flung her arms around his neck and hugged him. "Oh Gareth, your kindness is far more than I deserve."

He put his hands up to pull her arms away, for her closeness was too much for him to bear. "Alice, my dearest Alice . . . "

She drew back from him, realising that she hurt him still. "Forgive me, I am thoughtless."

He smiled, pretending to box her ears. "Never that, 'cariad'."

Morvina suddenly placed herself between them, her hands on her hips and a frown on her face. "*Sir* Gareth, what were you doing that you know so much about Pembroke's intentions?"

He sighed. "I was riding northwards from London to join the Earl of Warwick. I happened upon Pembroke and his prisoner riding south."

"So, you still persist in wearing the black dog's colours. Why is it, eh? You are now twenty-four – your father pledged you to Warwick's service only until you were twenty-one!"

Alice's lips parted as she realised the truth of what her maid said. She had not given it much thought these past years since she had known Piers, but now that it was pointed out . . . "What does it mean, Gareth?"

"It means only that I chose to remain with Warwick and know therefore what he was about. I was of more use to you doing that than in any other capacity. And the decision has proved a wise one, for I have saved you and Piers on more than one occasion." He was rightly reproachful.

Morvina looked disbelieving but Alice touched his arm. "You are right, we should not have doubted you for one moment."

The maid turned to Alice. "I have a request, my Lady." She glared at Gareth to tell him to leave the room, but he sat stubbornly where he was.

"What is it?"

"I wish to extinguish all light in the castle."

Gareth snorted angrily. "A pox on your dabblings and chantings, Morvina!"

"Why, Morvina?" Alice did not know what the maid meant.

"I wish to kindle needfire."

Alice's eyes went from one angry face to the other. "What is needfire?"

Gareth stood, pouring himself a draught from a jug. "Needfire is burned at times of stress. Those of the Old Religion believe that it draws the aid of the old gods and dispels evil. 'Tis a foolish and empty thing."

Alice was thoughtful. "Is it for Piers?" The maid nodded. "And is it what he would wish himself?" Again Morvina nodded. "Then do as you wish, you have my permission to extinguish all light in the castle."

Gareth stared at her. "You do not believe in all this rubbish?"

She would not meet his eyes. "It is for Piers."

Realization dawned upon him. "You mean that the Earl of Cornwall is of Morvina's persuasion?" He was incredulous.

"Aye," said Morvina coolly, "and if you had any wit you'd realise that the black hound of Arden is no Christian either!"

"Gareth . . . " Alice went to him. "Gareth, will you promise to help in this?"

"I am a Christian, Alice, I do not believe."

"All I ask is that you be content to sit in darkness until Morvina has done what she wishes."

He hesitated, but the pleading in her eyes moved him. "For you I will, but I wish to have no part in it."

141

"Nor will you have!" Morvina was abrupt, her tone intimating that she would not accept him anyway. "And neither shall you, Lady Alice, for you must take another draught of my preparation. You need more sleep, especially as I suspect that tomorrow we will be riding for Bampton. You would have slept on had you not been aroused by my kinsman here!" She jabbed verbally at Gareth.

Alice smiled. "Do not quarrel. We have need of each other. I will take your potion Morvina, and Gareth will behave himself admirably — will you not?" She turned her head to him, and he nodded his agreement.

Morvina was opening the casket again and already had taken out a small bunch of withered herbs. She mixed the medicine swiftly and held the small cup out to Alice.

Alice drank deeply and the maid hustled her back to the bed and then turned on Gareth once more. "Be gone, Sir Gareth, you have no place here."

He remained firmly where he was. "You be gone, Morvina, and commence your incantations. I shall stay with Alice until she sleeps."

"It is not seemly . . . " Morvina did not approve.

Alice's drowsy voice interrupted her. "Gareth can stay with me, do not worry so."

The maid closed the casket with an abrupt crash, gathered it beneath her arm and left the room. She paused in the doorway. "Gareth, remember to extinguish the candles presently." He inclined his head.

Alice could feel the potion taking its hold upon her again. She was vaguely and distantly aware of Gareth's lips upon hers in a gentle kiss before she lost consciousness.

Gareth settled himself in a chair and stretched his legs out. He had ridden long and hard, and was weary . . .

Two hours later Morvina returned, her mission accomplished and the needfire kindled for Piers' protection. She came quietly into Alice's chamber and stopped in horror at what she saw. Alice slept on, unaware, a tiny smile upon her lips. In his chair Gareth slouched, in a deep, exhausted sleep.

On the table, in a sea of melted wax, the candles burned on. There had been a light in the castle; all the while there had been a light . . .

TWENTY-THREE

BEATRICE of Pembroke smiled warmly at Alice as she dismounted after the tiring journey from Longmore. "Lady Alice, what a great pleasure it is to see you once more."

A manservant removed the dusty travelling cloak and Alice curtsied low to her hostess. Behind her Morvina, Gareth and Stephen dismounted too, and Stephen took charge of the remainder of Alice's party. They had travelled with about twenty of Stephen's most trustworthy men.

The June sunshine blazed down from a flawless sky, but the ancient house at Bampton was cool inside as Beatrice led her guests in from the hot summer day. With her own hand she poured a refreshing cup of mead which Alice drank thankfully.

Beatrice allowed herself the luxury of studying Alice closely. There could be no doubt that Gaveston's mistress was one of the most beautiful women in the realm. When first she had come to court she had been little more than a child for all her years, with a poor knowledge of how to dress to the greatest advantage. But now, after the passing of four years, Lady Alice de Longmore had blossomed into a lovely, graceful, accomplished young women. Beatrice nodded to herself from her seat by the window, her sharp little eyes taking in the willowy figure of the tall, red-headed girl. That waist was so slender that surely a man could span it with his hands and leave his fingers touching . . . well, perhaps not quite, but the impression was surely that. And that gown of silver-blue brocade was a delight to behold, with its costly undergown of dark grey silk embroidered with wine-red thread, and that same wine colour lined the long, pendulous sleeves of the overgown. Alice's hair was brushed into two loops over her ears and then coiled on the top of her head, and partially covered by a flowing headdress of silver silk; The headdress was held in place by a padded velvet circlet of dark grey, embroidered with the dragons of Longmore.

Beatrice sighed wistfully, for there had been a time when Aymer de Valence's plump wife had not been so plump. Aye, in her younger days Beatrice had been possessed of a dainty prettiness of her own. She stood and went to her embroidery frame, seating herself heavily behind it and taking up her needle again.

"Lady Alice, I must be honest with you and tell you that I do not know if I shall meet with my Lord's approval for allowing you to come here. He is very disapproving of your being . . . er . . .

Gaveston's mistress . . . " She blushed slightly and smiled shyly.

Alice put down her cup upon a table and turned to her hostess. "Would that I could be Piers' wife, but that is not to be."

The needle hovered thoughtfully. "You know do you not that the Countess of Cornwall has but recently borne him a daughter." She watched Alice carefully to see her reaction to this news.

Alice smiled, her fingers moving over the filigree silver buttons on her sleeve. "I knew that she was with child, but not that she had given birth to a daughter."

The needle jabbed at the canvass fiercely. "He has acknowledged the babe as his own!" Beatrice's lips were a straight, compressed line. Could nothing shake this foolish girl's loyalty to Gaveston!

"I knew that he would do so, for he is a man of honour, my Lady."

Beatrice rested her hands in her wide lap, shaking her head ruefully. "I had hoped that you did not know, Alice. I had hoped that he had not told you at all and that the knowledge would drive you away from here before he comes. You would be so much better without any further contact with the Earl of Cornwall."

Alice went to her, reaching down to touch the folded hands. "Beatrice, I pray most earnestly that I do not cause trouble for you with Lord Aymer, for such would be a sorrow to me. But I would tell you this . . . I would not have truly lived had I not met and loved Piers Gaveston."

Beatrice looked up into the steady golden eyes. "I am glad that he has brought you some measure of happiness, Alice . . . "

Alice squeezed the podgy fingers. "It is not merely some measure, Beatrice, it is all my happiness!"

The Countess smiled. "Then I perceive that nothing I can say will dissuade you from your foolishness. If only it could have been some other man, some other knight who stole your heart . . . " She could not hide her innate sense of outrage at Piers' position at Edward's court.

Alice straightened, divining Beatrice's thoughts. "Do not think unkindly of him, for he is none of the things you fear. Come, would it not please you to know that Lord Aymer is the only one of England's Earls whom Piers honours? He told me that he would surrender into your Lord's hands, and that he has done."

The Countess glowed in spite of her attempts to conceal her feelings. Try as she would she could not entirely dislike the King's favourite, for he had always been kind and tactful towards her. It was only the surly noblemen who felt the sting of the Gascon's cruel tongue. Aye, and he was so handsome . . . Beatrice sighed, and began to rethread her needle.

The moments passed in companionable silence before Beatrice looked up again. "I see that you have Warwick's lieutenant in your company once more."

"Gareth?"

"The same. I cannot imagine *where* his loyalty is truly placed, for he rides at so many sides."

Alice smiled. "Gareth is a true and loyal knight, Beatrice, and his loyalty is to me. He has helped me from danger on many an occasion . . . I owe even my liberty to him."

"But he still wears Warwick's badge! It would be as well to keep him from my Lord's sight, for Aymer abhors Warwick. I think we may thank God that Warwick has no knowledge of my Lord's plans, for I would not trust Beauchamp to honour any agreement."

Alice felt a distant coldness settle over her, for Beatrice's words were a faint echo of her own uncertainty. But if the Lords Ordainers had sworn oaths to uphold each other's words, then Warwick was equally as bound as the others . . .

Beatrice sighed. "It is truly a shame that not all the Lords Ordainers have the same purity of purpose as my dear Lord. I would place my Lord, Gloucester, Surrey, and the dearly remembered Lincoln on the side of honour . . . as to the others! Well, think on them; Lancaster, Warwick, Arundel, Hereford . . . Holy Mother, what a nest of venomous serpents!"

Alice turned to look out of the sun-filled window, over the sloping hillside. The trees and bushes shimmered in the heat haze, seeming to dance upon the hot earth, and in the distance the hills were a purple haze of warmth. The hedgerow flowers were in their fullest glory, bobbing their colourful heads to the merest whisper of scented breeze. Close to the window grew a thick lavender bush, and its heady perfume saturated the close air; butterflies flapped daintily around it, jewel-like and brilliant.

The Countess watched from the embroidery frame, smiling to see the soft eagerness upon Alice's face. So obvious was her anticipation, her impatience to be with her lover once more. "You know that he is wounded slightly, do you not?"

"Gareth told me, but he said it was not serious."

"Nor is it, merely a flesh wound. But it is in his thigh and this makes riding more than a little difficult, which is why the journey from Scarborough has taken so long. But I received word at dawn today that my Lord fully expects to reach Bampton tonight. You will not have long to wait now."

A warmth rushed through Alice's veins. Tonight! Tonight she would look on him again . . .

The long June evening was still sunny when the evening meal was finally cleared away in the hall. Alice sat in her room, the window thrown wide open. From here she could look down the dusty road where at any moment she would see Pembroke's retinue. Oh hurry, hurry . . .

Far below, the lavender seemed to renew its perfume twicefold, as with the gradual cooling of the evening the pungent essence filtered through into the small room. Alice breathed deeply, thinking that she would ask Beatrice for some of the plant to take back to Longmore . . .

Hoofbeats! Surely she could hear . . . yes, Pembroke was coming. The silver and blue banners flapped above the cavalcade in the fading light. The long, dark gold shafts of the dying sun threw strange shadows over the Earl's party as it approached Bampton. Her eyes searched the party, but she could not see Piers.

As Pembroke reined in outside, Alice hurried from the window and out into the passageway. At the head of the stairs she paused, for already Aymer was entering his house.

Beatrice was waiting to receive her husband. "Aymer, my dear Lord, it has been so long since I last saw you." Pembroke hugged his plump little wife, kissing her warmly.

She glanced behind him. "But where is your prisoner?"

Pembroke sighed, unfastening his cloak and handing it to a waiting servant. "Bah, we could only reach Deddington, some twelve miles away, before I realised that we stood no hope of reaching Bampton before nightfall. Gaveston's wound has been troublesome, and the pain was considerable. I could not force him to further effort and neither could I stay away from you another night, sweetheart!" He kissed her again. "I left him at the rector's house in Deddington, with a small guard, and then came on alone."

Beatrice was uneasy, and she remembered her conversation with Alice that very afternoon. "But is it wise to leave him alone?"

Pembroke misunderstood. "He is in no condition to escape, and anyway, he is a man of his word."

"That is not my meaning. What if Warwick should come to know . . . "

Aymer put his arm around her fat waist. "Warwick is a Lord Ordainer, just as I am. Besides, Edward has revoked the ordinances and so Gaveston is no longer charged with treason. He has willingly given himself into my keeping. You worry overmuch." He walked into the hall where servants had prepared a meal for him. Beatrice went slowly after him, but the very slowness of her gait told of her own doubts.

At the head of the stairs Alice stood in silence, and her excitement turned chill within her. Pembroke had left Piers alone, alone but for a few guards! The doubts struggled with one another, forcing to the surface of her thoughts, and now they would not be denied. She whirled about and hurried to Stephen's room where she knew she would find also Gareth and Morvina.

The two men were engaged in a game of chess, and Morvina leaned familiarly over Stephen's chair watching. They turned in surprise at Alice's hurried entry. The door swung back on its rusty hinges, creaking loudly.

Stephen stood, his face immediately wary. "What is it?"

Gareth leaned over to lift his leather coat from the bed where it lay. " 'Cariad', you are as white as snow."

She was almost weeping. "He has not brought Piers, he has left him alone at Deddington."

Gareth slowly put on the leather coat, fastening the thongs with infuriating deliberation. "Alone? Come, sweetheart, Pembroke would not be so foolish."

"But I heard him say so! Alone but for a few guards because he could travel no further on account of his wound." Alice wrung her hands.

Stephen smiled nervously. "But he will be safe enough. The ordinances . . . "

Alice exclaimed irritably. "The ordinances? What notice will Warwick take of the law? He hates too much, too completely!"

Morvina hurried to her mistress, leading her to sit down in a chair. Gareth sat on the arm of the chair and put his arm around her shoulder. "Do not worry so, Alice, for if Pembroke is so unconcerned then surely the danger must not be so great as you fear."

She pulled away from him. "And you are prepared to risk Piers' life on such a feeble conjecture? You guess, only guess, as do

147

I, but is it not better to be safe than to be filled with regret later?"

Stephen picked up a chessman, turning it in his hand slowly. "If Pembroke has only just reached here, then I doubt if anyone else even *knows* that Piers is left at Deddington . . . "

Gareth sucked in his breath suddenly. "D'Audley!"

"What of him?" Alice's eyes were wide.

"D'Audley had met Pembroke some short while before I did, Pembroke made some remark about the highway being alive with Warwick's creatures. If d'Audley met him then you can be sure that Warwick is in full possession of the facts."

Stephen tossed the chessman back on to the board. "There is no time to be lost! We have a chance of reaching Deddington before Warwick does." He grabbed his cloak and ran from the room. Alice's limbs were shaking with her fear for Piers, and her teeth chattered. Guy Beauchamp's face seemed to hover in the room before her haunted eyes, and that face bore an evil smile.

Morvina brought Alice's cloak and placed it about her shoulders. "You will go with us? But I have no need to ask you that, have I?" She smiled.

Gareth paused in the doorway. "We must persuade Pembroke to return, without him we stand little chance. The few guards he *has* left will not believe our tale."

The maid pushed him out, leading Alice by the hand. "I will stay behind and do what I can. We have no time to all try our hand at convincing him, and Lady Alice is in no state to convince him of anything. Hurry now, I can hear Stephen and his men outside."

Down the staircase they hurried, and out into the warm evening. The sun had sunk in the west, and the skies glowed red beyond the trees. The horses were refreshed, and stamped eagerly. Gareth mounted quickly, reaching down to swing Alice up behind him. Stephen had not brought her palfrey and now he frowned. "Is it wise to take her with us?"

Alice's voice was shrill. "I will not stay behind!"

Without further ado, they turned their horses in the direction of Deddington and soon the air was filled with the sound of hoofbeats.

Pembroke heard the commotion and hurried outside. He was in time to see the small party as it rode away into the night. He turned to his wife. "Who are they?"

Beatrice looked warily at her husband. "I think that it is Lady Alice de Longmore and her party."

Aymer dropped the chicken leg he was holding to the cobbles, staring after the now vanishing party. A slight worm of doubt gnawed at him. He turned and his glance fell upon Morvina. He recognised her immediately. "What do they intend? Are they seeking to take Gaveston?"

She shook her head. "No, they ride to protect him from the Earl of Warwick."

Pembroke picked at a fibre of chicken flesh which was stuck between his teeth. "Beauchamp does not know where Gaveston is, and besides, Warwick will abide by my word."

"By your leave, my Lord, I do not think that the Earl of Warwick will spare a thought for your pledged word, and he *does* have some idea of where you and your prisoner are for Sir Hugh d'Audley will have told him. Your prisoner is in great danger, my Lord, and I think that only *your* presence will prevent a terrible murder."

Pembroke glowered at her. "Murder? What do you speak of, wench?"

Beatrice put her hand on her husband's arm. "Aymer, I think maybe she is right. Warwick's personal hatred of Gaveston passes all normal bounds. If he sees an opportunity to rid himself and the world of Cornwall, then I greatly fear that he will take it."

Pembroke hovered in indecision. He was tired, he had ridden all day to be with his wife. He had not much faith in Warwick, it was true, but even Beauchamp would not dare . . .

Morvina could see that he was not yet convinced of the imminent danger. "My Lord of Pembroke, the Earl of Cornwall gave himself into *your* custody and yours alone. He trusted his life to you as a man of honour, and now you have left him without your protection in a part of the realm which is far too close to Warwick for safety."

The words took effect, and Pembroke gave orders for his men to prepare to ride once more. But it was well over an hour before he left Bampton on the road to Deddington. And an hour can be a long, long time.

TWENTY-FOUR

DEDDINGTON was quiet. The village was deserted in the early hours of the morning.

Alice's party dismounted and went on foot in the direction of the rectory. They crept quickly past the small cottages which were locked and bolted for the night. Not even a candle seemed to glow from within.

Outside the rectory they came at last upon signs of life. Four guards in Pembroke's silver and blue colours paced up and down before the door. Stephen sent one of his men around the back of the building and he returned with the news that four more men guarded the rear entrance.

Stephen leaned back against a wall, turning his head to whisper to the others. "I do not know what to do next. Pembroke's men will never accept our word of Warwick's probable approach. Our only hope lies in getting Piers out. But how?"

Alice bit her lip. Piers was there, within a few yards of her. They must save him! An idea crept into her head. She touched Stephen's arm. "I could perhaps gain entry. If Piers is wounded, then it is likely that his wound would be attended. Deddington would have a midwife, and she would be well skilled in such things. If I pulled my hood well over my face and stooped, then I could pass for such a woman."

Gareth's hand clasped hers. "No! Besides, what use will that be? You have still to get him out."

Stephen put his fingers to his lips. "Not so loud, Sir Gareth. I fear that I can think of no better plan for the moment. If Piers is warned of the danger he is in, it could be that he is well enough to make good his own escape. There is much ivy growing over the side of the rectory, and the twines look sturdy enough. It is so thick that it almost conceals a small window . . . there, can you see it?" He pointed and they all saw the black shadow behind the waving ivy leaves. "Alice, if you can gain entry, then you had best try to get him to whichever room lies behind that window."

Alice nodded, and before Gareth could make further objections, she was gone, pulling her hood forward so that her whole face was in shadow. She held her cloak together in the front to hide the rich silver-blue brocade of her gown.

She stepped into the roadway and into the full stream of moonlight. Boldly she walked towards the rectory. The guards took little heed of her until it became apparent that she was coming to the door which they protected. They crossed their pikes before her face and she halted immediately.

"What is your business here, Mistress?"

"I come at the behest of the rector, good sirs." She spoke roughly, her voice muffled by the cloak.

"At this hour?" They were surly.

"Aye, at *this* hour! I was sent for some time ago but was already attending a birthing. A babe cannot be hurried into the world. I am the midwife and the rector sent word that you have a wounded man here in need of my attention! Now do I gain entry or not!" She spoke roughly and forcefully, as she knew a midwife would for those good ladies were the scourge of many a village.

One of the guards removed his pike. He had met one such as this before and had no intention of crossing her. "Well Mistress, I doubt if the rector will be pleased for he took to his bed many a hour ago."

"Then leave him be! I have no need of *his* interference in my work!"

Unbelievably the door was pushed open for her to go in. She walked past the guards and the door closed behind her again. Her eyes took a moment to grow accustomed to the candlelight within. There were more of Pembroke's men inside, she counted five in all. Eight guards at the doors, and five inside the rectory. She poked one of them sharply with her finger. "I have come to attend a wounded man. Where may I find him?"

His eyes widened apprehensively as he heard the harridan voice emanating from the black-cloaked figure. "Aye Mistress, he is upstairs. His room is guarded, you cannot miss it."

She climbed the stairs unhindered, and along the passageway which faced her she saw the two guards. At the far end of the passageway was a small door, and she knew that beyond that door lay the room with the almost-concealed window.

The guards looked up in surprise as she approached. "Stand aside for me to pass, dolts, if I have to explain my reasons for being here once more then I swear I'll take a birch to your buttocks!" Alice was astounded at her own capacity for taking on the personality of a midwife.

They stood aside immediately. A pity on the unlucky prisoner to have his wound prodded by *this* old cat! They could tell a midwife when they saw one!

She lifted the huge latch on the door and pushed inside. The single candle flickered in the sudden draught, but she saw the curtained bed straight away. The curtains were drawn back and tied, and Piers had lifted himself on to one elbow to see who entered. "Who is it?"

She closed the door and pushed back her hood. "You do not know me, Piers?"

"Alice?" He fell back weakly against the mattress.

She hurried across the room, horrified at the faintness of his voice. The wound in his thigh had been poorly dressed and the flesh was red and angry. Blood oozed thickly from behind the dirty dressing. He took her hand as she came close and pressed the palms to his lips. "Sweet Alice, Pembroke is softening to have allowed you here."

She twined her fingers in his, feeling weak at touching him again. "Piers, we have got to get you out of here. We are certain that Warwick is coming to take you."

He shook his head. "But I am with the good Lord Aymer . . . "

"Pembroke has left you alone, Piers. There are fifteen men guarding you!" Jesu, and Warwick will come with five hundred! "You must try to escape. Can you stand?"

He began to struggle to his feet, but his face drained white as the pain lanced through him from the wound. He swayed and she put her arms around him to support him. She pushed him back on to the bed, her heart beating frantically as she sought an answer. He was not strong enough to overpower the two guards outside, and she could not do it herself. But if the guards remained, how then could she get him to the room at the end of the passageway?

She went to the window and peered out. The room where Piers was imprisoned was at the front of the rectory, and directly below she could see the four guards by the front entrance. Across the street a shadowy figure stepped out briefly from behind a small cottage. She recognised Stephen and was about to signal to him when he stepped hastily back into the darkness at the side of the cottage.

Hoofbeats drummed through the night air as a mighty force descended upon Deddington. Soon the street outside was filled with red and white and Guy Beauchamp rode in to seek his revenge.

Her fingers shook. There was no time. No time. Where was Pembroke?

Piers had heard the hoofbeats and his dark eyes were on Alice's face. "The black dog comes to bite, my love, do not let him find you here."

She went to him. There was nothing she could do now. But never would she leave him. She pulled his head against her breast and held him tightly. He seemed almost to be in a daze, as if he did not quite know what was happening. Her fingers stroked the damp black curls, and the silent tears ran down her cheeks.

The rectory was in a turmoil suddenly. Pembroke's men were caught unprepared and Warwick's superior numbers left them no chance. Footsteps hurried along to the door and it was flung open.

Warwick's men paused in surprise at seeing her there. They glanced at one another. Then Guy Beauchamp himself pushed his way into the room.

His piercing eyes recognised Alice immediately. "Well, the Lady of Longmore! Do you still adorn the Gascon squire's bedchamber then, my sweet Alice?"

She swallowed. "The Earl of Pembroke swore on the Host that the Earl of Cornwall would be safe . . ."

"Pembroke? I do not see Pembroke!" Warwick rolled his eyes expressively at the ceiling. "Take the traitor!"

Still she held Piers. "He is no traitor, the King has removed all charges against him!"

Piers stood, putting his hand gently to her trembling face. "Do not endanger your most precious life for me, Alice. I must go with them." He turned to Warwick. "I shall come quietly enough, I ask only that you allow the Lady Alice to go free."

"You are in no position to ask anything. She comes too." Warwick motioned to his men and they seized Piers and dragged him roughly from the room. Alice saw the spasm of pain which crossed the white face as the wound reopened and fresh blood spurted out.

"My Lord of Warwick, have a little pity. He is wounded. He cannot possibly escape from you now, I beg of you that your men are not so rough."

Beauchamp's lip curled unpleasantly as his jealous heart tightened its grip on him. "Oh, how you fight for him, how fiercely you protect your lover! Maybe it is true that he cannot escape, but your presence here leads me to wonder how many of your friends from Longmore are here too. He is to be guarded most carefully, and if that means being rough, then so be it." He gripped her wrist and pulled her behind him as he went down the stairs and out into the street.

She was thrust unceremoniously on to a horse and her hands

tied before her so that she could grip only the pommel of the saddle. Warwick himself looped the reins over the horse's head and led her.

Piers was tied in a like fashion upon another horse. Even in the uncertain moonlight the ghastly white of his face was plain to see. Once more he seemed to be in some sort of daze.

Warwick's unpleasant laugh sounded close by. "How dowdy the fine peacock is now! What a pitiful sight! Would that our pretty King could see his beloved Perrot *now!*" He glanced sideways at Alice's stiff face. "Would Edward wish to plant a kiss upon *those* lips?"

She looked at him, her eyes full of loathing. "The King will always love Piers as he would love a brother! Nothing will change that, not even the jealous whinings of England's nobility who so envy his position. Will *you* ever inspire such devotion, my Lord of Warwick? I think not." She was jerked savagely as Warwick spurred his mount forward.

From the shadows Alice's friends watched helplessly.

TWENTY-FIVE

THE apartments at Warwick Castle were luxurious enough, with their costly tapestries and beautiful carved chairs. And books! Alice was surprised to realise that Guy Beauchamp possessed books, for he did not seem the type of man to take an interest in such things.

She stood by the window trying in vain to see down into the courtyard where there was a great deal of noise as a large party rode in. This *must* be Pembroke! She closed her eyes with relief. Now Piers would be saved once more.

She turned back into the room, her face hardening as she saw the men-at-arms who stood around. The great Earl was making certain of his captive's whereabouts at all times. She had not been allowed one moment's privacy since first arriving at the castle at dawn.

Over an hour later footsteps approached the door and she turned eagerly as the door opened. But Guy Beauchamp was alone as he stepped into the room, snapping his fingers sharply to dismiss his men. When they were alone he turned back to face her.

"Well, Lady Alice, you have become a vastly awkward encumbrance to me."

She was triumphant. "Because you have to explain to the Earl of Pembroke how you came to have me in your custody?"

He grinned, enjoying playing with her taut emotions. "Pembroke? I have not seen that doughty Earl nor am I likely to for he chases his tail towards Elmley at this very moment, and your impertinent friends also with luck!"

She faltered. Unsure. "Then who . . . "

"Arrived but an hour ago? Why it was the Earls of Lancaster, Arundel and Hereford, come with all haste from Kenilworth."

Alice felt dull with dismay. As Beatrice had said, these four Earls were a nest of venomous serpents . . .

"We have tried your lover, and found him guilty." Warwick's malicious pleasure was horrible.

"Tried him? On what charge?"

"Treason. He has been declared a traitor by the King's own word. As a traitor he was tried and as a traitor he will die."

"But you cannot do this! The King has revoked all the charges . . . "

Warwick smiled again. "In Warwickshire the ordinances still run, Lady Alice."

She stared at him. "You have connived at this have you not? You know well enough that what you do is outside the true law and so you pretend that the treason charge is still legal!"

His smile faded a little. "What is this *pretence* you speak of? I have heard nothing of the King's mind-changing, and there is nothing you or anyone can do to prove otherwise. The Sheriff of Warwickshire has not informed *me* of a change in the law."

She could have wept then. "But the Sheriff of Warwickshire is *your* retainer, *your* creature! He will do your bidding."

"You make a serious charge of collusion, sweetheart, and I think that you will have great and virtually impossible difficulties in proving such a crime." He put his hand out to her face, stroking the clear skin gently.

She turned sharply away from him. "What do you intend to do now?"

"Oh come now, Alice, you disappoint me with such a foolish question. You know well enough the penalty for treason."

Oh no, not that, not that . . . She bit her lip, tears brimming in her eyes.

"Do not fear, Lady Alice, for to my great regret I cannot hang, draw and quarter him. He is of noble blood, is married to the King's niece and has Gloucester for a brother-in-law. Lancaster dares not execute him in any other way than by beheading him. The peacock is about to understand the strength of the black dog's teeth!"

"The King . . ."

He snorted in disgust. "Edward Plantagenet will weep a few tears and then forget!"

"But *I* will not forget." Alice's golden eyes were malevolent. Never before had she hated so much, never before had she so wished to take another's life . . .

His eyes moved away from such deadly contempt. "You are a mere woman, I do not fear *your* threats."

She noticed how his eyes wandered over her body, dwelling on the curves outlined by the clinging silver-blue brocade. Could she bargain for Piers? Could she use her body to win life for the man she loved? "I will do anything you wish if you will only spare his life. I will give you Longmore . . . and myself."

He came close, a dull red flush staining his cheeks as he looked at her. "Sweet Alice, you do not understand do you? I can have all I wish. I can be rid of the Gascon, and then return to take you and Longmore. You have nothing to barter with, Alice, nothing at all . . ."

A coldness clutched her stomach, twisting her jagged nerves. Was there nothing she could do? A half-forgotten phrase of Morvina's entered her frantic head. "You would take the life of one of your own kind then?"

He stepped back, his face wary. "What do you mean by that?"

"Oh come now, my Lord Earl, is it now my turn to be disappointed in *your* foolish questions? What is the penalty in your faith for taking the life of another believer?" She leaned towards him, forcing home her tiny advantage. "Twice you have been warned. *Two* spiders. What comes next?"

His face was suddenly white and his dark grey eyes were wide with apprehension.

More footsteps approached and the door opened to admit Lancaster, Arundel and the gloomy Hereford.

Lancaster's face was alight with triumph. "Well, Beauchamp, the time has come eh? Where is it to be then? The courtyard here?" He glanced briefly at Alice.

Warwick could not look away from her. "Here?" His haunted eyes swung at last to the others. "No. Not here."

Lancaster tutted irritably. "You do not change your price *again?* We have not come here upon a fool's errand I trust!"

Beauchamp passed his hand over his dry lips. "It is no fool's errand."

"Then why prevaricate about the venue of his death?" Lancaster's sharp little eyes were angry.

Arundel stepped forward, his elegant presence somehow out of place amongst the three other men who could claim no such beauty as he. He smiled at Alice, but the smile did not reach his china blue eyes. His bright golden hair swung as he turned abruptly to face Warwick. "Why draw back now?"

"Because I have done enough, involved myself sufficiently in this matter. Now I feel it is time for someone else to bear a little of the responsibility."

Hereford's face grew even gloomier as he sighed loudly and flung his gauntlets down upon a table. He sat in a chair and put his legs upon the trestle. "This argument could go on forever, Warwick. Surely the fact that he dies on *your* lands makes little or no difference. We are here, and by our presence we signify our involvement."

Warwick was not to be moved however. "It is not quite so simple, Hereford. *I* captured him. *I* imprisoned him. All you have done is ride here to join me. If he dies on my lands then my name is truly the only one to be held up before the King."

Lancaster laughed in his amazement. "The *King?* Jesu forbid, Warwick, you do not suddenly fear the King?"

Warwick could feel the net closing in more securely and he fought to be free of this final responsibility. "I tell you that I will not have him mur . . . executed on my lands." So nearly the true word slipped out from his frightened lips. His eyes slid back to Alice.

"Oh very well, I have no stomach for a continuance of this squabbling!" Lancaster kicked Hereford's legs down from the trestle. "Come on, we will take our 'charge' back along the Kenilworth road. My lands are only a short distance away. He shall die on the estates of the earldom of Lancaster! Does that suit your lily-white conscience?" He rounded back sharply on Warwick.

"I care not where he dies, merely that it is not on my land." Beauchamp's lips were almost white.

157

"Wherever he dies at your hands the crime will be outside the law." Alice made so bold as to touch Lancaster's arm.

With a grimace he shook himself free of her. "Madam, the justices of this county sat in judgement on him, and found him guilty. How then can it be outside the law?"

"Because the justices had no jurisdiction to try him on such a charge. The ordinances have been revoked."

Lancaster's pink and white face creased into a hollow smile. "My dear lady, it does not matter to me how or why the justices took it upon themselves to try him. The fact that they did so is quite sufficient for my ends."

Arundel sauntered arrogantly over to her, taking her hand and pressing it to his warm lips. "My Lady." He bowed with insolent exaggeration before turning and going towards the door.

She must stop them. "My Lord of Arundel, do you do this merely because the Earl of Cornwall tipped you into the mud at Wallingford? What a truly pretty knight you are, Sirrah!" His handsome face twisted savagely as he whirled about to face her, but she allowed him no moment to strike back. "I only pray, Edmund Fitzalan, that you are sober enough to remember the foul deed you are about to commit. I hope and pray that your nights scream aloud at the horrible crime which will stain your name forever."

Lancaster raised his eyebrows. "Madam, you spit most admirably."

She turned her attention to him then. "Aye, maybe I do, it is because I am loyal. Loyalty is perhaps a word you know nothing of. Edward will have cause to ponder upon your usefulness one day, my *Lord*."

Lancaster raised his hand to slap her, but Hereford surprisingly stopped him. "Leave her, Thomas, she can use only her tongue."

Alice was in a frenzy to stop them now. The moment they went from that room she knew that Piers was doomed. "My tongue is my only weapon, true enough. And is not that the only weapon Piers ever used against you? Never once has he meddled in things which did not concern him. He has not sought to influence the King against you and neither has he abused his power. It is your insufferable pride which leads you to murder him. Your pride has been pricked because he has risen higher than you."

Arundel smiled coldly. "Of course he has risen higher, sweetness, for the King will find no sodomist amongst his nobility! He needs must look to his Gascon squire for a bedfellow."

"That is not true and you know it," she whispered.

Lancaster grabbed Hereford's gauntlets and thrust them into that lord's hands. "Come . . . "

Still she tried to hold them back. "And when this day's work is done, my Lords, you will be divided. There is only one thing which unites you and that is the existence of Piers Gaveston. What price your unity when he is dead? Pembroke, Surrey and Gloucester will be alienated as soon as they discover what you have done. I look at Hereford and see that his heart is not in it. There are only two of you then . . . for I pay little heed to Arundel's poor shadow. You may be the most important magnate in the land, my Lord of Lancaster, but you are still lower than the King himself."

Lancaster had listened for long enough. He pushed Hereford towards the door. "Maybe so, Madam, but I am still strong enough to withstand my cousin Edward."

The door closed on them.

She turned to Warwick. "Save him!"

Beauchamp shook his head. "If they take him from here then I am absolved from taking the life of another of my religion. I will not lift one finger to save him."

She spat in his face then, and the spittle clung to his iron-grey beard. "You snake, Warwick. The scum of the sewers bears a sweeter smell than you."

There was a resumption of the noise in the courtyards and she ran to the window, leaning out as far as she could, but the door behind her opened and she was pulled back into the room.

Arundel's grip was firm as he held her. "We have decided that it shall be your privilege, Lady Alice, to witness the execution."

"No." Her fear rose sharply. She could not see him die, not Piers who was life itself to her.

"Oh come now, do you not want to see that he dies like a man? Or are you afraid that he will whimper and weep like a babe?"

Warwick was uneasy. "Arundel, is this not a little barbaric?"

Fitzalan sneered. "You have wriggled free of all responsibility, Beauchamp, and so do not now meddle in matters which are no longer your concern!"

"Lady Alice *is* my concern!"

Arundel dragged Alice to the door. "Then we shall return her to you — unharmed. You may do with her as you will — and I wish you good sport, Beauchamp."

In the courtyard the gathering waited in silence. Alice's frantic eyes sought the lonely figure of Piers. He was seated on a rough country horse, and the harness streamed with colourful ribbons. A peacock's feather had been stitched to another ribbon and this was tied around his forehead. His dark brown eyes were soft as he looked at her, but they hardened as he suddenly realised that they were going to force her to watch.

"Lancaster, you cannot do this."

"Can I not? Then you under-estimate me, Gascon!"

Piers' lip curled with contempt. "Nay, I think rather that I have sadly *over*-estimated you in the past! You play-act at being the man, Lancaster, and the role is far beyond your capabilities!"

"Your opinions are to count for little from now on!" Lancaster's sharpness showed that the taunting words could still bite deep.

"Still I reach you, brave Thomas, and shall reach you from the grave."

Hereford urged his horse forward. "Let us get on with this, to delay is foolish." His apprehension was obvious, and Piers seized upon it.

"Hereford, in this valiant gathering there are only two men with any semblance of honour — *I* shall not return, you will. I charge you to defend my Lady Alice." Hereford grunted uncomfortably, and Piers leaned forward more urgently. "Humphrey de Bohun, are you man or mouse?"

Hereford's gloomy face flushed with a surge of anger. "Very well, Gaveston, you have my word on it."

Piers glanced up and caught a glimpse of Warwick's face at a window. He wasted no opportunity, even now. "Does the black dog mean to skulk in his kennel then? Does he not wish to come and chew upon the poor bone?" Warwick's face vanished from the window immediately and Piers' mocking laughter rang around the courtyard.

Alice was almost fainting with grief. How could he jest at such a time? How could he gibe at these men who meant to murder him? But Piers' apparent courage was a shield, for beneath he was afraid, as any man would be who rode to his death.

Tears lay wetly upon her cheeks and she could barely stay in the saddle of her mount. Piers was led past her to the front of the procession, and he forced the man who led his poor horse to pause for a moment. The peacock's feather bobbed ridiculously above the dark curly hair. Lancaster and Arundel looked back angrily, but Hereford remained firmly at Piers' side and so they had to wait.

"Courage Alice, it is not long now, but how shall I bear myself proudly if I know you weep so bitterly? Help me, sweetheart."

Through her tears she gazed at him. "I am not strong enough to bear this." The feather swam sickeningly.

He made to touch her, but his hands were tied before him and he could not. "Know this, that I loved you above all others . . ."

Arundel's thin voice called back to them. "Have done with this whimpering!"

Piers was led on and Hereford leaned over to take the reins of her palfrey.

Through the streets of Warwick the procession wended its way, and the people lined the wayside to witness the passing of the King's favourite. Curiosity was in their eyes, curiosity and some laughter as they saw the ribbons and feathers. This crude humour they could understand. But Piers' dignified bearing they could understand too, and they admired the man who went so proudly to his death. Some cried to see him. Their inquisitive eyes looked at Alice too, wondering who she was who wept so bitterly for Gaveston.

The Avon curled lazily along its valley as they left Warwick behind and rode the dusty track towards Kenilworth. The humid day was overpowering, and a strange dull yellow light lay over the land as a storm approached from the south-west. Not a leaf stirred and not a bird sang. The dust billowed around the horses as they approached a solitary hill, the site which Lancaster had chosen for the execution.

"Blacklow Hill," murmured Hereford at her side, "And a black place it is too." He crossed himself.

She could not raise her head to look, and she hated herself for her weakness. Hereford looked unhappily at her, finding his task more and more onerous with each step they took. She should not be subjected to this torture; Humphrey de Bohun's chivalrous heart went out to her, but his fear of Lancaster was greater.

At the foot of the hill Piers forced the procession to halt yet again, and turned in the saddle to look at Hereford. "De Bohun, take her back to Warwick. Take her back, I beg of you." There was no hint of mockery in his voice now, only an earnest plea. The crowd muttered to itself, and necks were craned to see her more clearly.

Hereford came to his decision speedily and dragged her horse's head around sharply. He urged both animals to greater speed and they left the horrible scene behind them. Alice began to scream then, again and again she screamed for Piers. She swayed in the saddle, a faintness engulfed her. Hereford reined in and leaned over to her, plucking her from the saddle. Then he hit her roughly across the face and she slumped unconscious against his chest.

He continued on his way back through the silent streets of Warwick, his horse's hooves clattering and echoing upon the cobbles.

Alice did not hear the distant cheers a few minutes later as Lancaster's men severed Piers' head from his body. A blessed black infinity saved her from that.

TWENTY-SIX

THE women sat around the bed watching, while one of them dabbed Alice's face with a damp cloth. She lay motionless, her eyes staring sightlessly at the rich hangings. The embroidered Warwick badge of the bear and ragged staff twisted intricately over the dark red velvet.

Hereford stood uneasily at the foot of the bed, his dark face seeming to have aged during the past few hours. A fierce bruise marred Alice's pale face and he looked away miserably. Had he hit her too hard? But she would not stop screaming, and he could not bear to hear a woman scream. He could not suffer the sombre atmosphere of the room any more and strode out thankfully.

Outside the skies had darkened as the storm crept closer, and a distant rumble of thunder wandered across the low heavens. The clouds were still a strange mustard colour, and thick with rain.

Alice heard the thunder. How long had she lain here? Time meant nothing to her now. The darkness of the room could have been night or day. The heaviness of her heart was boundless. The cold cloth wiped her face again and she looked at the anxious woman who tended her. "How long have I been here?"

"Since noon, my Lady . . . some four hours now."

Four hours. Had he been gone from her for so long already?

Uneven footsteps halted outside the door and then it was flung open and Guy Beauchamp lurched into the bedchamber. He held a

162

cup in one hand and a small flagon in the other, and from the way he swayed he was more than a little drunk. He dismissed the women peremptorily and then wove his staggering way to a small table. Alice watched him warily, the morbid drowsiness dissolving rapidly as she felt the danger of his mood.

The flagon grated against the table as he sought to put it down steadily, and the red wine splashed over the brim. He turned, drinking deeply from his cup and staring down at her.

"Well, Alice, one score have I settled this day. Now there remains but one more." He grinned, but the muscles of his face seemed sluggish and lop-sided.

She drew away to the far side of the bed, her eyes watchful. "Have you to drink away your fears and guilt then? Can you not face the shadows?"

"My hands are unsoiled by his blood. See?" He deliberately placed the cup on the table and held up his hands towards her. "See?" He tried to grin again and moved unsteadily towards her.

"Keep away from me." Her voice escaped in a hiss.

He reached the bed and held on to one of the posts to maintain his balance. He allowed his eyes to wander over her as she crouched there against the wall, pressing herself as far away from him as she could. Her hair was loose, and the silver-blue gown was ruffled, spoiled. He could see the whiteness of her thigh before she covered it with the folds of her skirts. His tongue passed over his lips and he put his hand up to loosen the collar of his coat. His breathing became heavier as he looked at her once more, and then in a moment he was upon her.

He was immensely strong as he pinned her beneath him, ripping her gown with one hand. The thin summer brocade gave before him, and his eager fingers caressed the soft white skin of her shoulder. She felt his lips against her throat as she struggled, and she heard his voice murmuring her name over and over again.

Then suddenly he was gone. She lay there, not understanding what had happened until someone leaned over her and she saw Gareth's anxious face. Carefully he pulled a fur skin from the bed and wrapped it around her, then he pulled her to her feet and she saw that the room was filled with the men of Longmore. She recognised their faces, but they wore Guy Beauchamp's badge upon their breasts. She stepped towards them and her foot struck something warm and solid. Looking down she saw the senseless form of Warwick. Blood oozed from his forehead where he had been struck.

She frowned. It was hard to think. To think. "How have you got in here?"

Stephen smiled kindly. "You forget, Gareth is still officially one of the Earl's lieutenants, although after this work I doubt if he will continue in such a post. It was easy enough for him to lure enough of Warwick's men outside the castle to a place where we could ambush them, tie them up and steal their clothes."

Gareth put his arm around her shoulder. "We would have come more quickly, but we followed a false trail to Elmley. When we realised we had been deceived we doubled back, only to find Lancaster, Arundel and Hereford still here. They left a short while ago and we seized our opportunity."

"And Aymer de Valence? Where is he?" Alice hated Pembroke in that moment.

"He rides back from Elmley behind us, but his speed is slower. Stephen's men are used to fleeing through the night at great speed." Gareth's heart ached for her. She was like some beautiful blossom, broken from the bough and trampled upon.

Morvina pulled a small knife from her purse and stood over Warwick. "*You* are responsible for all this, a thousand curses on you for your evil-doing." She raised the knife to stab him, but Stephen grabbed her arm hastily.

"Leave it now, my lovely, for we have yet to get out of this cursed place, and I will not have you murder him in cold blood."

"Let me finish him!" Morvina's little figure twisted out of his grasp.

He moved after her, holding her more firmly. "No. Do as you are told!" His voice was hard. He turned back to Gareth. "You had best lead the way again."

Gareth pushed open the door and peered out in the passageway. There was no-one to be seen and so he beckoned them to follow him. Warwick's men paid scant attention to Sir Gareth ap Llewellyn as he walked through the castle at the head of the party. It was not until they reached the great hall that they encountered a little trouble.

Seated by the empty fireplace, whittling at a stick with his dagger, was Sir Hugh d'Audley. They did not see him at first for he was alone and moved very little. They were half-way across the hall before he shifted his feet and they heard the shuffling noise. Stephen froze immediately, and Alice gasped, stifling the noise but too late. D'Audley stood, his eyes wide as he saw who stood there.

"Llewellyn? What's amiss here?"

Gareth took a deep breath. "You see nothing, Hugh, do you understand me?"

D'Audley's good-looking face changed ridiculously. "You will be caught."

"We stand a chance if you hold your clacking tongue."

Stephen grinned horribly. "I can still his clacking tongue now if you so wish."

Hugh stepped back hastily. "There is no need, I have no quarrel with the Lady Alice. My eyes are blind to your passing."

Gareth's eyes were cool. "No doubt you are wildly happy tonight, Hugh, for you see your way clear to the Countess of Cornwall's heart."

D'Audley flushed quickly and looked away.

Alice went to him. "You have achieved your goal, Sir Hugh. Piers is dead and his wife a widow. Do you have a hope that she will wed you?"

His eyes were wary as he looked at her. "I love her, Lady Alice, and that you may believe."

"Then if you wish to become her husband you had best keep your lips closed now, for I swear that the King will forbid any such marriage, I will see to that."

"I have given my word, my Lady. I have seen nothing. But if you remain here for much longer then I cannot see how you hope to survive in Guy Beauchamp's stronghold."

Stephen touched Alice's arm, sliding his hand to hold her fingers. "Come, Lady Alice, he will be as good as his word, the more so for your threat. Come." Gently he pulled her away. Hugh watched in silence as they left the hall, then he sat down again in his chair and whistled quietly to himself as he whittled away at the wood.

In the courtyard the horses waited where they had been left. They mounted and rode unchallenged out of Warwick Castle.

The early evening sky was almost black above them and the wind was beginning to rise, whipping up the dust into eddying clouds. The first drops of rain were beginning to fall as they came face to face with Aymer de Valence. One of Stephen's men had remained on the road to waylay the Earl, and now they awaited the fugitives from within Warwick's nest.

"I am by far too late am I not?" His unease was evident. His oath had been broken and he knew too that his action in deserting his prisoner was open to a great deal of criticism.

Gareth nodded. "By far, my Lord."

"May God forgive me, then, for I must bear the blame. My scouts have informed me that Lancaster, Arundel and Hereford have not long since ridden back towards Kenilworth, although I gather that Hereford was extremely vexed and heart-weary of it all. I am surprised that they so took the law into their own hands — Warwick I can believe it of, but not Lancaster. He is too conventional."

Alice raised her head, pulling the fur more closely about her shoulders as the rain fell more heavily. "Piers was murdered on Lancaster's lands, by Lancaster's men, and the good Earl smiles to himself because he knows he was apparently within the law. But for Warwick's machinations and collusion with the Sheriff of this county, then Piers would still be alive. You are right, Lancaster would have been too conventional to murder, but he will close his eyes to the bending of the law."

Pembroke stiffened. "How do you mean, bending the law?"

Alice explained all Beauchamp's plottings with the Sheriff to disguise the truth. "Lancaster knew what had been done, but he will deny the knowledge, and who can prove him a liar?"

Pembroke's shoulders slumped. " 'Twas well planned, and I can see Guy Beauchamp's devious mind at work in it. Well, I shall ride to the King's side now, for I will not lend my name further to the affairs of the Lords Ordainers. I curse the day I ever believed in their aims."

Alice's eyes brightened a little. "May I accompany you to the King?"

"No, Alice, leave well alone now. Please." Gareth pleaded with her.

Pembroke pulled his hood over his lank hair as the rain soaked them all. The horses stamped in the muddy puddles, and small riverlets streamed down the slope towards Warwick town. Thunder rattled overhead and the horses tossed their heads nervously. Aymer took a deep breath, looking closely at her. "Do you think your presence will do anything to oil the stormy waters?"

"I do."

"How? You can only be a sharp and poignant reminder to Edward of Piers Gaveston. *I* must gain all the support I can now to hold back the King's anger, for make no mistake his first instinct will be to raise an army against the murderers of Blacklow. It will

166

mean civil war truly unless the more moderate men around the King can prevail upon him."

"Let me go with you. I have much to explain to the King, things which Piers would want me to tell him. I think that my presence will do infinitely more good than harm."

Pembroke nodded at last, rubbing his neck as the raindrops lay coldly against his skin. "Very well, I will put my trust in you. But the Lord have mercy on you if I find that you go merely to incite Edward's wrath further against the men who killed your lover." The words were sharp, to the point. Then the Earl glanced at Gareth. "I think, Sir Gareth, that in your own interests you had best work to dissociate yourself completely from Warwick's name."

Alice smiled at Gareth. "Go to Longmore, Gareth, it is ever your home. I shall come there as quickly as I may, but first I *must* go to the King. Do not worry for me, the Earl of Pembroke will protect me."

Gareth bit back the retort. As Pembroke had protected Piers? He looked away.

She rode away with the Earl's party, leaving her friends behind.

TWENTY-SEVEN

THE gates of London were barred against them. Pembroke had great difficulty in persuading Edward of his good intentions and it was many an hour before at last the King believed the messages sent by the Earl and allowed him in.

Humphrey de Bohun arrived at the gates, but Edward would not allow him in. Alone of the Blacklow Earls Hereford was filled with remorse, but was denied the opportunity of throwing himself on the King's mercy. Lancaster and Warwick remained fast on their estates, while Arundel scurried around the land in a frenzy of indecision. His nerve had deserted him now, but he was still too frightened to come to London.

The Palace of Westminster was a worried place. Everywhere men talked in groups, their faces anxious, concerned. What would be the outcome of all this? Pembroke was shunned by some, who turned their backs pointedly on the man who deserted his hostage.

Along a corridor they came face to face with the Earls of Gloucester and Surrey.

Gloucester's young face was more than a little unfriendly. "De Valence, I wish you joy of your interview, for he is in no mood to be pleaded with."

Pembroke inclined his head, knowing that he deserved the reproaches of his fellows. "Nonetheless, I must go to him."

Surrey's light grey eyes fell on Alice. "Lady Alice?" He took her hand and kissed it gently, squeezing the cold fingers. "I cannot sufficiently express my horror at what has happened, nor sufficiently express my distress at your loss."

She withdrew her hand slowly. "Maybe I should thank you, John de Warenne, but I cannot. You and your fellow Lords Ordainers hunted Piers as if he were an animal . . . but I think maybe that the animals were in pursuit and not pursued."

He smiled faintly. "There are grades of animals as there are grades of man, Lady Alice. Even I do not deserve to be placed side by side with Lancaster and his accomplices."

Gloucester stood aside for them to pass. "I pray that you succeed, de Valence, for if you do not then I fear greatly for the safety of England. The Scots have not lived idly while England tore herself apart with political intrigues, they have remustered their strength and merely await a suitable moment to strike. At the moment *that* is all which must matter, for if England descends into civil war she will be at the mercy of the Scots."

Edward's apartments were quiet, almost deserted. Walter Reynolds sat at his desk, staring at a quill which he turned between his nervous fingers. He should be triumphant, exultant, for his chief adversary was dead and the way to the King was now clear. But his heart was heavy. His fox-like face lightened as Aymer de Valence entered.

"My Lord of Pembroke, God be praised you have come. You must do something!" He stood, the jewelled cross around his neck swinging wildly on its chain. "Already he issues orders for his army to muster. The country will be torn limb from limb unless he can be stopped."

Pembroke shuffled. "You all appear to think that he will listen to me! Jesu above, *I* am probably one of the last men he wishes to set eyes upon at this moment."

Reynolds began to finger the priceless cross. "You are the only one left, my Lord. Even the Queen has attempted to reason with him, but he ordered her from his presence! She left in great distress a few moments since." His eyes wandered to a small doorway which Alice knew led directly to the Queen's apartments. "She is in her rooms, Lady Alice, perhaps you could go to her. There is no-one else and she is greatly upset." For the first time he noticed the fur which Alice clutched around her body.

Alice's lips parted in amazement. "Me? My Lord Bishop, do you think she would welcome *me?"*

"Someone must attend her, Lady Alice. She trusts only Queen Margaret who is ill in her bed. There is only Gloucester's wife, but she is little more than a girl. The Queen expects her first babe within a few months, it could be that such a child is the very balm needed to soothe so troubled a land. If her distress should bring on an early labour . . . "

Alice slipped away through the tiny doorway and soon found herself in Isabella's luxurious apartments. The little Queen sat stiffly in a chair listening to a lady who read from a book of Arthur. Tales of the great king's deeds gave Isabella no pleasure and she stared unhappily at the floor. She heard the door close softly and turned to see Alice. "My Lady?"

Alice came forward, aware of the quietness which fell upon the room. The tales of Arthur dwindled to a vague halt. "Your Grace, I came to see if I could be of any assistance to you . . . "

Isabella stood, her hand resting protectively against her swollen stomach, and then she turned towards her visitor. "Your misfortunes are great, surpassing even mine, Lady Alice." Her dark eyes were cool. Was she remembering the many slights she had suffered at Piers' hands?

Alice bowed her head. "He is dead, Your Grace." It seemed so easy to be able to say these words. Was she to shed no tears for him?

The Queen nodded. "It is as I said, my Lady, our misfortunes are akin, for I shall never fully possess the man I love." Her hand pressed more firmly upon her stomach.

There was no mistaking her meaning. Alice was surprised even more than she believed possible. Isabella loved her husband. After all she had suffered from his thoughtlessness, she loved Edward Plantagenet! The Queen swallowed and Alice could see that the tears were close again. She hurried forward and took Isabella's hand, leading her around the chair and gently seating her. The other ladies glanced at one another. Here was a strange sight, Gaveston's mistress offering sympathy to one of Gaveston's most implacable enemies.

The Countess of Gloucester stood suddenly, ushering the others before her from the room.

When they were alone, Isabella looked up at the tall English girl. "Will the Earl of Cornwall be between my Lord and me for the rest of our life together? Now Edward cannot even look at me without remembering that I was directly the cause of Piers' first banishment because of the letter I wrote to my father. He thrust me from him when I went to him." The tears forced their way out into the world.

Alice put her hand on the trembling shoulder. "You were not at fault, had I been in your position I too would have written such a letter."

Gratefully Isabella clutched at the hand. "Why did Piers make my life so unbearable from the first? I could not harm him, and probably would never have complained to my father if he had not made his dislike for me so personal and so hurtful?"

"If I tell you the truth I do not know if that will be a good thing." Alice suddenly wanted to help this pathetic Queen.

"Tell me, for it is my right to know why he despised me." The red-rimmed eyes were lifted to Alice's face.

"Piers believed that your father was responsible for the death of his mother."

The puzzlement in the Queen's face told Alice that she knew nothing whatsoever about the matter. She was innocent. On impulse Alice told her everything. "His mother was burned at the stake for witchcraft."

Isabella gasped. "So terrible a death?" She stared at the rushes and then at the discarded book where the lady had left it, and the thoughts tumbled about in her head. So *that* was what lay behind it all! "So suddenly it becomes clear, no wonder he hated me. I could think only that he hated me as a jealous mistress would hate a new bride, and I believed what I was told by the wives of the English Earls who were envious of him." She blushed a little, biting her lip. "It was not until very recently that I realised that it was not Piers of whom I should be jealous, but . . . others . . . When first I set eyes upon the handsome King of England I was overcome with joy that he was to be my husband. I loved him from the outset, and I still love him. If I could come into his heart then I would surely be the happiest of women. I know that he is not perfect, and I know that he is the victim of a . . . malady, shall we call it? . . . but the good things about him far outweigh those faults."

She stood suddenly, turning to Alice. "But we talk only of *my* unhappiness, what is to become of you? What shall you do now?"

"There is nothing for me here. I shall return to my estates in Gloucestershire."

Isabella smiled warmly. "There will always be a place for you at my side, Lady Alice. I shall not forget your kindness in coming to me in the midst of your sorrow. I am truly sorry that he is gone, Alice, and I shall pray for his soul." The Queen dropped the more formal use of Alice's title and spoke to her as one woman to another.

The Countess of Gloucester came into the room, dropping a hasty curtsey. "Your Grace, the King wishes to see the Lady Alice."

Isabella looked quickly at Alice and then nodded. "If you ease his heart as you have eased mine this day, then my indebtedness to you will be infinite."

Alice followed the Countess from the Queen's presence.

Edward was alone in the small chamber, He stood by the window gazing out over the Thames. The tide was at its flood and the many boats rode high on the swell. Swans floated in a white cloud around the jetties outside the old palace, flapping their wings threateningly at the various craft which tried to navigate the crowded waters.

He turned his head as she was shown into his presence. For a while he did not speak, then he said: "How can everything move onwards so normally, Alice? How can nature itself not realise that he is gone from us?"

His voice was almost breaking and Alice was struck dumb. The words which she had so carefully remembered vanished from her mind as she looked at him.

He shook his head slowly, leaving the window and coming closer to her. The cloth-of-gold of his brilliant coat caught the dying rays of the sun, flashing richly in the dark room. His golden hair was touched with orange as the shaft from the window crossed his head. "I could have told him not to fall into Warwick's hands . . . " The words sounded harsh, unfeeling, but she knew that they disguised the anguish in his heart. His blue eyes were sad as he looked at her. "I should not have left him at Scarborough, for by my presence I gave him protection. He was wounded and could not travel swiftly, and I went to raise support in York. Scarborough was impregnable I thought." His long fingers played with the heavy chain which lay across his broad chest, moving over the precious gems with which it was studded.

He noticed the fur she held about her, and held out his hand, She released the fur and handed it to him. His blue eyes hardened as he saw the torn gown beneath. "Warwick?" She looked away and did not answer him. "Poor Alice, you have suffered a great deal."

He walked away from her and she watched him. He went to a casket which he opened and took out a small hairbrush which he brought back to her. With his own hands he began to brush the long tangled hair. At last he finished and the dark red tresses shone like beaten copper. He stared at her and put his hand out to take a curl between his fingers. She heard the heavy rings clink faintly as his fingers moved. "He loved to see your hair thus, Alice." His hand twisted convulsively in the hair and he turned his face away to hide the emotion which seized him.

He freed his hand at last and turned his back on her, leaning his hands on a table and staring down at a bowl of comfits which stood there. "I shall have their hearts wrenched from their loathsome bodies for what they have done. England shall echo to their dying screams, and by all that is Holy their deaths shall be slow! It takes my every strength not to go to where Hereford skulks at this very moment and put these hands about his traitorous throat!" He held his hands up before him.

At last Alice's strength returned to her and she remembered all that she must say. "That is not what Piers would have wished, Your Grace. I loved him as much as you, and so I make bold and beg of you not to pursue your present desires. He came back to England to give his life for you, for England."

The brilliant blue eyes swung disbelievingly on her. "I cannot believe what you say."

"It is true, and you *must* believe it. Think of him, think of how he was. Can you not see that he had to do it. He said that his existence would always be a cause for rift between you and England's nobility. The gap could not be spanned. He died for the safety of your crown and your life."

His face twisted with pain. "You would put the blame on me?"

She took his hand and laid it against her cheek. "No, I want only for you to understand, and to see that you must withhold your anger now."

"What shall we do without him, Alice? How shall we live?" He pulled her close to him as if by doing so he dragged Piers back from the dead. She rested her head wearily against his chest, closing her eyes.

"I cannot even give him a Christian burial, did you know that? That fool Canterbury placed him in excommunication and did not reverse it. Piers died excommunicate and so I cannot bury him on consecrated soil." Edward laid his cheek against the dark red hair.

Alice said nothing. Edward could not know that Piers would not have wished for a Christian burial.

For a long while they stood together in silence, drawing comfort from one another. Then he released her and lifted her face towards him. "You counsel me to follow the advice of Pembroke, Gloucester and Surrey then? You would have me stay my hand from my murderous nobility?"

"If you do not then he will have given his life for nothing."

"You have me trapped, sweet Alice, trapped by the love I bore for Perrot. If he died so that I could live at peace with my quarrelsome, contemptible Earls, then that is the advice he would have me follow. As always I will follow Perrot's advice."

Alice remembered Isabella. "Your Grace, in one thing Piers was very wrong."

"And what could that be?"

"He did not counsel you sufficiently strongly to be kind to your bride."

"I will hear no words on her behalf! She is in every way a daughter of France and in every loathsome way a niece of cousin Lancaster!" He was sharp, unwilling to listen.

"You are wrong, and so was Piers. He blamed her for something done by her father.'She had nothing to do with his mother's death, nothing at all."

Edward looked a little dazed. "I cannot follow all this. Fathers, mothers, all the relatives under the sun appear to be involved!"

"Did you know that Piers' mother died as a witch?"

"I did, but it was not a fact which could be safely bandied about in *my* court."

"Well, did you know that the King of France was involved in her death?"

"No, that I did not."

"Piers was wrong to blame your Queen for his mother's terrible death. As wrong as it would be to blame the daughter Piers left behind for some crime committed by Piers himself. It is the one matter in which I must frown upon Piers' actions."

The King took a deep breath, glancing at Alice and then away again. "That does not alter the fact that she worked to aid the barons who wished to be rid of Piers."

"She was alone, very young, and very much in love with you. She used the only weapon she had to strike back. Can you blame her? Piers was the cause of most of her unhappiness, not all I will admit, and he took a cruel pleasure in wounding her whenever the opportunity arose."

"You defend her, Alice, why?"

"Because she loves you, because she is to bear your child, and because she does not deserve to be left outside your heart. Three very good reasons why you should be at peace with her."

He smiled slowly. "And that is all it ever could amount to. At peace. I can never love her . . . or any woman . . . you know that." He continued to smile. "A man cannot conceal his nature, cannot stifle the truth forever. You can call me immoral, call me a pervert, preach to me of Sodom and Gomorrah, but the facts will not alter. I am what I am, and poor Isabella must face this. Piers may be dead and gone, but *he* was no obstacle to her, not in that way."

Alice felt desperately sorry for this unhappy King. "Isabella has already faced this, Your Grace, and she loves you yet."

He bent forward and kissed her cheek gently. "For you I will be kind to my Queen." He walked to the door. "I shall go and countermand my previous orders, will that satisfy you?"

Suddenly Gareth's name came into her head. "Your Grace, I have one favour I would beg of you."

"Ask and it shall be granted."

"The Earl of Warwick's lieutenant, Sir Gareth ap Llewellyn. He rescued me from Warwick Castle at great risk to his own life, and by doing so exposed himself to the Earl's revenge. Will you extend your protection to him?"

Edward nodded. "Beauchamp shall not touch Sir Gareth, Alice, you have my word on that." Then he was gone.

Alice stood alone in the small chamber, and her glance fell upon the casket from which the King had taken the hairbrush. The brush lay upon the table and she picked it up and laid it on the thick green velvet which lined the box. As she closed the lid she saw that a coat of arms had been worked in enamel upon the top. Green and gold eagles shone in the fading light. She passed her cold fingers lovingly over Piers' badge, and at last the tears came.

She sank to the floor beside the table, holding on to the leg for support, and she wept bitterly for all that she had lost.

The room was in darkness when at last Isabella found her.

TWENTY-EIGHT

"I am commanded to a banquet in London." Alice placed the royal parchment carefully on the table in front of Gareth.

He picked it up, read, and flicked at the broken seal which hung from it, before tossing it back upon the table and looking at her. "Well? Shall you go?"

She turned away and looked at the brazier which glowed in the centre of the room. Stephen stood by it, warming his hands against the fierce heat. It was more than a year since Piers' death, more than a year since she had left London behind and returned to Longmore. And now, suddenly, there came this letter from the King. Her presence was required at a great banquet at Westminster . . .

"I do not think that I can refuse him. The mere fact that the King himself takes up a quill to write personally speaks volumes of his desire to have me there."

Gareth scowled at the parchment. "Aye, he wants you there, and you know why!"

She would not meet his eyes. Events had proved turbulent in England during the past year. For a long while Edward had refused to even meet the Earls who had caused Piers to be so heinously murdered, and in a like fashion those same Earls refused to admit that the ordinances had not been running in Warwickshire. Hereford had made his peace with Edward, but the other three were adamant. They demanded that they be believed as being within the law that terrible day at Blacklow. If he agreed to their demands now, Edward would have to virtually admit publicly that Piers had been a traitor, and this he would never do.

As in chess, it seemed that the whole affair had reached a stalemate, but then Queen Isabella gave birth to a son. England rejoiced at the advent of an heir, and the hearts of the people swung perceptibly back to their King. Edward's position was further strengthened by the death of that fervent supporter of the Lords Ordainers, the old Archbishop of Canterbury. Immediately Edward put forward before the Pope his own nominee; none other than the ever-present, ever-faithful Walter Reynolds. Reynolds. So warned-against by the watchful Piers. Now the most powerful representative of Holy Church in England was Edward's own man. Reynard was come into his own.

The Earls' position weakened. They clung to their estates fearfully, and the King made known his lack of concern at their predicament by leaving England with his Queen to travel to France for the knighting of Isabella's brothers.

In the middle of July he returned, and three months later the Earls of Lancaster, Warwick and Arundel made a public apology to him at Westminster Hall. They received in exchange full pardons for themselves and their adherents.

Edward was victorious. He had won their capitulation, they had admitted finally that they had committed a crime. Piers Gaveston had not been lawfully executed, he had been murdered.

This uneasy peace between the King and the Earls was a poor, frail thing. It rested on shoulders which were unprepared to fully support it. The King still thirsted secretly for true revenge for Piers, and the Earls' simmering anger was only just concealed beneath the surface. For the sake of England, however, both sides attempted to work together.

Now the King was giving a banquet, and all his nobility were invited. The peace was to be sealed publicly by this show of amiability.

Gareth stood and went to her. "Alice, you do know why the King wants you there, don't you?"

She took a deep breath. "He invites all the nobility . . . "

He turned her to face him. "Come *on* now, 'cariad'. He wants to have you there to impress upon the Earls that Piers is the silent victor in all this. By bringing Gaveston's mistress to court he makes his revenge a little sweeter."

She removed his hands from her arms. "Gareth, has it not occurred to you that perhaps my own thoughts are in accord with the King's? Maybe it could be that I too wish to flaunt the past in front of them."

He moved back a little, glancing unwillingly at Stephen who stood immobile by the brazier, pretending that he heard nothing. "He lives on so strongly in your heart, then?"

"Yes, Gareth. Even so small a vengeance as this banquet is better than no vengeance at all."

Without a word he walked from the room, slamming the door behind him. Stephen turned slowly and looked at her as she glared at the door. "Lady Alice, you do not choose your words with care, I fear."

Angrily she went to sit close to the fire, gripping the arms of the wooden chair fiercely. "I have no need to choose my words."

"Have you not? He has been with you constantly this past year and has been of great comfort to you . . . and you know it! He has worked hard to protect you from curious eyes wishing to stare at the Earl of Cornwall's paramour."

She set her lips stubbornly. "Then he had no need to do so, Stephen, for I am well able to conduct my affairs in my own way. He seeks to run my life for me and I do not like it, not at all. Sir Gareth ap Llewellyn has no right to interfere in my affairs."

Stephen frowned. "Lady Alice, you do not sound well with such words upon your lips. He has long since made reparation for any past fault."

She was furious. "Since when does my steward join in with unasked-for advice? Am I surrounded by unskilled advisers? I shall go to London, and I shall attend the banquet! And if I have further cause for embarrassment such as I experienced yesterday on account of your activities as Malcolm Musard, then I shall deal with you too!"

Stephen blinked. "What are you talking of?"

"I speak of my meeting with the Abbot of St. Peter's who much laments the loss of a number of his sheep! He tells me that the outlaw Malcolm Musard was recognised! A man of Saxon colouring, he called him, and vastly like my steward at Longmore! I was not fool enough to mistake his sly meaning, and my embarrassment was great."

Stephen absently put his hand up to his pale golden hair, deeming it prudent to change the uncomfortable subject of his illegal activities. "And how shall you travel to London, my Lady?"

Her lips were a tight line for a moment before she decided to drop the topic too. "Perhaps Sir Thomas Berkeley is also journeying to the banquet. Send a messenger to Berkeley and tell him that if he is going, then I would much appreciate the opportunity of

177

travelling with him. There is safety in numbers in these lawless days, especially with so many brigands roaming the land!" She scowled crossly at him and he made good his exit.

Sir Thomas Berkeley's dappled stallion drank deeply from the clear waters of the stream, snorting a little and shaking its head. He pulled his cloak more tightly around his thin shoulders, shivering in the winter cold, and his breath froze in a pearly cloud.

Alice had dismounted to stretch her legs, and Sir Thomas watched her. "You are by far too thin, Lady Alice. As your neighbour and friend for these many years, I make so bold as to tell you. Grief cannot last forever, but if you nurse it as at present then you will waste away."

She flushed quickly. "Sir Thomas, I have lost the man who was everything to me, so I pray you do not wag your finger at me for . . . " She broke off as they heard the sound of another company approaching from behind. Her heart froze as swiftly as her breath as she recognised Guy Beauchamp.

Warwick reined in in surprise as he saw the party who refreshed their horses by the stream. "Sir Thomas? Lady Alice? How provident that I should meet two such close acquaintances upon the King's highway." His grey eyes glittered as he bowed.

Sir Thomas returned the salute, but his fear overcame him and he lapsed into a timid silence as always he did when meeting Beauchamp. The Earl had terrorised him for so long that he could not think clearly when face to face with him any more.

Warwick's highly-strung charger pranced impatiently, its sharp hooves sounding noisily upon the frozen earth.

Morvina sat upon her small dark palfrey and watched him, and somehow her presence seemed to agitate his horse. It tossed its head nervously, rolling its eyes in her direction. The maid did not move, but kept her steady gaze upon Beauchamp's face.

He tried to calm the animal, and then decided such efforts were useless and made to urge it across the stream instead. Its hooves danced around and the harness jingled. Then it turned sharply and its hind quarters brushed against the sharp glossy leaves of a holly bush. The pricking startled it further and the foolish animal nearly tossed its rider to the ground.

A small brown bird fluttered from the holly, squeaking its fear, and in a trice it was dashed beneath the capering hooves. Suddenly the stallion was calmer, shaking its magnificent grey head. Warwick stared down at the trampled bird, dismounting.

To Alice's surprise he bent to the tiny feathered creature and picked it up, stroking it gently. His face was full of concern.

"A wren, my Lord of Warwick?" Morvina's voice was detached.

Sir Thomas leaned forward to peer at the Earl. "Does it live?"

"No." Warwick's voice was sorrowful and he placed the small corpse upon the ground.

Morvina laughed and the sound was somehow blood-chilling. "Have you killed the hedge-king, my noble Lord?"

Warwick's eyes were full of a strange pain as he looked at Alice's maid. "Have you done this?"

The Welsh girl shook her head. "There was no need. Those who do evil shall be visited by evil themselves. That is how it is, how it always will be."

He glanced down again at the dead wren and then remounted, but Alice saw that his hands were shaking. His party rode across the stream with much splashing, and disturbed the water for those who remained behind. The horses lifted their heads from the muddy stream.

Alice returned to her palfrey. "What is so important about the killing of a wren?"

Morvina seemed to pull herself from the strange mood which had overtaken her. "The wren is the hedge-king, and to kill it is unlucky. The king of birds must not be killed or harmed in any way, for to do so means that the culprit will be visited by some dreadful accident or misfortune within the year."

Alice mounted and began to ride across the stream. She had heard Morvina's words before. At Bamburgh she had almost believed, but no more. The needfire had not protected Piers, so why should she now believe that Warwick's killing of a wren meant anything.

They rode on towards London.

TWENTY-NINE

MORVINA stood back to admire the result of all her work. Her mistress was to shine at tonight's banquet.

Alice wore a magnificent gown of dusty rose velvet, which

179

trailed so far behind her that the maid had to drape the folds over her arm. Lifting the skirt thus left the soft apple-green silk undergown revealed. Tiny silver buttons decorated the tight green sleeves, and the overgown was trimmed with delicate white fur. Her hair was parted in the middle and bunched in two silver nets over her ears. Now she glanced sideways at Morvina.

"Do you think I look well enough?"

"There will be few ladies at the banquet able to stand side by side with you."

"You do not fully approve of what I do, do you?" Alice could feel the reservation in her maid's voice.

"I think it will do you no good, my Lady."

Alice was resentful. Why did they all think so badly of her? She caught sight of Morvina's herb casket, and her resentment bubbled over. "What of your religion? Do you still believe so fervently in its power? Two years ago at Bamburgh we all tossed pebbles into the flames, and yet you made no mention of one being damaged. You kindled a needfire. But still Piers is dead."

Morvina went to the casket and opened it, taking out a tiny leather pouch. She loosened the thongs and dropped the contents on to a table. Out fell fragments of stone, black and smoke-stained.

"This is the Earl of Cornwall's stone, my Lady. I found it in the ashes of the fire and I told no-one. As for the needfire, well when I returned to your bedchamber I found that Gareth had fallen asleep and left the candles burning. For needfire there must be no other flame nearby."

"Why did you not tell me?" whispered Alice, her eyes large as she stared at the pieces of pebble.

"What good would telling you have done? You would have been fearful of his life with each passing moment. He knew well enough what must happen to him, and he made no enquiry about the Hallowe'en pebbles. But the pebble showed the truth, for within the year he was dead."

Alice turned towards the door, pausing to look back. "Warwick killed the hedge-king . . . "

Morvina gathered up the pebble and replaced it in the pouch. "The Earl of Warwick will be dealt with, you may be sure of that." She fingered the bunches of herbs lovingly, a small smile on her face.

Westminster was ringing with the sounds of the great banquet, and Alice suddenly realised that she must be a little late. But this was surely the time that Edward had commanded her to attend; perhaps he had made a mistake . . .

One of the King's heralds announced her name and the noise in the hall was stifled immediately. The minstrels' music was suddenly the only sound. Close to her side a large hound chewed upon a discarded bone, its teeth crunching loudly. All eyes turned towards her and she felt her face begin to grow hot.

The King sat at a raised table at the head of the great hall, with the Queen at his side, and all the Earls grouped around. He stood and held out his hand to her.

"Lady Alice, you are truly welcome. Come, we have a place for you." He indicated the vacant chair at his left.

Her lips parted. She could not sit there! To do so would be to place herself above even the Earl of Lancaster. The insult would be too great . . .

Edward's hand was steady as he led her towards the dais. She saw Pembroke's face drawn into a frown as she passed him, and Beatrice kept her eyes firmly upon a white sugar sublety before her. Surrey's good-looking face bore a quizzical expression as he watched her walk past. Warwick scowled at his plate, ignoring her pointedly. Lancaster sat at Isabella's side, his face bereft of expression, and he steadfastly took no notice of either the King or Alice. Arundel's handsome face was a picture of mixed emotion. Hereford pedantically took up a napkin and wiped the corners of his mouth, sniffing loudly and then looking at his fingernails. All this she noticed in those brief seconds before Edward himself drew back her chair for her to take her place.

Isabella leaned forward and smiled a welcome. "Lady Alice, it gives me much pleasure to see you again, your absence has been a source of concern to me." Her face was kind, her voice gentle. There was a new softness about the Queen and as the banquet progressed Alice noticed how Isabella's face lit up with pleasure whenever Edward spoke to her.

Edward made much of his Queen, laughing at her little jokes and touching her hand often. He was striving to please her and no-one but Alice could see how great was the effort he made.

On Alice's other side sat the Earl of Gloucester, now one of Edward's closest adherents. He was pleasant and made himself congenial to his new neighbour. Alice guessed that this was why he had been placed by her, any other Earl might have made his feelings more obvious . . . except perhaps Surrey who now raised his glass to her.

181

The many courses passed before her dazed eyes in a confusing succession, each dish seeming more rich and succulent than its predecessor. But she could take no delight in them. She realised now that Edward had deliberately told her an incorrect time at which to make her appearance, and she knew that she had been used as Gareth had warned. She realised too, that her determination to avenge Piers could not stand up to such enormous pressure. How she wished she had remained at Longmore.

Gloucester smiled at her untouched plate. "You have no appetite, Lady Alice?"

"Would you, my Lord?" She could not hide her unease.

He took a jug from a waiting page and carefully poured out a cup for her. "You knew what you did when you accepted the invitation."

"No, not really. I did not know that I was to be Piers himself tonight."

He smiled. "If you eat nothing, then you will be faint later on from hunger." He looked at her face, seeing the sudden surprise which crossed it. He followed her glance and saw that she looked at his sister, the Countess of Cornwall, and Sir Hugh d'Audley, who sat together, leaning close and familiarly. "They are soon to be betrothed."

The golden eyes swung back to him. "It comes as no surprise to me really, it just seems . . . so wrong . . . "

"Piers did not care for my sister, nor she for him. They were honest in their dealings with one another, that much can be said of the marriage. My sister loved Hugh before she married Piers, and the love endured. It does not seem wrong to me that they should wish to wed now."

She bit her lip. "It is wrong, for Hugh d'Audley told Warwick that Piers had given himself into Pembroke's keeping, and he also told him which route Pembroke was taking southwards. He knew that the Earl would waste no opportunity of seizing Piers, and he told him in the hope that by doing so he would rid himself of your sister's spouse."

Gloucester's face changed and his eyes narrowed as he looked at the laughing couple. "What you say puts Hugh in an unsavoury light, but proving it would be impossible, as well as ill-advised in view of the reason for tonight's banquet. We are all supposed to put Blacklow further behind us with each mouthful we sup."

The banquet limped along painfully now, Alice's arrival having successfully dampened the small flame of camaraderie which was burning. Only the music of the minstrels saved it from total disaster. The Fools who capered before the royal dais found themselves hard put to raise a smile from the sullen faces of the Earls, and only the King and Queen laughed and clapped their hands.

As the tables were cleared away at last, Alice thankfully moved away towards the shadows at the side of the hall, choosing a spot between two torches where their light was weakest. But Edward's sharp eyes followed her.

He held up his hands to quieten the minstrels, and the hall became quiet. "Let us dance now, my Lords, Ladies." He turned to Isabella, holding out his hand, but she shook her head, laughing.

"I cannot, my sweet Lord, for I am by far too full of the good things we have eaten!"

He smiled, and then turned suddenly to where Alice stood. "My Lady, you shall be my partner then."

Her heart seemed to jump. This was terrible. Why, oh why had she come here . . . ? Edward crossed the floor, his long cloth-of-gold sleeves brushing against the rushes.

The minstrels began to play once more as the King and his partner reached the centre of the floor. The Earl of Gloucester led his young wife out to join them, and Surrey too. Soon quite a number moved to the music, but all the other Earls remained in their seats. Pembroke refused Beatrice's pleas; he did not approve of what Edward had done tonight, and he showed his disapproval in the only way he dared.

Warwick slouched in his chair, stroking the banded grey feathers of a peregrine falcon which was on his wrist. Occasionally his eyes wandered over Alice's slender figure as she danced. He remembered the whiteness of her throat, the softness of her skin . . . The falcon screeched loudly, flapping its wings, as he stood abruptly and replaced it upon its perch. Again it screeched, angry at being put aside. He snapped his fingers at a page who hurriedly removed the complaining bird from the hall. Its calling could be heard long after it had gone. Warwick stood by a doorway, his scarlet coat brilliant in the smoky light. He did not take his eyes off Alice now, watching her continuously before pushing his way past the men who guarded the entrance and leaving the banquet.

The music played on. The dance seemed never to end. Alice could have wept at her foolishness. At last the final chord sounded and the dancers bowed to one another before moving away. But

Edward held Alice's hand and she had to remain with him. They were alone in the middle of the room, with all eyes upon them.

He opened his purse and took something out, something which flashed like blood in the torchlight. He did not speak loudly, but so deathly was the hush that his words carried plainly to every corner. "It is good fortune, Lady Alice, that you have chosen to wear so beautiful a gown tonight, for I have here a gift which will gladden your heart. It is a gift from Perrot, a gift which he dearly wished you to have and which he willed you." He opened his palm and there rested the circle of rubies which had once belonged to Piers' mother.

She could hear Piers' voice now . . . 'It is all that I have which was hers' . . . Tears pricked her eye lids, blurring the beautiful jewel. Edward pinned it to her shoulder himself.

A squabble broke out between two hounds at the far end of the hall, and a Fool pretended to conduct the fight according to some unknown rules. Laughter rippled around the gathering, and the scene in the centre of the floor was forgotten.

Alice put her fingers over the ice-cold rubies, but her eyes were reproachful as she looked into Edward's face. "Your Grace, you have done me a great wrong by all that you planned tonight. It was unkind of you."

He seemed taken aback, as if he had not heard correctly. "Unkind?"

"Have you no thought of *my* feelings at all? I wish that I had feigned illness and not come, for you have raised me in the image of Piers in order to provoke all those here who were responsible for his death. It was very wrong of you." Her voice was low and breathless, for she knew that she should not speak to the monarch in such a way, but her embarrassment and hurt were very great.

Edward was perturbed, leading her to a corner where the crowd was less dense. "I would have expected, Lady Alice, that you would have enjoyed all this, enjoyed their discomfort at being reminded of their misdeeds." His tone was abrupt.

"Maybe so, but not in so flagrant a manner. To place me above your cousin of Lancaster, to ask me to dance with you as being second only to the Queen . . . "

He took her hand and raised it to his lips, clasping her fingers warmly. "But Alice, you *are* second only to the Queen, You were the beloved of Piers and he was second only to me. For his memory I place you in your rightful place."

She stared at him. He meant what he said, believed it completely, and was honestly surprised at her reaction. To him Piers was still everything, grieved for endlessly and loved forever. Through Alice he sought to reach that beloved memory, warm a little life into the vanished ghost. Edward Plantagenet was not fickle in his loves.

Her anger was suddenly no more, and she returned his handclasp. Like Piers, she could not stay angry with him, she could only love him.

He was pleased now, and his pleasure showed upon his face as he led her to speak with Queen Isabella.

THIRTY

AT the end of the evening Alice walked back through the rambling palace of Westminster to the room which had been set aside for her. It was in the oldest part of the building, down a narrow, low passageway lit by a few torches.

She pushed open the door and went in. It would be good to be free of this gown and to have her hair brushed by Morvina's soothing hands . . . The room was silent. "Morvina?"

She looked around but could see no sign of the maid. The curtain was drawn across the far end of the room where the bed was, and she drew the drapes aside and peeped in. Perhaps Morvina was asleep, after all the hour was late . . .

The dusty curtains smelled damp as if steeped in winter chill, and the brazier had burned low. A candle flickered upon the low table, but of Morvina there was no sign.

"You shall not find your serving wench, Lady Alice, for she is well taken care of!"

She whirled about, her breath catching in her throat as she saw the scarlet coat of Guy Beauchamp.

"What are you doing here?" Her fingers held on to the old curtains tightly.

"I have come to finish that which was once begun."

A coldness settled upon her, a hand of fear and loathing. "Get out of here." She could only whisper.

He grinned and slowly closed the door, turning the key in the lock and then putting the key into his purse. "We have much unfinished business, Alice."

She cowered back against the curtains, her eyes wide with terror. He stopped close, enjoying her fear. "I once promised you that there would come a time when I would know there to be no danger of interruption. That time has come."

"You would do this here? When I am under the King's protection?"

This seemed to amuse him. "The protection of Edward Plantagenet? I do not think that *that* amounts to very much, sweetheart. He could not even protect his lovely Perrot, so I doubt vastly if he can protect you!"

She shrank away from him, this time she knew there was no escape. He put out his hand and turned her face towards him. "You have flaunted yourself before me all your life, Alice. To have been forced to give you to my womanish nephew was galling, but I had a wife and could not take you for my own. My nephew's death came at a time when I was without a wife, but you took yourself off to the Gascon squire!" His face twisted into an ugly mask. "What you could find in that prinked pervert? What could *he* give you that I could not?"

Her lips moved but no sound came out. She was petrified, and fascinated as she saw the depth of his feeling. Gone was all pretence, all posturing. He had wanted her for all these many years.

He straightened and began to unfasten his coat. "Even as a child you were beautiful, I could see the faint beginnings of your loveliness then . . . Oh, I shall savour every sweet and blessed moment of this, Alice, for I have waited long enough for you."

Her knees became water and she sank to the floor. If she could have found voice to scream it would have availed her nothing. The walls were many feet thick in this part of the palace, and the oak door would muffle any sound.

His coat hung loose and he moved towards her, stopping as he caught sight of the ruby pin on her shoulder. His tongue passed over his lips quickly and his eyes widened slightly, but his desire for her overcame all else. "Come here."

She could not move, her limbs were heavy as if deep in molasses. He grew irritated. "Very well, I shall come to you! He reached down and snatched at the silver net which held her hair. It came away painfully as the pins dragged at the roots of her hair. The dark red tresses tumbled down, warm and scented, and he grew more excited, fumbling roughly with the fastenings of her gown.

She bowed forward, her arms tightly clasped around her chest, drawing the rose velvet gown tight so that he could not manage the fastenings. His fingers grasped the rich stuff and he ripped it. The sound was loud, but was deadened immediately by the stone walls. The undergown of apple silk was her only protection now and he stood back to look at her. He was breathing very heavily.

"Stand up!" She did not move. "*Stand up!*" His senseless rage frightened her into action and she scrambled to her feet, whimpering a little, and leaning back against the nearest wall, her eyes wide and hunted.

As if to steady himself he took a huge breath, holding it for a while before exhaling slowly. The calmness returned. "Turn around that I may unfasten your undergown."

Silently she turned her back towards him, leaning her forehead against the hard stone. He seemed suddenly imbued with infinite patience as he released each small button, but at last he was finished.

He pulled aside the curtains which concealed the bed, and then tossed his scarlet coat to the floor. He lay on the bed, putting his hands behind his head and surveying her as she stood there.

"Now the moment is right, Alice. You shall come to me now."

"No." The word was a feeble defiance.

"But you will, Alice, you will. Your disobedience will only antagonise me, and that will be no beginning to our relationship, will it?" He was so reasonable that her fear could only mount.

"There is to be no relationship, my Lord. Tonight is the beginning and end of any association between you and me."

His teeth gleamed white in the dim light of the candle. "Then by all means let the beginning and end commence . . . " He held out his hand to her.

She pressed her trembling lips together and stayed where she was.

A frown creased his forehead and he ran his fingers through his iron-grey, curly hair. "Alice, I am fast losing patience. I ask you once more."

"I spit on you, you toad! I shall never come to you, I would as soon die!"

His nostrils flared with anger and he sat up, his eyes glittering. "Very well, if you wish to make a battle of this, so be it!" His speed trapped her as he got up from the bed and caught her wrists, dragging her back to the bed. With a slithering sound the silk fell to the floor and she was naked.

He released one hand and she immediately clawed at his face, her nails dragging his skin so that he cried out in pain. Blood sprang to the surface. Again and again she jabbed at him before he caught her hands and twisted both behind her.

He pressed his lips to her mouth, in complete mastery over her now. She twisted and squirmed beneath him, dragging her mouth away at last and sinking her teeth deep into his shoulder.

But then she screamed out in her own pain as he took her.

He stood at last, bending slowly to pick up his coat. He looked down at her as she lay then on the bed, her face buried in the mattress and her hair spilling about her shoulders. Her skin was bruised and there were scratches on her back. "Well Alice, you made the battle, not I." He stared at her as he fastened the coat.

She pushed her face further into the softness of the bed as if by doing so she hid herself completely. Tears trickled from beneath her closed lids, but she made no sound.

A sudden thundering on the door brought life into him and he whirled about his eyes widening. Who was this? Someone was shouting *his* name! He glanced back at Alice but she did not seem to have heard the disturbance.

He took out the key, drawing the curtains across the room before opening the door. The Earls of Lancaster and Arundel burst in, and Lancaster's round face was red with fury as he stared at Warwick. "You imbecile! What have you done?"

Warwick smiled slowly. "What I have done is *my* business and mine alone."

"You think so? Would you undo all these past months' negotiations? We have achieved a peace of sorts with the King and in one blind urge you endanger everything!"

Morvina pushed her way past Arundel and hurried towards the curtains. Lancaster heard her cry of dismay as she saw Alice. He went to the curtain and glanced in, turning back to look long at Warwick. "By All the Saints, you *are* an animal! And how do you suppose we are to stifle her when she recovers her senses properly? I curse the day I found you as my accomplice!"

Arundel idly tossed two coins in the air, jingling them together as he too went to the curtain. His eyes slid warmly over Alice's body and he smiled. The smile vanished as Morvina cursed him in Welsh and tossed a jug of icy cold water at him. Angrily he closed the curtains, and the dust which flew from them settled on the droplets of water on his jacket. He flicked irritably at the richly embroidered cloth, his handsome face flushed.

By the bed, Morvina gently turned Alice to face her, pushing back the damp red hair from the hot face. An iron-grey hair clung to Alice's shoulder, and Morvina took it swiftly between two fingers and hid it in her casket.

Warwick was unabashed. "How did you discover what was happening?"

"The maid got free and decided that I was the wisest choice of rescuer for her mistress." Lancaster scowled at Beauchamp.

Warwick laughed at that. "Rescuer? You? You were only too pleased to have her witness Gaveston's death, I doubt if you could be termed 'rescuer'!"

"Do you not realise the danger that lurks over the border in Scotland? Further wrangling and quarrellings in England will achieve nothing but a Scottish victory! The King's acceptance of us is a fragile thing, Warwick, and will be shattered forever should he discover what you have done. Jesu, Beauchamp, your foolishness staggers me! Tonight Edward singled her out for his especial favour, he set her up as high as he dared. He could not have been plainer had he shouted aloud! I took heed of the warning, as did Arundel and Hereford, we dare not upset our hard won amnesty. Think what will be lost if the Scots over-run us. Edward may not be our greatest King, but he is still King and the country must unite under him at a time like this."

At last Warwick's grin faded. He glanced down at the floor and then back at Lancaster. "What is to be done then for I cannot turn back time."

Lancaster glared furiously at him. "I think that you had best take yourself away from here, many miles from here! Now!"

Wordlessly Warwick left the room, closing the door quietly behind him, and Lancaster turned to Arundel. "Do you think we shall be able to reason with her?"

Arundel shrugged. "How should I know? She has been raped, I doubt if there are many more unpleasant experiences for any woman. Do you want me to speak to her?"

"You? Jesu above, no! You cannot keep the lechery from your eyes even now! Any sweet words from you will no doubt make matters worse."

Again Arundel shrugged, the coins jingling in his hands. "Then what do you suggest?"

Lancaster pulled aside the curtain and glanced in, seeing that

Morvina had pulled a coverlet over Alice. He beckoned to the maid. "How is she?"

"She will recover my Lord, that is about all which may be said."

"May I speak with her?"

Morvina stood aside. She had deliberately chosen the Earl of Lancaster to aid Alice. He had more to lose than anyone by Warwick's actions, and if he was a vain, unscrupulous man of little ability, he was at least adept at fighting to retain his immense wealth. She understood well enough the dangers of civil war if Edward's mercurial temper should be aroused, and for the moment the risk must be averted. Her dark eyes narrowed as she thought of the iron-grey hair in the casket.

Lancaster sat uncomfortably on the edge of the bed. "Lady Alice?"

She opened her eyes. "Have you come to gloat?"

He shook his head. "No, I have come to plead with you."

Her eyes closed again. "Of what?"

"That you seal your lips about what has happened here tonight."

She tried to laugh but grimaced in pain instead. "Why should I protect Guy Beauchamp?"

"Because if my cousin Edward comes to know then we will be back to the time immediately after Blacklow. Civil war. War from Scotland. Bloodshed such as has never before been witnessed. Believe me, I have great sympathy for you . . . "

"Sympathy? You make me vomit, Lancaster! You could not experience so human an emotion! You despise me, and always will, and it is only the risk to your own fat neck which brings your scuttling feet in my direction now." She pulled herself up on to her elbows.

Arundel decided that Thomas of Lancaster was not making a great impression upon her, and he pulled aside the curtains and came closer. She stared up at him. "What you say is true, Lady Alice, and we cannot deny it, but it is also true as my Lord of Lancaster tells you. One word from you now could crush England's shaking safety."

"You are still asking me to protect you."

Arundel sat down. "Aye, and we have done little to merit your protection. But in this one thing we are innocent. Warwick's lust for you has simmered for many years now, that is a fact which cannot be denied . . . but are *we* to blame for that?"

Alice's head throbbed and her throat was cracked as she

swallowed. Morvina pushed a cup of wine against her lips. As she sipped the wine, she stared at Arundel.

The anxiousness in his blue eyes could not be hidden, and his fingers played nervously with the coins in his hands. Lancaster's tense body was stiff, apprehensive. How sweet it was to have them at her mercy like this, how full the pleasure of knowing that she could condemn them out of hand if she so desired . . .

"You have a silver tongue, Edmund Fitzalan, I am almost persuaded."

He smiled. "Pray God that you are fully persuaded."

She drained the cup. "You are so trivial a man, Edmund, mean and spiteful, a sheep which scurries after its master. And you, my Lord of Lancaster, are the chief bell-wether! You bleat and the flock hurries to you. You are both well-matched in your total lack of merit. Your ally Warwick is unspeakable, a beast which would sully even a pig-sty. Three of you whose lives will be made easier for the silencing of my voice."

Lancaster could barely hide his anger, but he forced himself to sit quietly and hear her out. There was nothing he dared do to stop her. Arundel pursed his lips, maintaining his smile. "Say all you wish, Lady Alice, but still think on what I have said."

She thought. She thought of Edward's contorted face as he cursed Piers' murderers. 'I shall have their hearts wrenched from their loathsome bodies for what they have done!' And Piers would still have died for nothing if civil war should break out now. The silence grew heavy.

"Very well, for the sake of the Earl of Hereford I shall say nothing."

"*Hereford?*" Arundel's mouth dropped in surprise. Lancaster blinked.

"Yes, he alone of all of you showed me a little kindness. Rough he may have been, but at least he revealed a semblance of honour when you had descended into the Pit. For his sake, and his alone."

They left her shortly afterwards, Arundel once more jingling the coins in his hand. They paused outside the door and he tossed the coins high into the air. "A thousand blessings on Hereford, eh?" He grinned in the darkness at Lancaster, and the coins clattered noisily to the floor.

THIRTY-ONE

THE night was still. Frost hung in the air and clasped its tendrils around everything. Alice stood by the window of her bedchamber at Longmore and looked out over the well-loved scene. The Severn was a strip of shining silver curving away into misty grey-black distance, vanishing at last beyond the cold horizon.

It was two months since she had returned to Longmore, two months since Guy Beauchamp had treated her so brutally. Even now she shuddered at the thought of him. She had been true to her word and had said nothing to Edward as she took her leave of him. He suspected nothing and saw nothing odd in her quietness; but Isabella's knowing eyes had seen the disguised bruises and dark shadows beneath the golden eyes. Nothing was said, but Isabella wondered greatly at the change in Alice.

Now Alice shivered in the February night air, and drew her cloak more closely around her shoulders, rubbing her face against the warm fur lining. The moonlight which shone so piercingly through the narrow aperture showed clearly the scratches and bruises which still marred her skin.

She remembered how pleased she had been to see Gareth once more, and she had surprised him by running into his arms on her arrival back at Longmore. But she had not told him of Guy Beauchamp. Morvina was sworn into silence, and so not even Stephen knew. Oh, how she wished to forget everything, forget the past . . . But she could not set Piers' memory aside so easily, and she could not ever forgive Guy Beauchamp.

A furtive movement on the bank of the river caused her to pause. Someone was down there, creeping along the narrow path which wandered the river's edge. Her brows drew together as she saw yet another figure, then another. What was going on?

"Morvina?" she called softly, going to the adjoining door and peeping at the maid's bed. It was empty. There could be only one explanation, some ceremony of the Old Religion was to take place. She did not stop to think further, but went immediately to her wardrobe and selected a thick winter gown. The gown was unbelievably difficult to put on without the aid of Morvina, and most of the fastenings had to be left. She picked up the fur-lined cloak and pulled it tightly around her and then hurried from her rooms.

The guards did not question the lady of the castle as she hurried out into the bitter cold and across the courtyard. She went through the kitchens and buttery until she came to the tiny postern gate in the south-west wall, then she slipped outside and down the steep curving path towards the river.

Many of the villagers were also on their way to the river, and she pulled her hood forward to hide her face. Down the path they sped, black shadows moving in the silver white moonlight. The ground cracked beneath their feet, the grass crunching and splintering as the ice was broken. An owl called across the valley, a long low wavering cry. Above the pearly orb of the moon shone from a black sky, and the stars glittered like diamonds.

The ground was slippery as the slope quickened and suddenly Alice's feet slid from beneath her. With a startled cry she fell from the path and down the grassy bank. Winded, she lay still for a while before sitting up. She had done no damage to herself but her arm felt bruised.

A pair of eyes glowed close by and she gasped with fright. The eyes were steady and unblinking, then they moved as their owner came closer. She leaned back towards the grass, but then almost laughed with relief as a thin tomcat padded into a patch of moonlight from the shelter of the bushes where he was hunting. His pale green eyes looked reproachfully at her and she knew that the noisiness of her arrival had disturbed his chances of a meal for some time now. He sat down and put his ears back in disgust.

She stood and scrambled back up the bank, slithering a little on the grass and smooth frozen mud. Once back on the path she found herself completely alone. All the others had long since vanished. She hurried on down towards the river.

The land flattened out, and she hurried on for more than a mile before at last reaching the edge of a small grove of oak trees right on the bank of the river. In the grove she saw an immense gathering, and recognised so many of the faces. There must surely be few villagers still in their beds tonight. She crept closer until she reached the sturdy trunk of an oak.

Tonight there was something different about the meeting. They were all so quiet, almost stern. An unlit bonfire had been built in the centre of the grove, and now everyone took a seat in a huge circle around the fire. Bedith was there and soon his strange pipes were making their music.

Morvina stepped into the centre of the circle, and Alice's eyes widened as she saw that her maid was not wearing white, but black.

The little Welsh girl was inexpressibly graceful as she danced, and Alice watched. But something jarred tonight. There was something unnerving about the dance, and the music. There was no joyfulness in either, but a menace, a threat. Alice found herself clinging to the cold trunk of the oak tree. The circle of watchers began to sway in unison to the unholy rhythms.

Overhead the trees rustled in the slight breeze which sprang up. The bare branches cracked and creaked complainingly as the frost's grip was disturbed. She glanced up and saw a golden-green ball of mistletoe only a few feet above her head. The white berries shone like pearls.

The music stopped suddenly, and the rustling of the trees became immediately loud. The silent river moved stealthily past, so near, yet unheard. Morvina took two tinder-dry twigs of oak and began to rub them together. The world seemed to hold its breath in excitement as it watched for the spark of fire. A wisp of bluish smoke rose and was whisked away by the playful air. Morvina held the twigs to the straw-packed bonfire, and soon the pale moonlight was joined by the roaring redness of the scarlet and orange flames. The bonfire blazed loudly with life.

Morvina closed her eyes as Bedith's music began again, slowly, oh so slowly. She twisted her body to the dance, circling the bonfire. Her dark hair streamed out behind her, and the black robes fluttered like bats' wings. Once as she passed she bent and swiftly took up a small wooden box which lay on the ground close to the fire.

She opened the box, still dancing, and two objects were taken out and the box tossed away. In her right hand she held what looked to Alice like a small doll. A sigh rippled around the circle as she held it aloft.

Alice stared. Even from this distance there was no mistaking the crude effigy. Red and white paint was daubed over it in the pattern of Guy Beauchamp's badge. But what she could not see was the wiry, iron-grey hair which was pinned to the doll. The music stopped as Morvina began to walk around the circle, close to the onlookers, holding out the effigy for all to see. She began to whisper a name. "Beauchamp, Beauchamp, Beauchamp . . . Bee-cham . . . Bee-cham . . . Bee-cham . . . " They all took up the chant and the Earl of Warwick's name hung on every malevolent lip.

Morvina sprang back towards the fire, her finger to her lips. The chanting ceased as she held the doll up again, holding her left hand high too. Then she spoke.

194

"This is an evil man. He takes life. He has taken the life of one of us, one who has joined us, here." The crowd hissed angrily, like a thousand snakes. He has been warned, but has not heeded the warnings, and so by the purification of fire we shall destroy him and his vile influence." The hissing was renewed.

Morvina's left hand moved suddenly as she tossed something into the fire, and Alice saw the silhouette of a spider. The third and final spider. The maid walked slowly around the circle again, holding the doll out for all to see. "Beauchamp, Beauchamp, Beauchamp . . . Bee-cham . . . Bee-cham . . . Bee-cham . . . "

A shriek split the night as the hated doll was tossed into the heart of the fire.

Alice could watch no more and turned to run away from the grove. She scrambled blindly along the path, and did not stop running until she reached her own apartments.

And when Morvina returned an hour later, Alice feigned sleep, and the following day said not a word of what she had seen.

THIRTY-TWO

ONLY weeks later, as spring began to warm the land, a small party of horsemen galloped up the slope towards Longmore just before dawn. The drawbridge was lowered speedily as the party was recognised and soon they were inside the sheltering walls.

Alice sat up in bed on hearing the sounds of their arrival. She got out of bed and pulled on her robe. Morvina's bed was empty yet again.

In the great hall Alice came upon a scene of confusion and noise and laughter. The new arrivals drank wine and ate as if they had not seen food for a month. They did not see her at first and she was able to survey them at her leisure. Gareth was there. And Stephen. And Morvina. Morvina? The maid was dressed like a man, with her hair pushed up into a cap!

"What is going on here?" Her voice rang out across the hubbub.

Gareth paused as he raised a cup to his lips, and his face blushed at her tone. Stephen coughed as a crumb of bread caught in his throat. Morvina's eyes widened with dismay.

"My . . . my Lady . . . "

"I think that some explanation is called for! You have been out in the night and come back at dawn with as much noise as an invading army! What has been going on?" Her eyes swept around the unruly crowd and came to rest on a hood clasped in the hands of one man. She recognised it. "So, the mighty Malcolm Musard has been raiding the countryside again has he?"

Stephen put down the crust of bread and stepped forward. "Yes, my Lady, we make no denials."

"Gareth? You too?" Alice could hardly believe that Gareth, *her* Gareth, would ride on such night raids.

"Yes, Alice. I have been with them." For the first time she noticed that his hand was covered in blood.

"What has happened to your hand, Gareth?"

"We . . . er . . . we were surprised on the lands of the Abbot of St. Peter's, and my horse stumbled. I was thrown and my mount trod on my hand. 'Tis nothing."

Alice walked slowly into the centre of the hall. "Am I to understand then that Longmore is being used as a home by a band of outlaws?"

Gareth winced as his hand brushed against a table, but his eyes followed her. "Yes, 'cariad', you may understand that. And it has been thus ever since Stephen became your steward. Many is the time that you have eaten the Abbot's mutton, Sir Thomas Berkeley's venison, even the Earl of Warwick's game . . . "

Laughter rippled around the crowd, but Alice was not at all amused. "Be silent! How dare you, how *dare* you take such liberties. This has all been without my knowledge and certainly without my approval. I will not have Longmore used to such low purpose!"

Gareth's green eyes flashed angrily. "You did know, Alice, and have always turned a blind eye because it suited you. Even Piers knew what went on, and smiled at what we did. Such an expression as I see on your face now ill becomes you!"

Stephen's eyes widened and he pursed his lips, glancing at Morvina.

Alice's face whitened with fury. "What right have you to speak to me in such a fashion?"

"I have every right, *my Lady!* I speak to defend Stephen, Morvina, and all these men here. You should be ashamed of yourself!"

She almost stamped her foot with frustration. "I will forbid any further activities."

He raised his eyebrows and leaned forward towards her. "You will not!" She raised her hand to strike him but he caught her wrist. "You will not, Alice, because I am telling you that you will not. The activities of Malcolm Musard are a legend in these parts, a legend which is loved by everyone except the landowners whose game is poached. Many a starving peasant family has been fed because of Stephen here, and so who are *you* to play the tyrant and say he must stop?"

Angrily they glared at one another, but she knew she was in the wrong. She lowered her eyes to his wounded hand. "Your hand must be dressed," she said quietly.

The change of subject was taken by the outlaws as a sign of resignation, and the chatter broke out again. Morvina hurried away to bring her casket.

Gareth sat down again, smiling up at Alice suddenly. Gradually she returned the smile, and he took her hand and kissed it gently, before turning away as if his action embarrassed him.

Morvina carried her heavy casket to a trestle, opened it and then turned to look at his hand. She glanced back at the array of herbs as if to decide which preparation was required. Alice went to her, looking down into the box with interest, reaching to touch the crisp, dried leaves and the tiny bottles of liquid.

"Which one do you want?"

The maid frowned over Gareth's hand. "The smoked glass bottle, I think. There on the right."

"This one?" Alice picked up a bottle.

" 'Diawch!' Do you want to kill him? That is a deadly poison. No, the bottle next to it. Yes, that's right." She took the second bottle and turned her back on Alice to administer the potion.

Stephen joined them, handing a brimming mug of ale to Gareth; "I thought the mighty Warwick had us then, Gareth."

"Warwick?" Alice caught the name and her voice was urgent.

Morvina glanced at her swiftly, detecting the sharpness.

"Aye, we were surprised by the great Earl himself as we poached merrily of the Abbot's fleet-footed sheep!"

"What is he doing here?" She was dismayed. He was certainly not dead. He was well enough to ride. Morvina's incantations had not worked. Disappointment surged through her; she knew that if

Warwick had been seriously ill word would have reached Longmore . . . but the knowledge that he was apparently completely untouched by the magic still came as a bitter pill.

Stephen gulped his ale, smacking his lips. "Oh, I had word that Beauchamp is staying at Gloucester Castle . . . most probably he comes to terrorise the Abbot on some matter or other."

Gareth was thoughtful. "Aye, but that still does not account for his presence up in the hills before dawn. He knew that we would be turning our attention to that particular flock and he was lying in wait."

Stephen stared at him. "Are you saying that we have a Judas in our midst?"

"Well, the suspicion must be there, must it not? How else could our whereabouts be known?"

Placing his mug down next to the casket, Stephen gazed around the noisy hall, his glance falling on first one face and then another. There seemed to be no uneasy soul, no eye which slid away before his stare. "Gareth, we have to tread with care. Warwick got his man into Longmore before, how, we do not know. It could be that he has wormed a spy in here again. We shall keep the King's peace until a more opportune season . . . by which time I will have dug out the guilty man."

In a corner a small, dirty little man sat quietly sipping his ale. He had a narrow face, minutely freckled, and his fine brown hair receded from his forehead. His fingers shook slightly and he tightened his hold upon the mug to conceal the trembling. He could see the look on Stephen's face as he surveyed the room, and he knew that he was in mortal danger if the steward of Longmore should discover that he was not only the castle's blacksmith, but also Guy Beauchamp's man.

Alice watched Stephen's good-looking face as he pondered upon the unpleasant knowledge that there was a spy in their midst. Again and again the hard, bright eyes rested upon each face in the hall, returning finally to the small figure in the corner. The blacksmith. He had come to Longmore at about the time the Earl of Cornwall came to Tintagel, and Warwick had discovered what was happening then . . . For a blacksmith, Jack Byalls was uncommon scrawny . . . Stephen's strong fingers drummed upon the trestle and he gazed steadily at the blacksmith.

Byalls' eyes were terrified as he realised that Stephen's suspicions were directed towards him. He wiped his shaking mouth with the back of his hand and stood. He must get out somehow. He began to walk from the hall, but Stephen's shout sent three men after him. In a moment he was grabbed and brought roughly before the steward.

Morvina stopped her ministerings and stood quietly watching. Gareth turned in his seat, his eyes narrowing as he saw the identity of the culprit.

There was little need to question the blacksmith, for his obvious fear and guilt was written large across his white face. Stephen motioned his men to remove him from the hall, and his whimpers of dread and his pleadings were heard until the door closed behind him.

The mood of the outlaws changed subtly. Gone was the urge to laugh and make merry, to poke an imaginary tongue out at the unseen Warwick. The Earl's plottings and schemings had come uncomfortably close to them, and the knowledge cooled their enthusiasm.

Morvina continued dressing Gareth's wound, while Stephen poured himself a further mug of ale. His glance met Alice's for a brief second.

She looked from the face of her unusual steward to the box of herbs. Warwick touched her, even here in Longmore, his evil fingers curled around her. She swallowed with difficulty, for her throat was dry. All the hatred and loathing came rushing back, and she found herself staring at the smoked-glass bottle which lay still amongst the herbs.

Morvina saw her and slowly closed the casket. Alice turned away her golden eyes large and pensive.

THIRTY-THREE

ALL through that fine spring day Alice was in a grip of excitement. Her strangeness did not catch the attention of Gareth or Stephen, but Morvina sensed the change immediately. But Alice did nothing unusual. She rode out in the afternoon to see the elver catch, and rode slowly back along the river bank towards Longmore, pausing a while in the village to order some new slippers from Bedith.

As night fell, a solitary figure slipped out of the postern gate and down the narrow path, skirting the base of the hill and back towards the village. The cloak was pulled tightly around its head and shoulders to conceal its identity, but the occasional splash of turquoise silk as the cloak flapped could only have belonged to Lady Alice de Longmore.

She slipped past the first few rough cottages until she came to Bedith's home. He was too old now to row the swift current at Stonebench and lived alone in this tiny cottage. He opened the door quietly as she tapped upon it.

"I have the mare waiting for you, my Lady, are you certain that you do not wish me to accompany you? I have another horse . . . "

"I am sure, Bedith. My business is private."

He led her around to the back of the shabby cottage to where a bay mare was tethered to a post. The saddle was old and worn, and the mare was not the most elegant of mounts, but Alice was glad enough to see the beast.

Silently she mounted, her voluminous skirts gathering uncomfortably about her legs. Bedith pulled the heavy folds aside carefully, his fingers lingering over the priceless silk. Such fabrics, such magnificence . . . He sighed wistfully, glancing down at the rough wool cloth of his own coat.

Alice turned the mare's head towards the north and the hidden city of Gloucester. The land before her now was marshy and dangerous, and could be traversed only by those who knew their way. Many a traveller had lost his life in the murky, water-logged bog. But Alice was confident. As a child she had ridden this way often, though her father would have beaten her had he known.

The mare picked her careful way along the narrow causeway which was the only path. The hooves sank into the ooze, and the beast snorted slightly as an owl's call carried over the barren scene. The moon was stifled tonight, hidden by the miasma which hung over the marsh. The reeds sprang back eagerly after the mare had passed, pointing their dark green heads towards the dull sky. Occasionally she heard a frog croaking in the mist, a horrid, jarring sound in the loneliness.

Alice put her hand inside her cloak to her purse, and she felt the cold, hard outline of the smoked-glass bottle.

In the castle life hummed on normally. No-one had missed Alice as yet. Gareth played chess with Stephen close to the fire in the great hall, leaning down occasionally to stroke the head of the large brown and white hound which sprawled across his feet. Stephen scowled at the chessmen as he pondered his next move.

Morvina came into the hall with her casket. Spring was upon them now and the herbs would have to be sifted carefully, the old tossed away to make room for the fresh. She sat down, the casket on her lap, watching the game of chess for a short while before opening the lid and taking out the first few bunches of leaves. Then her fingers stopped their movement. Something was wrong. A bottle was missing.

Her mind worked quickly as she realised which bottle it was. So dangerous and deadly a poison could kill a thousand men . . . She glanced around the hall, puzzled. She had not seen Alice for some time now, and Alice had shown so great an interest in that particular bottle. Silently she put down the casket and hurried from the hall towards her mistress' apartments. They were empty.

Morvina's alarm was heightened by the discovery that Alice's cloak and a pair of heavy slippers were missing too. Seizing her own cloak, the maid ran back through the deserted passages to the hall.

"I think, gentlemen, that we had best ride for Gloucester as quickly as we can."

Stephen turned in surprise. "In this mist? Whatever for? I told you that we would remain inactive for a while . . . "

Morvina was exasperated that he did not immediately understand. She explained.

Gareth picked up a white pawn. "You have merely mislaid the poison, Morvina. You should take more care."

"*Mislaid* it? You are foolish to think that I would do such a thing. Her cloak is gone and I can find no sign of her. The poison is missing, and Guy of Warwick is in Gloucester."

"But how is she expecting to reach Gloucester? She has taken no horse!"

Stephen stood. "Why should she have cause to poison Warwick? He might have been responsible for Piers' death, but surely she would not . . . "

"There is more, much more. Suffice it that Lady Alice has another, far more personal reason for hating Warwick, and if that is placed alongside the other black marks against him, then she has reason enough. Believe me. I think she has gone to administer that poison to him, and I know that she will in all probability succeed only in being caught and recognised."

201

Gareth pushed the boarhound aside suddenly. "I believe you. She could have got a mount from the village if she so desired. We shall ride now."

They ran from the hall, rousing the castle into activity.

The gates of Gloucester were still open as Alice at last left the unsafe causeway and rode up on to the hard road. The lights of the city were a welcome sight after the perilous journey across the marsh. The mare snorted and tossed her head, and Alice put out her hand to steady the animal.

A solitary cart was creaking slowly towards the still-open gateway and she urged the mare forward to follow the cart. Southgate yawned black before her and she saw the impatient guards beckoning the dawdling cart to make haste that they could observe the curfew time.

She did not notice the hoofbeats thundering up behind her, for her mind was dead to all thoughts but the final extinguishing of Guy Beauchamp. The hatred welled up to exclude all else.

A small chestnut pony appeared beside her and a hand seized her arm. "Give me the bottle, my Lady."

"Morvina!" Alice stared in dismay. She had been discovered.

"Give me the bottle, you must not do this!" The maid's voice was commanding.

"Let me ride on, Morvina, for it has to be done. What you did did not work, *it did not work!*" Alice was almost weeping now.

Realization dawned across the maid's face. "You saw us in the oak grove?"

"Yes, I saw everything. It was weeks ago now, but he is still alive!" Alice took out the bottle and handed it to Morvina. There was no point in continuing, not now . . . "He should be dead," she whispered.

"But my Lady, you do not understand. What you saw was not everything, and the magic can only work if the Earl of Warwick *knows* what has been done. It is the discovery of the spell by the victim which works the magic, not the spell itself. I was going to acquaint him with the knowledge myself . . . " She broke off as more hoofbeats filled the air. The larger mounts of Gareth, Stephen and their men were more cumbersome and unsafe across the marsh causeway. The maid's pony was swift and sure-footed.

Ahead the cart rumbled on towards the gateway.

Gareth reined his foaming, fearful horse in, reaching out to take her hand. "Jesu, Alice, we have risked our vain necks in so headlong a gallop across that land! Why did you do it, 'cariad'?" His fingers were warm and safe.

"I wanted him dead, and would have done it had not Morvina reached me in time . . . " She twisted to look at the maid but there was no-one there. Her eyes fled up the roadway towards Southgate and she was in time to see it close upon the cart . . . and upon a small figure on a chestnut pony. Morvina had gone on into Gloucester and she had the poison with her.

Stephen was dismayed. "Morvina . . . "

Gareth lifted Alice from the saddle and placed her before him on his horse. "There is nothing we can do, Stephen, the city will not open its gates to us now. Do not be fearful for her, she will be safe enough . . . you know Morvina."

Stephen ran his agitated fingers through his straw-coloured hair. "Aye, I know her. She has gone to finish what the Lady Alice began. If she should be caught at such an act . . . "

"She will not be, Morvina never is. She will return to you, Stephen, I tell you the truth."

Alice buried her face against Gareth's coat as the hot tears flowed afresh. He put his arm around her and held her tightly, laying his cheek against her hair. "Come, we will return to Longmore, Morvina will come in the morning."

Slowly they turned back towards the marsh.

Gareth watched Alice's anxious pacing in the great hall. He leaned to toss a fresh log on the dwindling fire, and the noise disturbed the hounds. Sparks wandered up, mingling with the thick black smoke. Stephen's face was white with worry for the girl he loved. He stared at the arched portion of sky visible through a slit window. Dawn was creeping across the heavens now.

They did not hear Morvina come quietly into the hall. The hounds saw her first and stood to greet her, their tails wagging. A falcon heard her approach and cocked its head on one side to listen, fluffing its grey-barred feathers proudly.

"It is done, my Lady . . . once and for all it is done . . . " Morvina walked up to her mistress.

Stephen closed his eyes with relief, taking her hand as she paused next to him and laying the cool fingers against his lips.

Alice could say nothing. For her, the Welsh girl had taken an enormous risk, a risk which could have cost her her life. Alice felt small.

The maid picked up a black knight from the discarded game of chess, looking down at it as it rested in her hand. "Guy Beauchamp has breathed his last, and with his passing Piers must be allowed to rest. His death has been avenged, and your own suffering has been avenged. In the Old Religion we take a life for a life, as it says in your Bible, and then we put aside all memories. You must do the same, and look to the future now."

The Severn glittered in the warm spring sunshine and the two figures sat on the high bank and stared downstream. Their horses nibbled the fresh green grass behind them, their tails swinging to brush away the first of the summer insects.

"Morvina said it would come before an hour had passed." Alice watched excitedly. She was never tired of the bore.

Gareth pulled a blade of grass and dragged it between his fingers. "Whatever Morvina says, then so it will be."

Alice lowered her eyes from the river and looked at him. "Forgive me for all that I have done, Gareth, please." A slow flush took her as his green eyes turned to her.

"There is nothing to forgive, sweetheart, for I deserved to lose you. I should have fought for you long before Piers challenged me."

She touched the curling brown hair and smiled. "But you have not lost me, Gareth, not now."

A rushing, splashing noise filled the air as the bore swept upstream. A silver torrent spread across the wide quiet river, drawing nearer with each second. The horses lifted their heads from the grass to look, moving away from the strange sound. The wave swayed almost out of the banks as the river curved close to them.

Alice closed her eyes and leaned back against the bank as Gareth kissed her.

"Soon after Gaveston's execution the Earl (of Warwick) died mysteriously; it has been suggested that he was poisoned by Gaveston's mistress."

from the Official Guide to Warwick Castle.